mW

Sandy stiffened involuntarily

"Offer your assistance?" she asked angrily. "Is that what you were doing back at my apartment when you threatened to throw me in jail if I didn't cooperate?"

He paused with his spoon halfway to his mouth. "Keep your voice down, Alessandra. If you're upset because you think I've arbitrarily taken over your investigation, then let's get something straight right now. Bert was a seasoned veteran. I didn't worry about protecting him. I was wrong—he's dead. I'm not going to make that mistake again. I happen to think Mr. Vanish exists and that he poses a threat to anyone attempting to unmask him. Therefore, I'm going to watch over you the whole time like a she-bear with a cub. With luck, we'll both come out of this alive."

Sandy's cheeks warmed with embarrassment. She'd had no idea what they would both be facing....

ABOUT THE AUTHOR

While writing for Harlequin Intrigue as Edwina Franklin, Arlene Marks also enjoys an active career as a professional nonfiction writer. Last year she took the plunge and started her own small publishing house, Summit Educational Services. She lives outside of Toronto with her supportive husband and two bright and energetic sons.

No Pain, No Gaine

Edwina Franklin

Harlequin Books

TORONTO • NEW YORK • LONDON
AMSTERDAM • PARIS • SYDNEY • HAMBURG
STOCKHOLM • ATHENS • TOKYO • MILAN

For David,
whose loving support
extends my grasp
as well as my reach

Harlequin Intrigue edition published October 1990

ISBN 0-373-22148-7

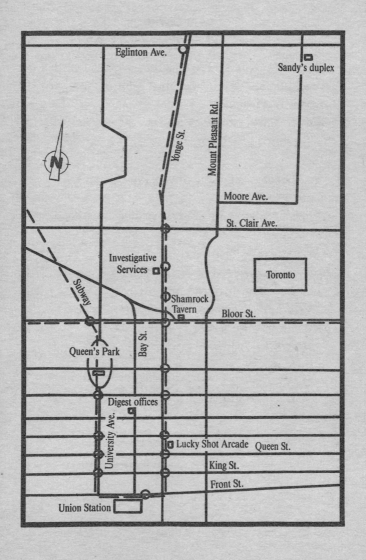

CAST OF CHARACTERS

Alessandra (Sandy) DiGianni—Spunky and vivacious, she stumbled onto a lethal string of unsolved crimes.

Detective Sergeant Ted Gaine—Meticulous and by-the-book, he protected against a faceless killer.

Mr. Vanish—Figment or elusive master of disguise?

Charlie—Was selling secret police files his nine-to-five job?

Allen Storm—Disorderly orderly.

Lou Parmentier—His rising political star fizzled when he was murdered in a bizarre case.

Sergeant Joe Wegner—Loyal partner, he was better than man's best friend.

Paul Rudd—A boss who barked orders while chomping a cigar.

Prologue

Tuesday, May 8

Happy Hour was a misnomer, Sandy decided as she glanced around nervously at the quietly murmuring clusters of people in the Shamrock tavern. They were mainly mixed groups of white-collar workers from the neighboring office towers on Bloor and Yonge Streets, quaffing an after-hours beer or three while waiting for rush-hour traffic to thin out. For the most part, they looked like a commercial for Molson's Golden.

But off in the corner sat a pack of young men, about six of them, wearing skin-tight jeans and crudely graffiti-covered T-shirts, passing a bottle around and whispering suggestively among themselves. Each time one of them looked at Sandy, she winced and shifted restlessly on her stool. She stirred the remaining slivers of ice in her Tom Collins, asking herself for the tenth time why she was still here. It was bad enough that she'd broken one of her cardinal rules and agreed to meet in a bar with someone she'd only spoken to once, on the phone; but this Charlie, whoever he was, was now half an hour late. She glanced up and caught the bartender gazing sympathetically at her. Five more minutes, she decided. If Charlie wasn't here by then she would leave.

Suddenly the stool beside hers creaked as a man sat down. After thirty minutes of leering attention from the boys in the corner, it took all the self-control she possessed to remain calmly seated while she sized him up.

He was short, with light brown hair and cracked, dirty fingernails. Flashing her a brief grin, he ordered a whiskey. Then, as though they'd been conversing for hours and he'd suddenly remembered to remind her of something, he turned to her and said, "Bert always paid for my drinks."

Sandy's back stiffened momentarily. Bert Waldron was the writer she had replaced at *Police Digest* magazine. So this unprepossessing little man was the one who had phoned her earlier today, who had chuckled chauvinistically when she'd confirmed that the "A. DiGianni" on the magazine masthead was Alessandra DiGianni, a woman, and had laughed out loud when she'd demanded to know what was so damned funny about that? Who had then dared her to meet him alone in a bar to find out how he could make or break her writing career? Her feminist dander dangerously high at that point, she'd taken his dare and angrily hung up on him.

And now here they were, exchanging baldly appraising stares, and the bartender was looking expectantly at her, poised to pour the shot of whiskey. After a beat, she nodded at him to go ahead and serve the drink.

"You must be Charlie," she said conversationally to the man beside her.

"Yep. And you're the newest staff writer over at *Police Digest*. It took some guts to meet me here. I'm impressed."

"Why? Because I'm a woman?" she said, beginning to bristle.

"Nah. Because you're a totally green rookie. I noticed your name on the masthead three weeks ago, and I did some checking. Until Rudd hired you, you were nowhere."

"I was with a leading women's magazine."

"Same thing." He paused to down half of his whiskey, apparently impervious to the daggers she was staring at him. "So I set up this meeting to find out whether you'd have the nerve to show up."

"I see. And have I passed your little test?" she said, snapping the last two words at him like whips.

He gave her a sly grin. "With flying colors, doll. Let's move to a booth so we can talk business."

Too busy wondering what he considered "business" to object to being called "doll," Sandy left a couple of bills on the bar, and she and Charlie carried their drinks to one of the booths at the back of the room. Once he was satisfied that nobody could overhear their conversation, he reached inside his windbreaker and pulled out a flat white envelope.

"Some of this isn't even in police records," he boasted quietly. "Call it research, if you like. But I have access to stuff that you'd never find out on your own. Hot stuff. Up to the minute. And absolutely factual. Before he died, Bert paid me by the month to feed him information for his articles."

Sandy nearly inhaled a mouthful of Collins. "Bert died?"

"Yeah, back in March. Boating accident." Charlie cocked his head curiously at her. "Nobody told you?"

Sandy shook her head, feeling a rush of heat to her cheeks. Nobody had told her, and she hadn't even thought to ask. She'd just assumed the collage of photographs on the office bulletin board was a sentimental leftover from Bert's retirement party. Some investigative crime reporter *she* was going to be!

"So how about it?"

"How about what?"

He sighed impatiently. "How about making me your confidential source? You're going to need one if you expect to make it into the big leagues, babe, and I'm the guy who can boost you up there. Listen, I deal in information, and I have plenty of eager customers. If they want to know what's *really* going down on the streets, they come to Charlie. I supply leads to every city desk in Toronto."

"Then why did you bother calling this 'totally green rookie' if you're so busy?" she asked.

Charlie paused, picking his words. "Because Bert was a good guy... and he was one of my regulars, so I figured I'd offer my services to his replacement, as a professional courtesy. However, since you're not interested—"

"I didn't say that."

A smile trickled across his face. "Okay," he said at last. "You just got the go-ahead on a series of articles about past unsolved crimes, right? And you've visited the newspaper morgues and the library, and collected a few scraps of information from the police...."

She frowned. "How did you know that?"

"Even though I'm not big on history," he went on, ignoring her question, "just to show my good faith, I went ahead and dug up some exclusive info on unsolved crimes for you, right here." He patted the envelope proprietarily. "You'll really like the murders," he added with a conspiratorial wink.

Sandy stared at the envelope, gnawing her lower lip uncertainly. She had a bad feeling about this. Instincts she hadn't needed since her rebellious teen years were telling her Charlie was flypaper—the kind of unsavory character who would stick to you, refusing to be shaken off once you'd touched him. And yet ... Paul Rudd had warned her that crime journalism was a tough field to break into, that she would have to be stronger and more aggressive than she'd ever been before. That she would have to get her hands dirty digging up information ... dealing with sources who ate and breathed and slept in that dirt ... sources like Charlie.

"All right," she said finally. "But I'd have to see the information first."

"Huh-uh. Money up front."

"I may be a rookie, but I'm not *that* green, Charlie," she warned him.

He scowled at her for a second. "Okay, okay," he grumbled, tearing open the sealed envelope. "I'll show you a sample, but that's all. You are really stretching my professional courtesy, lady."

The envelope contained a thick sheaf of loose-leaf paper. Charlie yanked one page free and thrust it across the table at her.

MERCANTILE BANK ROBBERY, was typed at the top, and then half a page of point-form notes, specifying the number of perpetrators, the make of the getaway car, even the exact wording of the robbery note. The bank job had taken place eight years ago, and neither the suspects nor the stolen fifty thousand dollars had turned up since.

This was perfect for her first article—*if* Charlie had his facts straight. Well, it would be easy enough to verify his information, since he had also provided the full names of two of the tellers and the assistant manager who had been on duty that day. In fact, Paul would insist she verify it with two independent sources—her new managing editor was a stickler for corroboration of all reported facts.

Sandy drew in a long, steadying breath, then touched the flypaper.

"Okay," she said with a nod, "how much are you asking?"

Charlie leaned back in his seat. "A hundred bucks for this package, and then a hundred bucks a month to keep it coming."

"Wait a minute, I can't afford—"

"Yeah, yeah, I forgot, you're a rookie," sighed Charlie, and sat up straight again. "Okay, just this once. A bargoon. Fifty bucks for what's in this envelope."

"Can I write you a check?" she asked hopefully.

"Lady..." he groaned.

"Sorry." Grimacing, she pulled a ten and two twenties from her wallet, thinking of all the hot-dog-and-macaroni dinners she'd be eating for the next week, and handed the bills over.

Charlie pushed the envelope toward her and stood up to leave. "Here's my phone number," he said, dropping an open matchbook onto the table. There were figures scrawled inside the cardboard cover. "Give me a call when you need some more research done. Any kind of research. I'm a versatile guy," he added with a smile.

Furtively, Sandy tucked both the envelope and the matchbook into her purse. Then, sipping slowly at her Collins, she waited until the tavern's swinging doors had finished echoing Charlie's exit before leaving the booth to make her own.

THREE WEEKS LATER, Sandy was on the phone, trying to get one of Lou Parmentier's associates to confirm or deny the hour at which Charlie claimed Lou had left a cocktail party on the night he was murdered. And Charlie wasn't flypaper anymore; as far as Sandy was concerned, he was a legitimate informant.

His information had been right on. Independent sources—some of them initially speechless at being contacted by a reporter, some of them uncooperative, even hostile, until she told them what she already knew—had eventually corroborated the facts of all twelve of Charlie's 'unsolved cases.' The details of those cases, placed side by side with the much older ones the police had given her, would make her articles gripping and relevant; would give them the "punch" Paul had said he was looking for.

And she'd even found a bonus lead, some references in Charlie's notes to a hit man nicknamed Mr. Vanish, who might or might not exist. Sandy loved puzzles, and this one promised to be fascinating. She decided to stir him into her second article in the series. A phantom killer, able to baffle the most sophisticated police forces, would certainly liven up a piece about unsolved murders.

Sandy consulted her notes for that article. The police had given her two of the four cases she was writing up—The Marchand-Florion serial killings, and the mystery of the frozen Mountie. Far more interesting, though, were two more recent murders: Lucas James, a farmer in the Credit Valley; and Lou Parmentier, a Toronto businessman and City Councilman-elect who had apparently been executed on the very night of his victory at the polls. The story had been national front-page news for days, and had shaken Toronto Council to its core. Whoever solved this murder, Charlie's notes suggested, would probably get a medal, a cash reward, *and* a key to the city. Not to mention a terrific scoop for the magazine, she thought with a grin as she peered at the details of the Parmentier investigation.

Sandy leaned back in her chair with a sigh. With a confidential source feeding her leads and three weeks' worth of dirt under her fingernails, she was finally beginning to feel like a pro.

Chapter One

One glance at the computer printout sitting on her desk was enough to send Alessandra DiGianni storming into Paul Rudd's glass-enclosed office cubicle.

Planting her feet firmly on the worn gray carpeting and her fists firmly on her hips, she tossed her mane of dark brown hair and demanded hotly, "How *dare* you change me into a man?"

On the other side of the cluttered oak desk, the managing editor of *Police Digest* magazine shifted his well-chewed cigar from the left to the right side of his mouth and gave her a questioning stare.

"Don't play dumb, Paul," she warned. "You promised me a byline on my first feature article, and then you went and changed it to Tony Bryant."

"Yes, I did."

"I turned down an associate editorship at *Lady of the House* magazine to come and work for you. I was going to break new ground, you said, be a role model for other women writers. So how am I supposed to do that if everyone thinks I'm a man?"

Paul Rudd sighed wearily. "Sit down, DiGianni." He chomped hard on his cigar and pointed imperiously to the extra chair beside his desk. Sandy noted the stern glint in his eyes and decided to sit.

"I changed your byline because the article became a collaboration between you and me." Raising a hand to still her objections, he explained, "I had to rewrite the piece to keep us out of trouble with the PMRC. You remember the Police Media Relations Committee, the public-affairs branch of the Toronto Police Department and official source of authorized police information in this city? Only a publication with a death wish would deliberately get on the bad side of those people, Sandy. And that's what your article would have done to us if I'd let it go through the way you'd written it."

"I worked hard on that article, Paul," she pointed out, "and I was careful to stay within editorial guidelines."

"I know," he said, and blew out a long, exasperated sigh. "Look, Sandy, you brought me an outline for a series of historical pieces—Great Unsolved Crimes of the Past. You were going to go right back to Confederation to compare the methods used by police then and now, and speculate on whether our modern techniques might have solved those unsolved cases. It was a nice, tame little assignment, perfect for someone just learning the ropes—until you decided to move them into a mine field!"

He was leaning across his desk now, his cigar jutting ceilingward like a warning beacon. Icy dread seeped down Sandy's spine. This was not the reaction she had been expecting from him.

"In our business, history means when all the possible suspects have died," he went on, his voice sharp enough to make her wince. "There is no statute of limitations on indictable crimes in Canada, Sandy. Police files can remain open, and their contents confidential, for fifty years or more. As long as there are suspects still alive, the case can still be solved—but not if some irresponsible writer leaks key details to the public. You know what I'm talking about.''

Sandy swallowed hard. "The kidnapping."

"And the bank job. An eight-year-old robbery, for chrissakes! And you put in the exact wording of the robbery note. There's no way the police would have given you that for publication, if they gave you anything about the case at all. That's why I had to rewrite your first instalment—to delete all the references to those two crimes. And that's why I've decided to put a senior staffer on this series with you—under his byline."

He was demoting her to research assistant on her own articles. Heat crept into Sandy's cheeks, forcing her gaze downward.

"Look," said Paul gruffly, "I hired you because you are a hell of a writer, Sandy, but in this corner of the profession things are different. We don't do pieces on furniture antiquing or rose gardening; so your previous experience doesn't count for much here. If you want topical feature assignments you'll first have to prove to me that you can handle them without getting yourself or us in trouble. Okay?"

A lead weight settled slowly at the bottom of her stomach. Paul was right. She was a green rookie and everyone knew it, even Charlie. Silently, Sandy nodded and got to her feet.

Her editor cleared his throat loudly. "I understand you've filed two more articles," he growled. "I'll be editing the second instalment on Monday. If there's nothing in it that would get us in hot water with the PMRC, and if the writing is up to your usual high standards, I might be willing to reconsider my decision about the series."

Sandy began to smile. And then it hit her. The second instalment! She'd even hand delivered it to make sure it arrived quickly. Suddenly her legs felt weak and she had to sit down again.

"We may already be in hot water, Paul," she told him reluctantly.

"What?"

"Well, I needed to check out some of the information in the second article, so . . . I took a copy to the police department for verification. It's the instalment about unsolved murders."

Mouthing a curse, Paul swiveled his chair and activated his computer terminal. He called Sandy's article up onto his screen and read it silently, his teeth locked so tightly around the stub of his cigar that she thought he would bite it in two. Then, with a discouraged sigh, he swiveled back to face his errant staff writer.

"First Waldron, then you," he muttered darkly as his eyes darted toward the message spike on the corner of his desk. "Damn . . ."

Sandy frowned, confused. "What was that about Bert?"

"Never mind Bert!" snapped her editor. "This is *your* article we're talking about, DiGianni."

He settled back in his chair, visibly searching his mind for the right combination of words. "My God, Sandy," he said at last, "the Parmentier case? You have reconstructed, in painful detail, a murder that is less than a year old. A murder that is probably still under active investigation. And even if it wasn't, it would still be a Homicide Squad file; and Homicide Squad files are always strictly confidential. Didn't you know that?"

There went her scoop. Sandy shook her head slowly. She could feel the weight of everything she still had to learn bowing her shoulders like a heavy yoke.

"The PMRC is going to give us a rough ride on this one," he warned her. "There's no legal way you could have got hold of any detailed information about this murder, unless..." Pursing his lips around the tattered cigar, Paul scowled at her across his desk. "Your source wouldn't happen to be inside the Toronto Police Department, would it?"

Sandy tried to visualize Charlie in a blue uniform, but the image just didn't fit. "No..."

Paul shifted his cigar again and bit down hard. "Thank God for that," he muttered. "The last thing this magazine needs is to trigger a Department scandal. What about a witness? Did your source actually see the murder go down?"

"I don't think so."

"Maybe he talked to someone else who did. Or maybe he found a way to steal the information from police files."

Paul sounded strangely matter-of-fact about this last possibility. "Are we in trouble?" she asked, her frown deepening.

"Only if you knowingly purchased information stolen from the Toronto Police. Did you?"

Sandy swallowed hard. "No, I— He wouldn't let me see it until after I'd paid him."

Her editor snorted past the cigar teetering on his lips. "You bought a pig in a poke, in other words. Oh, Sandy, Sandy, Sandy," he groaned. Paul clapped a hand to the bald spot at the back of his head and polished it slowly with his palm.

"Okay, kid," he sighed at last, "you're probably in the clear. As long as you didn't ask this source beforehand to get you the information—"

"I didn't."

"—and you'd never used him for anything before—"

"Never!"

"—and I'll vouch for the fact that you're an ignorant rookie who wouldn't recognize sensitive information if it cried tears all over her desk, then I doubt whether they could charge you with anything. Remember that when you have your little chat with Sergeant Gaine later on."

"Sergeant Gaine?" she echoed weakly, wondering whether she'd missed part of this conversation.

Paul leaned forward and yanked a scrap of paper off the bottom of his message spike. "The call came in early this morning. I was about to give it to you when you barreled in here and jumped down my throat. Detective Sergeant Ted Gaine, Homicide," he read, then tossed the scrawled message onto the growing pile of paper debris on his desk. "Obviously, Media Relations spotted the confidential information in your article and passed it along. Sergeant Gaine will probably ask you to reveal your source. You, of course, will adhere staunchly to the journalist's code and refuse."

"Even if he stole the information from police files?"

"Even if he mugged your grandmother the day before," said Paul sternly. "It isn't his business ethics you have to worry about, kid—it's ours. If you're using a source, even if he's a criminal, you have to protect him. Look, this confrontation between the press and the police isn't that big a deal. In fact, it's the best-choreographed routine in the news reporting industry. Ted Gaine has probably been through it a hundred times."

Sandy felt a sudden chill. "Is that supposed to be re-assuring, Paul?"

"What I mean is, he knows the drill by heart. Okay? He will be expecting you to say no. However," he added, causing something to drop with a thud to the pit of her stomach, "he's one of the toughest, smartest cops around. He knows you can't reveal your source, but that won't stop him from trying to force or trick or even charm the information out of you. So be careful."

"How about if I just don't phone him back?" she offered nervously.

Paul shook his head. "My people don't play hide-and-seek with the police. Besides," he added, glancing at his watch, "according to the message he left, Gaine isn't interested in talking to you over the telephone. He wants a face-to-face in about twenty minutes in that little Greek café just across Yonge Street. Don't be fooled by his informal choice of location, by the way. Smart detectives know that a cozy chat over coffee is a great way to get a suspect to drop his guard and maybe let something slip—so I'd keep my defenses up if I were you. Oh, and Sandy? Don't lose your temper with this guy, okay? He understands Italian."

Sandy left Paul's office and walked directly to the washroom, where she spent the next fifteen minutes splashing cold water on her face and doing breathing exercises. Nothing worked. Her cheeks continued to burn, her heart was beating a tattoo inside her chest, and her limbs were humming with adrenaline. She felt like a gladiator about to enter the arena, but armed with a pen instead of a sword.

And against tough, smart Sergeant Gaine, who would apparently stoop to any dirty trick to pry the identity of her source out of her, Sandy wanted a sword. No, she sighed as the last of the water gurgled down the drain, what she really wanted was a reprieve.

As she dried her face with a paper towel, Sandy surveyed herself critically in the mirror. If she *had* to go to this meeting with a guilty-looking flush in her cheeks, then the rest of her must project utter calm. Fortunately, she was wearing green, a cool color, and the simple lines of her straight skirt and matching tunic gave her a businesslike air. She would need it, she thought disgustedly, if she hoped to convince this Ted Gaine that she was old enough to vote.

In school, Sandy had been the envy of her friends, with her flawless olive complexion, her large brown eyes fringed with naturally curly, dark lashes, and her thick, wavy hair that looked professionally styled with no more than a vigorous brushing. It was a look all the other girls had to sleep on rollers and spend hours in front of mirrors trying to achieve.

At sixteen, Sandy had blessed her good luck. Now that she was twenty-seven and about to have a close encounter with tough-as-nails Ted Gaine, she realized that she'd been culturally deprived. Other women could paint cool sophistication on their faces when they needed a new persona. They generally carried the equipment with them. But all Sandy found in her handbag was a half-used tube of lip gloss and an atomizer bottle of Silken Shoulders cologne.

With a sigh, Sandy smoothed the lip gloss on her naturally rosy mouth and sprayed some fragrance on her wrists and the base of her throat, able to draw some comfort from the fact that Paul Rudd still considered her one of "his people." Not only had Paul not fired her, but he'd complimented her for being "a hell of a writer," and her editor didn't hand out compliments lightly.

"I'm a hell of a writer," she told herself in the mirror, screwing up her face in an approximation of Paul Rudd's habitual scowl. Then she gathered up her belongings, gave her hair one last pat and her tunic one last tug, and hurried to confront Sergeant Gaine before her nerve completely failed her.

THE MIDTOWN CAFÉ was a modest, family-run place specializing in light lunches and takeouts. The menu was handprinted in grease pencil on a long Arborite slab mounted behind the counter, and the daily special was always a Greek dish, meaning that even at ten-thirty in the morning, the café held a tantalizing mixture of aromas. Today the chef was preparing moussaka, and the air was redolent with lamb, tomatoes and tangy feta cheese.

Sandy stood just inside the door and glanced around at the dozen or so small tables with their burgundy cloths and polished chrome napkin holders. All the tables were empty but one. Tucked into the far corner of the café, sitting with his back to both walls and frowning into a coffee cup, was a disgruntled-looking man in a gray two-piece suit. Could this be Ted Gaine?

She could tell from the way he filled his chair that he was a big man, well over six feet, and broad-shouldered. His coloring was Mediterranean, like hers, although his closely trimmed hair and mustache were several shades lighter than Sandy's own nearly black hair. It occurred to her briefly that this man in the gray suit and charcoal-and-blue tie might not be Ted Gaine at all, that she might be agonizing about walking over to some accountant or insurance salesman who had wandered into the café. And then he looked up, eyes as gray and hard as steel locking commandingly with her startled brown ones, and Sandy knew, as the knot in her stomach turned to ice, that this was Sergeant Ted Gaine, exactly as Paul had described him—tough and smart, and not about to let her off the hook.

Sandy licked her lips nervously and began walking toward him. He got to his feet with surprising ease for a big man who'd been crammed into a corner behind a little round table.

"Ms. DiGianni?" Before her eyes, the stubborn glower melted into an expression of watchful neutrality. His official police face, Sandy realized, was not exactly honey, but certainly not the vinegar she'd first seen on his handsome features—and they *were* handsome, she had to admit, classically proportioned and perfectly regular, like a Roman statue come to life. There was Italian blood in his veins, she would bet on it.

"Sergeant Gaine?" When he nodded, she took the seat he'd already pulled out for her.

"Would you like a cup of coffee?" he offered, in a deep, warm voice that seemed to pour lazily over her senses.

This was the honey, she decided, a breath away from giving in to the sheer pleasure of being wrapped in that velvety baritone. And then common sense cut in with a ruthless reminder that the tall, good-looking man across the table was tough, smart Sergeant Gaine, her adversary in a matter of professional ethics; and the velvet turned to snow against her skin.

"No, thank you. I'd rather just get down to business." Sandy almost cringed at how flat and cold the words sounded.

For a moment, the gray eyes looked hard enough to spark. "As you wish," he replied, his voice still surprisingly soft. "I've read your article about the unsolved murders. You write very well."

She nodded stiffly, not trusting her voice to acknowledge the compliment.

"I was particularly interested in your reconstruction of the Parmentier case," he went on. "You went into some detail, describing his personal life, the nature of his partnership with Vermeyer, the way he was found in the back seat of a one-year-old Dodge, even the amount of money he had in his wallet at the time. Is all that factual?"

"I don't know. I submitted it to the police so that you could tell *me*."

Sandy thought she glimpsed a flicker of amusement in his eyes before they settled back into steel again. "You do realize that Homicide Squad files are strictly confidential, even after they've been closed?"

"I do now."

"Your covering letter contained a request that we verify the reliability of the information provided by your source."

"That's right."

"Would you care to name this source?"

His question might be the raison d'être of this interview, but according to Paul Rudd it was a formality, nothing more. Emptying her voice of all emotion, Sandy gave the formula answer: "No, sir, I cannot. As a journalist, I have an ethical obligation to protect my sources."

"Well, Ms. DiGianni, your obligation places my department in a rather difficult position. You see, your article contained certain facts about the Parmentier case that appear only in our files."

He was waiting for her response, watching her face carefully, his cold gray eyes like bullets locked onto a target. *Dio,* what difference did it make how warm and wonderful a man sounded if he looked at a woman like that? Sandy had to force down a nervous flutter in her throat before she could reply with any semblance of composure, "Really? I guess that proves my source is reliable, then."

"All it proves, Miss, is that you know more about the murder of Lou Parmentier than an uninvolved civilian is supposed to know."

"Quite true," she agreed. "I got the information from my source."

"Whose identity you refuse to reveal?"

"Whose identity I cannot reveal, Sergeant—there's a difference."

"Even if I told you that the knowledge your source possesses could place him in danger?"

"That's right."

"Or if I told you that by passing the information on to you, he might have placed *you* in grave danger?"

Sandy had to swallow hard to force the butterflies back down to her stomach. "Not even then."

Her voice faltered for only an instant, but Ted noticed it. In fact, very little about her had escaped his notice from the moment she had entered the café, too nervous to stand still even for the ten seconds it took her to locate him in the corner. Wide brown eyes under delicate brows, lustrous dark hair, full lips compressed into a hyphen of determination on a flawlessly oval face— without a trace of makeup, he realized suddenly. She was probably one of those women who would always look younger than her age. If she took care of her skin she would still be attracting admiring looks when she was well into her fifties. Was she as beautiful inside as she was outside? he found himself wondering—then immediately banished the unprofessional thought to a corner of his mind.

"How long have you been writing for magazines, Miss?"

"Altogether, six and a half years."

"And how long have you been working on this article?"

"About two weeks."

"Then you've known the gentleman at least that long?"

"You make it sound as though we have a personal relationship," she protested.

The corners of Gaine's mouth twitched briefly. "Sorry. How *did* you get together?"

"I had begun researching some past unsolved cases for a series of articles, and he . . . got in touch with me."

Gaine's forehead contracted in a frown. "He knew about your research?"

"That's what he said, Sergeant."

"Interesting. How did he contact you?"

"He phoned me at the office."

"He gave you the information over the telephone?"

"No, he requested a meeting," said Sandy uncomfortably. Was she giving Ted Gaine too much information? Had he decided to worm so many little details out of her that in the end it wouldn't matter whether she revealed a name or not?

"So you met him face-to-face," declared the sergeant. "Where and when exactly?"

Sandy hesitated, frowning. Would the bartender remember her from that far back? Was Charlie a regular at the Shamrock? He and Bert had apparently met there quite often.

"About a month ago, in a public place," she replied at last, challenging Gaine with a direct stare.

His lips twitched again. "And he just approached you, out of the blue?"

Sandy shrugged. "I guess..."

"Weren't you curious as to why?"

"He...probably had his reasons. With a source, some things are a matter of trust, Sergeant," she informed him stiffly.

"It's not safe to be too trusting, Ms. DiGianni. He was probably setting you up as a decoy."

"For what?"

"The informant either witnesses the murder or knows someone who saw it. When he decides to come forward, he needs a patsy, a decoy to draw the murderer's fire once it becomes known there was an eyewitness to the crime. And what better patsy could there be than a crime reporter eager for a scoop?"

"That's ridiculous!" she blurted.

"He's a friend of yours, isn't he?"

"Of course not," she bristled. Charlie was any number of things, but certainly not a friend of *hers*.

The sergeant wore a faint, smug smile now. "What did he tell you? That he admired your work and wanted you alone to tell his story?"

"I told you before—"

"Or maybe that he admired your legs, and wanted you alone to tell his story?"

She blushed fiercely, her anger rising. "He didn't witness either of those murders, Sergeant," she retorted.

Gaine leaned back in his chair, still smiling. Suddenly Sandy felt a trickle of perspiration on her back, like a finger gently tracing the length of her spine. At the same moment she became aware that her entire body ached with tension. Paul had warned her about her temper, and now she knew why. In the heat of anger, she had just let slip some information about her source.

With a concerted mental effort, she pulled back and collected herself once again. She mustn't reveal any more.

Sandy drew in a steadying breath. Then, as casually as she could manage in a voice half an octave higher than usual, she said, "If you aren't going to arrest me, Sergeant Gaine, I've got things to do before lunch." And she rose to her feet to end the interview.

"Maybe I *should* arrest you, for your own protection."

Poised to turn away, Sandy halted and stared at him in confusion.

"It's dangerous to traffic in street rumors, Ms. Di-Gianni."

"Street rumors," she echoed. "Such as?"

"Such as the one you speculated about in your article—the phantom hit man, Mr. Vanish."

"Your own police department maintains that Mr. Vanish doesn't exist," she reminded him.

A frown wedged itself between his brows. "For the moment. Look, I'm not going to argue with you. There are some kinds of criminals whose activities are best left to the police to handle. So you can take this as an official warning. I don't want you playing detective, understand?"

"I'm not going to argue with you, either," she informed him sharply. "Playing detective, as you call it, happens to go with my job description, Sergeant. I am an investigative reporter."

"So was Bert Waldron."

The room was deathly still. As their eyes locked, Sandy felt a chill ripple down her spine and knew she hadn't imagined the threatening undertone in Ted Gaine's quiet statement. This interview was definitely over. Fighting to keep her hands from shaking, Sandy pivoted away.

"You'll be hearing from me again, Ms. DiGianni," came the soft voice over her shoulder.

Fervently hoping he was wrong, she quickened her stride toward the street.

FOR RESEARCH and reconnoitering, he preferred a partial disguise—a mustache, tinted contact lenses, some powder in his hair and eyebrows, and a couple of props that would make a strong, and misleading, general impression. Over the years, he'd come to depend especially on them. People were so accustomed to swallowing stereotypes whole these days. Several times he'd even considered making his kill in a crowded place, with only the props to disguise him. Perhaps he would eliminate this Alessandra DiGianni that way. A well-timed push off the subway platform, maybe, in front of hundreds of horrified witnesses. He understood she used the public transit system every day, and rush-hour crowds in a city the size of Toronto could be *so* unruly....

As he approached the busy intersection, his keen eyes took in the size of the aging brick building just north of Gerrard Street, the location of its front entrance, the distance between the row of windows stenciled with *Police Digest*, and the roof, two stories above. There were plenty of brick edges exposed; climbing would be a simple matter, if it came to that. Perhaps he would come on her in the editorial office a half hour before deadline, with a small-caliber pistol in his hand. Everyone and no one would see him fire.

Pausing at the newsstand on the corner, he thoughtfully stroked his graying mustache while pretending to survey the selection of magazines for sale.

There was a disturbing trend beginning here, he reflected—two reporters in less than a year, and both of them working for the same publication. Obviously he'd failed to completely eradicate the first investigation. He would have to be much more thorough the second time.

Suddenly his eyes were drawn to the purposeful gait of the dark-haired, grim-faced young woman who had just crossed Yonge Street and was now striding firmly in the direction of the magazine offices. Alessandra DiGianni, in the rather attractive flesh. With a faint smile, Mr. Vanish shook his head apologetically at the magazine vendor and strolled away.

HER FOOT WAS WELL AND TRULY in it now, mused Sandy as she stared bleakly at the text on the screen of her computer:

Between them, Eliza Marchand and Florion, her lover, had concealed the murdered bodies of eleven trappers in the isolated bush north of Nepean. There were no witnesses, to the killings or the burials. In fact, not until an intuitive Hudson's Bay Company clerk made a connection between Florion's suddenly teeming trap lines and the mysterious disappearance of eleven men were the authorities called in.

Retracing the paths the trappers must have taken to the trading post, the provincial detectives eventually located several of the bodies. But by then the remains were skeletal, yielding little in the way of forensic information to the relatively unprepared

local surgeon. The Crown never did manage to make
a case against Marchand and Florion. If Eliza hadn't
left a confession in her will, the full truth about these
murders might never have come to light.

If forensic science had not been in its early stages
of development, if there had been more reliable lines
of communication, if Ontario had not been such a
wilderness—in short, if these crimes had occurred in
more modern times—they would surely have been
solved quickly. Or would they?

Consider a more recent example, the murder of

The murder of whom? All the recent murders in her
research files were out of bounds. She would have to re-
structure the article, transporting modern detectives and
forensic specialists into the past and putting them to work
on those much older cases. But, *Dio,* not today. After her
interview with Ted Gaine, Sandy was scarcely able to
frame a coherent sentence, let alone revise an entire article.

She was even having difficulty typing. Every time
Gaine's honey-smooth voice intruded on her thoughts,
her hands clenched into fists. There was no way to shut
out those remembered fragments of conversation, or the
residual feelings of frustration that accompanied them.
Ted Gaine had had an effect on her, all right, along with
her poorly digested lunch. Her mind and stomach were
both churning angrily.

*He's a friend of yours... Or maybe that he admired
your legs... ?* Suddenly Sandy's teeth were grating together. How *dare* he insinuate such a relationship between her and Charlie? Just because Gaine was a police
detective and her professional ethics demanded that she
protect a thief!

For Sandy was certain now that Charlie had stolen at least some of his information. "Some of this stuff isn't even in police files," he'd told her. How could Charlie have known what was and what wasn't in police files unless he'd seen them? He wasn't a cop; of that Sandy was certain. So he had to be a thief. A very helpful thief, she reminded herself. Bert Waldron had even kept him on a monthly retainer.

And Bert Waldron was dead. Lately it seemed as though every time Sandy tried to follow a train of thought, it always ended up on that same ominous note. Bert was dead and nobody had told her, and now it was blindingly obvious, from her contacts with Charlie and Sergeant Gaine, and from Paul's reaction to her second article, that she was following in the footsteps of her predecessor, whose boating accident Ted Gaine, at least, seemed to consider suspicious. And maybe Paul did, as well. Why hadn't he told her? Had he assumed she already knew? And what exactly had he seen in her article that morning?

Questions circled maddeningly inside her head, growing as they fed on one another, until there was scarcely room in her mind for another thought. Finally she couldn't stand it any longer. Punching the keys decisively, she logged off the computer and strode to Paul Rudd's office.

At the sound of his door opening and closing, Paul glanced up from his computer screen. "So how did it go?" he demanded gruffly.

Sandy sat down on the extra chair and deliberately folded her arms over her chest. "I asked you a question this morning and you ducked it," she said. "What *was* that about Bert?"

With a heavy sigh, Paul swiveled away from the computer. "I was hoping you'd missed that. It was just a reference in your article to something Bert had been working on. It . . . never panned out. That's all."

There was more to it than that, thought Sandy with a surge of curiosity. A dead lead shouldn't have elicited from an editor the reaction she'd witnessed that morning.

"Why didn't it pan out?" she persisted, sliding forward on her chair as Paul leaned back in his, polishing his bald spot with one hand. "Come on, Paul, I want to know. From what I hear, Bert was the best in the business. So why didn't this story work out for him?"

"All right," he said at last. "If I don't tell you, you'll probably try to dig it up on your own and get into all kinds of trouble. It's this Mr. Vanish thing." Paul sighed again, obviously losing a debate with himself over whether to say more. "Bert latched on to it years ago. He was sure he could prove Mr. Vanish existed. So he began gathering information—"

"Playing detective," Sandy murmured, recalling her parting exchange with Sergeant Gaine.

"It became a part-time obsession with him. He put together a huge file of stuff—names, dates, places—kept swearing he was *that close* to solving the riddle of Mr. Vanish, but he never did. The file just kept getting fatter and fatter."

"And where is it now?" she asked, trying to sound only casually interested and failing utterly.

"Gone," Paul replied darkly. "The Mr. Vanish file disappeared from our computer the same day Bert died."

"How? Did anyone else know about it?"

Paul shook his head. "Only Bert and me. Because of the possible danger involved—and to protect the scoop for the magazine—we decided to keep it a secret."

"Danger?" Sandy leaned forward tensely as an idea slipped through her mind, leaving a mixture of dread and anticipation in its wake. "You mean from Mr. Vanish?"

"Maybe," Paul conceded. "In our business it's best to play it safe, even when you think you already are. Bert was a pro, and look at what happened to him."

"So you're suggesting there might have been a connection—?"

"I'm not suggesting a damned thing, DiGianni," he growled, parting the air between them with his cigar. "And you can just get that gleam out of your eye. If there was a connection between that file and Bert's accident, that's all the more reason for you to keep your pert little nose out of it."

Sandy straightened in her chair, momentarily speechless with indignation. She'd always suspected Paul Rudd was a male chauvinist, but . . . *pert little nose*?

"Too dangerous for a poor, frail woman, is it, Paul?" she sniped.

All at once he was standing over her, speaking in a quiet voice that conveyed, a deeper, colder anger than any bellow could have done. "Listen here, *Miz* Di-Gianni. When Bert was killed, I decided to let his investigation drop. It's going to stay dropped. That's an order from your managing editor. If you're not prepared to abide by it, you can go clear out your desk right now."

His very adamance made Sandy feel suddenly fragile. There was no way she could win a confrontation on this issue, she realized. Paul was obviously refusing to assign her Bert's unfinished business because he didn't think she could handle it. In order to satisfy her now-burgeoning curiosity, she would just have to show him he was wrong.

Chapter Two

At two-fifteen the following afternoon, with very little progress made on her second article, Sandy was finding out why the small flashing block on her computer screen was called the cursor. Muttering a few unladylike epithets, she pressed the keys again, one at a time. Each time she tried to send the little block to the right, it went left. Or up two lines. Or down three. Finally it landed at the bottom of the screen and spewed out a line of symbols that bore no resemblance at all to the Roman alphabet.

"Your résumé said you could type," Paul remarked dryly over her shoulder.

"It's not me," she shot back. "There's something wrong with this machine."

"Maybe it doesn't like being pounded on."

"I'm a touch typist, Paul. I don't pound the keys."

Suddenly the telephone in Paul's office shrilled. He turned with a scowl to go answer it, leaving Sandy locked in grim and solitary battle with her keyboard.

"DiGianni!" he bawled a moment later from the door of his office. "A word with you, please?"

Sandy shut down her terminal and strode rapidly across the room to join him.

Paul was leaning back in his swivel chair, absently fingering the stub of his cigar as she stepped through the door. "Close it, would you?" he murmured.

He waited to speak until she had shut the door and was sitting comfortably in the extra chair beside his desk. "That phone call was from Sergeant Gaine. He wants another meeting with you, at three this afternoon, at Investigative Services. I told him you would be there."

Instantly, a flock of butterflies broke loose in Sandy's stomach. Another go-round with tough, smart Sergeant Gaine? There would be no pleasantries wasted on her this time, she was sure.

"I'm not going, Paul," she said tightly. "He's already asked me to name my source and I refused. There is nothing more to discuss."

Paul puffed on his cigar, eyeing her with disapproval. "Obviously he disagrees. And before you go flying off the handle, let me point out that you work for this magazine, which depends heavily on the goodwill and cooperation of the police department. Whatever respectability we have in the news community is the result of those official connections. So when a police officer requests an interview with a member of my staff, DiGianni, that writer cooperates."

His logic was undeniable, but the butterflies refused to settle down. Stubbornly, Sandy shook her head. "I can't."

"You mean you won't," he corrected her, his hand holding the cigar mooring him to the desktop as he swiveled back thoughtfully in his chair. "Why do I get the impression that something else happened between you and Gaine yesterday and you just don't want to talk about it?"

"Nothing happened, Paul. I did not reveal the name of my source," she told him, her voice rising defensively, "and I don't think I gave Sergeant Gaine any useful information."

Her editor glanced up sharply. "But you did tell him something?"

"Nothing specific—just that I knew my source hadn't witnessed either of the murders in my article. He got me angry, and it just kind of popped out," she apologized.

"Well, you'd better brace yourself for more of the same," said Paul grimly, perching his cigar on the rim of the cheap foil ashtray on his desk, "because that's probably why he wants to talk to you again—to see what other interesting tidbits he can get you mad enough to throw at him."

She shook her head again, even more vigorously than before. "I'm not going, Paul. Forget it."

"I'd love to, kid, except that Ted Gaine happens to be one of the most tenacious investigators in the department, and he's on your case. If you don't go to him, he'll come looking for you, guaranteed." Paul paused to inspect the end of his cigar. "He's like a bloodhound. As long as you have information he wants, he'll track you down, wherever you are. Just how far do you feel like running to postpone this interview, DiGianni?"

Sandy breathed a bitter sigh. If Paul was right and her only choice was between sooner and later, it made more sense to get this ordeal over with now. "Okay, Paul, you win," she said, frustration and resignation warring within her as she stalked out of his office.

Frank Leslie, one of the senior staff writers, looked up curiously from his terminal as Sandy slammed open and then slammed shut the drawer containing her handbag.

"The old rhino hasn't fired you, has he?"

"Not yet," she muttered darkly, rifling through her purse for the little wallet containing her subway pass. "I've been summoned to another meeting with Sergeant Gaine."

"You lucky soul," Frank chuckled. He ran both hands through his shock of salt-and-pepper hair on his way to a lazy, back-arching stretch. "By the way, did I also overhear you losing an argument with your terminal?"

"I'm afraid so," she sighed, finding the subway pass at last. "It's probably scrambled my file."

"Well, I'll be leaving a little early today, so if you return here this afternoon, feel free to use my terminal to access your backup file."

Backup file. Suddenly the thought was just there, begging to be tested. Was it possible? Paul said he and Bert had been extremely cautious about that particular investigation; what if Bert had taken an additional precaution and hidden an extra copy of the Mr. Vanish file somewhere?

And what if Sandy could find that file, and maybe even prove that Mr. Vanish really existed—*Dio,* what a coup that would be, for her as well as the magazine! Paul couldn't refuse to give her challenging assignments after that.

Of course, she would have to be twice as secretive as Bert, and present it to Paul as a fait accompli... No, wait, she was getting ahead of herself, Sandy thought with a shake of her head. First she had to find the file.

No, she amended bleakly, remembering the subway pass clutched in her hand, first she had to go see the tenacious Ted Gaine.

SEEN FROM THE SUBWAY entrance, the tall brick structure on Yonge Street that housed the Investigative

Services branch of the Toronto Police Department was
only a building, like half a dozen other high rises on this
block and the next. Still, as soon as she'd identified it,
that building became different; and as she approached it,
Sandy felt uncomfortably like a fox paying a visit to the
hounds.

She wished she'd had time to go home and change her
clothes. In her bleached denim skirt and checkered blouse
she looked like a high-school student on a day off between final exams. Before yesterday she might have considered using her youthful appearance to try to stir
Sergeant Gaine's sympathies. Today Sandy knew better.

Her footsteps echoed ominously across the terrazzoed
foyer. Reluctantly she stepped into the elevator, feeling
the familiar flutter at the back of her throat as the doors
sighed shut, and a responding flutter from the pit of her
stomach as she felt herself lifted, ready or not, to the
eighth floor.

The elevator doors opened again on a featureless beige
hallway. But off to her right was a small reception area
tucked discreetly into an alcove.

The receptionist was a blonde, about Sandy's age,
wearing a cream-and-peach outfit and a carefully casual
short hairstyle. Mounted on the wall over her head was
the crest of the police department, with the words
INVESTIGATIVE SERVICES in raised gold letters on the
bottom half of the plaque.

As Sandy approached, she saw that the reception desk
shared the alcove with a compact three-seat sofa; and
sitting at the far end of the sofa was a tidy, rather compact man wearing a tweedy brown sports jacket.

He watched her keenly with pale blue eyes as she identified herself and signed the receptionist's logbook. Then

he got to his feet, smoothing back a rebellious lock of straight blond hair.

"Ms. DiGianni? I'm Sergeant Wegner, Sergeant Gaine's partner. Would you come this way, please?"

Sandy followed him along a side corridor, down a flight of stairs, around a couple of corners and through a plain wooden door into a medium-size classroom equipped with a portable blackboard, easel and overhead projector.

"Have a seat, Miss," Wegner offered with a polite smile. "Sergeant Gaine will be with you in a moment." Sandy nodded vaguely, then suddenly realized that he was on his way out of the room.

"Oh, Sergeant!" she called abruptly. He spun around with a questioning expression on his face. "As Sergeant Gaine's partner, are you investigating the Parmentier case, also?"

"That's right."

Sandy licked her lips and pinned on a smile. "Then will you be coming back, as well . . . to interview me?"

"No, Miss," he said, his pleasant tenor voice tinged with regret. A moment later, the door closed behind him, and she was alone.

Like a prisoner exploring the boundaries of a new cell, Sandy walked around the classroom, studying every stick of furniture, every piece of equipment, every square foot of stark, painted wall. Her restlessness increased with each minute that straggled past—and there were quite a few of them.

Suddenly the door opened behind her.

"I'm sorry to have kept you waiting," he said tersely, impatiently, as though he was the one who'd been cooling his heels, not Sandy.

Dry-mouthed, she forced herself to turn around slowly. Sergeant Gaine was wearing the same suit as yesterday, with a crisp white shirt and a gray tie that looked like silk. From the neck down, he looked cool and businesslike. From the neck up, however... His brows were drawn tightly together, tension whitening the little weathered lines she hadn't noticed before at the corners of his eyes. A storm was brewing in those eyes. Sandy could feel its chill breezes halfway across the room.

She'd been right, she thought with a shiver. Today *was* going to be much worse than yesterday.

Ted saw her chin wobble and immediately felt his resolve do the same. His superiors wouldn't approve of what he was about to do. Ted wasn't altogether sure he approved of it himself. But he had to do something. Since yesterday, for reasons he preferred not to examine too closely, he'd found himself thinking often about this woman's safety and coming again and again to a single conclusion: Alessandra DiGianni mustn't die as Bert Waldron had done.

For a moment he let silence stand between them like a wall of glass. Then he spoke, deliberately sharpening each word and loading it with disdain: "You seem to think that solving murders is some sort of game we play here, Ms. DiGianni. It isn't. It's serious, it's dangerous, and it's not for amateur detectives like you. You also seem to think that having a press card gets you into the game. It doesn't. All it does is turn you into an obstacle and a hazard to the trained personnel carrying on the investigation. You think you're special? Think again. You're one of a thousand scheming reporters in this city, all climbing over one another to get a scoop. You're just another fly on the dung heap, Ms. DiGianni.

"The only difference between you and the rest of them is that they're going to live a lot longer because they know what they're doing," he went on grimly. "You're in way over your head, lady. If you want to play hardball with the big boys, you're going to have to make all the right moves just to stay alive. One mistake, just one, and you end up like your unfortunate colleague, Bert Waldron."

Her spine straightened at the mention of that name. "Are you making a threat, Sergeant?" she demanded.

"Take it as a warning, Ms. DiGianni. An example not to follow."

"You're not going to frighten me off with macho noises!" Her chin was jutting a challenge at him . . . and trembling at the same time.

Ted sighed inwardly.

"Frighten you, Ms. DiGianni?" he echoed wearily, strolling between the desks toward her. "Perish the thought. I said it because it happens to be the truth. Bert Waldron was a seasoned professional with years of experience. You're a rank novice with everything to learn. But you do have a few things in common. Bert played detective; now you're playing detective. Bert was investigating Mr. Vanish; now you've shown an interest in Mr. Vanish. Bert is dead. I want you to think about that."

Think about it? He wanted her to have nightmares about it!

"I want you to think about it," he repeated emphatically before she could recover her balance, "and I want you to do the following: Stop playing detective. Stay away from the Parmentier case. And forget about investigating Mr. Vanish."

All by itself, Sandy's head began to shake no. He was telling her not to do her job; he might as well instruct her to resign from the magazine. She had already accepted philosophically that the Parmentier case was out of bounds for reporters, but rebellion ignited inside her at the very thought of giving up Mr. Vanish.

"As long as I don't interfere with an ongoing police investigation, you can't order me not to make inquiries about someone your own department says does not exist," she informed him.

The gray eyes narrowed. "But what if they've guessed wrong? That would mean there's a ruthless, highly intelligent killer on the loose. As long as there's even a remote possibility of danger, I won't allow a woman to tackle him alone."

"You won't allow?" she repeated incredulously as a storm of indignation swept away all her remaining uncertainty. "Let me tell you something, Sergeant. I've been on my own since I was twenty-one. And like most women, I can handle a heck of a lot more than most men think I can."

He stopped and inhaled deeply before continuing, his chiseled features settling into an even harder mask than before. "All right," he said, "since you're so sure you're up to this, let me tell you what we already know about Mr. Vanish—assuming he exists, of course. The name first came up ten years ago in connection with a rash of execution-style murders in several large cities. Nothing definite, just a lot of unsubstantiated rumor. And in case you're wondering, none of those cases has been solved yet.

"We call him Mr. Vanish because nobody knows what he looks like, or what he's going to look like. The few street people who aren't too terrified to admit that they've heard of him tell us he's a master of disguise. So he can get close to his victim, make the hit at his convenience, and then disappear. And we can't even start looking for him. That's Mr. Vanish's edge, his protection. And a man like that, assuming he exists, would go to any lengths to hang on to it. He would kill anyone who'd witnessed one of his hits, and then go after anyone the witness might have spoken to, just in case.

"Maybe Bert Waldron was one of his victims. Maybe Mr. Vanish knows that you're interested in him, too, Ms. DiGianni. Maybe he's just waiting for you to make another move in his direction so he'll have an excuse to pop you, as well."

Ted saw a flicker of fear cross her face and then fade as her features set with determination. Too late—the seed was planted. He'd wanted to throw a real scare into her, one that would keep her awake at night and glancing over her shoulder during the day, but it appeared he would have to settle for gnawing doubt. Considering how stubborn and independent she was, perhaps doubt would accomplish the same thing—make her think twice about pursuing a story. He could only hope it'd keep her out of risky situations.

"All right, Sergeant—" he heard her sigh "—you've made your point. I'll tread very carefully, and I'll try to keep my fingers out of your pies."

She still wasn't making any concessions. Ted could feel his jaw muscles flex as he replied in as neutral a voice as he could manage, "I'll settle for that now, Ms. DiGianni. But be advised that if I catch you interfering with any police investigation whatsoever, I'll arrest you. And if you continue to endanger your life by hunting for Mr. Vanish, I'm going to treat it as attempted suicide—which happens to be against the law—and arrest you. Do we understand each other?''

Her lips pursed momentarily. "I'm afraid we do, Sergeant. Please don't bother seeing me out." And she spun around abruptly and headed for the door.

Frank Leslie had already gone home for the weekend when she returned to the magazine's editorial department. Good. Sandy dropped her handbag into her desk drawer on the way to Frank's terminal.

Every staff writer was assigned a password to protect his or her work prior to publication. When Bert died, his official password would have been deleted and his work-in-progress reassigned; but Sandy was betting that Bert had put a copy of his secret file under another password, one that nobody else knew about.

Ted Gaine had tried to frighten her out of continuing Bert's investigation; Paul had ordered her to leave it alone. How could a true investigative reporter ignore a double challenge like that?

Then Sandy gasped as it suddenly hit her—Ted Gaine knew that Bert had been investigating Mr. Vanish. Paul swore that he and Bert had kept the file a secret, and yet Sergeant Gaine knew. And if Gaine knew, others might.

With a mounting sense of urgency, Sandy logged on and began trying out passwords: the obvious ones first— anagrams of Bert's name, and VANISH, HITMAN, SECRET—then the less obvious.

PASSWORD NOT FOUND, the computer kept saying.

Finally, with a small, exasperated noise, Sandy swiveled Frank's chair away from the terminal. What if Bert had drawn on some personal memory, some private facet of his life, for the password? Clearly Sandy would have to find out more about him before trying again.

"YOU'RE THINKING ABOUT A MAN."

Her mother's triumphant voice snapped Sandy out of her reverie and brought a guilty flush to her cheeks. "Don't be silly, Mama. I'm not even seeing anyone," she mumbled, and stuffed a forkful of lasagna into her mouth.

"I didn't say you were seeing a man—I said you were thinking about one," her mother pointed out, her words sharpened by a slight remaining Italian accent.

Sandy shrugged defensively, knowing exactly where this conversation was headed. "All right, I was thinking about a man. I think about lots of men. It's no big deal."

"You can't spend your life thinking, *cara*. You don't earn a living by thinking. You don't put a meal on the table by thinking. You don't get a man—"

"Mama!" protested Sandy.

Her mother smiled benignly and sank a fork into her own serving of lasagna. "I read in the paper the other day, there was a stabbing. A young woman, your age, in an apartment building a few blocks away from yours."

Angela DiGianni was several inches shorter than her daughter and generously proportioned. But her mother's figure wasn't the only thing that conformed to Italian tradition.

She had opposed Sandy's decision to move to her own place six years earlier and still refused to let the matter rest. Each time the family got together, as now, her mother would revive the issue with fresh arguments. And Tommy, Sandy's younger brother, would sit as he was sitting now, eyes and ears wide open, glancing bemusedly back and forth like a spectator at a pingpong tournament.

Sandy sighed with exasperation. "She surprised a burglar in her living room and attacked him," she explained to everyone at the table. "It was a foolish thing to do."

"She lived alone. It's dangerous for a woman to live alone in the city, especially in that neighborhood," declared her mother heatedly.

Sandy felt the edges of the fork handle biting into her clenched fingers and forced them to relax. She knew where this argument was going. "I don't want a roommate, Mama."

"And I don't want to read about you in the newspaper!"

With a sigh, Sandy glanced across the table at Uncle Hugo. He sat placidly munching black olives, apparently oblivious to the tension in the air.

Hugo Savarini was her mother's older brother, taller than her mother and with white hair instead of gray. He'd stepped in with financial assistance after her father, Joseph DiGianni, was killed, and always sat at the head of the table whenever they had a family meal. But that was as involved as he was willing to become with the DiGiannis.

The result was that Tommy's adolescence had been stormier than most. Hugo could have made it easier on them all by giving Tommy a strong father figure to measure himself against; instead, he'd reinforced the emotional wall between himself and his nephew and let the boy find his role models elsewhere.

"So, tell us about this man," coaxed Angela.

Sandy shrugged uncomfortably, wondering how much she could safely tell her mother about Ted Gaine. "He's just a police sergeant I've met a couple of times, that's all. I wrote an article about the Parmentier murder, and he was one of the investigating officers on the case. He insisted on talking to me about it."

"He insisted?" echoed her mother, her eyes widening anxiously. "You're not in trouble, are you?"

"No, Mama," Sandy sighed, adding silently, *not yet, anyway.* "It was just standard procedure."

Her mother digested this for a moment, then remarked, to nobody in particular, "A policeman would be a good choice for a roommate."

"Mama..." warned Sandy.

Her face a picture of slandered innocence, her mother slid her chair back and got to her feet. "Alessandra, *per favore*, the dishes?"

This was it, Sandy thought. Her mother only needed help clearing the table when there was something she wanted to discuss in the kitchen. Or to continue to discuss, in the kitchen.

Sandy stood up and began scraping and stacking plates as her mother brought in a huge bowl of fruit for dessert. Noticing Tommy's sullen expression, Sandy could guess what her mother wanted to talk to her about. Lately, most of her Friday evenings had been spent in serious sisterly discussion with her wayward younger brother. He'd made a couple of new friends a few months earlier, two kids named Vito and Dooley, who called themselves "the Knights of the Night," and Mama was certain they would all three go to prison, if they didn't end up in hell first. Sandy had seen Tommy with the Knights a couple of times, had watched from a distance as her brother slipped easily into the swaggering gait and threatening manner of a street hood looking for trouble. She'd scarcely recognized him then. Mama was right to worry, Sandy thought, but without Hugo's involvement there was little either woman could do.

"Okay, Mama, what's wrong?" Sandy sighed, setting down the pile of plates and cutlery on the tiny kitchen counter.

Wordlessly, her mother turned and showed her a blue gift box from Birks Jewellers. Inside, resting on a bed of black velvet, sparkled a gold bracelet set with rubies.

"Tommy gave me this. For all the birthdays he missed." Snapping the case shut, her mother dropped it on the counter as though it had burned her hand. "He has no money, Sandra. I can't give him allowance. In February he was fired from his job after school. How would he buy such a thing?

"I ask him and he looks at me with eyes like stones. But he listens to you. *Per favore, cara,* talk to your brother. Find out what he has done. Please!"

Sandy took a steadying breath and walked back into the living room. Behind her, her mother was making a nervous clatter with the cutlery. Twilight was sifting into the little apartment through the yellowing slats of the venetian blinds, along with the reassuring growl of traffic from the street below. The smell of tomatoes and spices still hung in the air, or perhaps in the eight years that her mother and Tommy had been living here the delicious cooking aromas had permeated the walls and furniture.

Tommy had wedged himself into a corner of the sofa and was reading a car magazine. It was hard to believe he was seventeen already, and in his final year of high school. But Sandy could see the dark shadow of whiskers on his lower jaw, and his shoulders and chest were filling out. When Tommy stood up, he was inches taller than his sister. He wouldn't be a boy much longer. Would she still be able to get through to him when he was a man?

Or would he interpret her interest in his life as unwarranted interference and throw it right back in her face?

Suddenly Sandy felt a sharp cramp deep in her stomach. For the first time in her life, she had indigestion from her mother's lasagna.

Chapter Three

The next day, Sandy trotted down the steps of her duplex, emerging from the cool shadow of the entrance-
way into the cheerful warmth of a summer morning. She
flinched and pressed her sunglasses firmly up the bridge
of her nose, then began walking purposefully toward the
bus stop at the corner.

The discussion with Tommy the previous evening had
been strained and futile; and now, after her second
sleepless night in a row, her senses felt bruised. Her eye-
balls ached, and her tongue tasted like cotton wool
dipped in vinegar. Normally she would be back in her
apartment, in her pajamas, with the color comics on her
lap and a cup of espresso within easy reach. Instead, she
had thrown on a pair of blue cotton slacks and a seer-
sucker shirt and was on her way to the Lucky Shot Video
Arcade to have a serious talk with its manager, Uncle
Hugo.

A fresh breeze stroked her face, and as she lifted her
head to enjoy the unexpected coolness, Sandy noticed the
man standing at the bus stop across the road. He was
average-looking, wearing a casual denim suit and a Blue
Jays baseball cap, and he was staring at her with almost
mesmerizing intensity. No, she decided, trying to ignore

a sudden sensation crawling just under her skin, staring wasn't the right word. He was studying her, with emotionless eyes, like a scientist examining a specimen ... or a collector about to capture one. All at once alarm bells were going off inside Sandy's head, and she knew that she didn't want to cross the road, didn't want to ride the bus with that man, whoever he was.

Eglinton Avenue stretched between them and the light was still red. Sandy veered left across Bayview and strode briskly toward Yonge Street, still feeling the pressure of those eyes between her shoulder blades. Was he following her? Did she dare turn around to look? She quickened her pace, nearly breaking into a jog.

Storefronts were barely noticed blurs, pedestrians became flashes of cloth and costume jewelry as Sandy passed them. At least she wasn't alone on the street. If he *was* following her, if he caught up to her before she reached Yonge Street, there would be witnesses.

Dio, she had to know. As she passed a china shop, she halted abruptly, as though her attention had been snagged by something in the display window, then cast a cautious glance sideways.

He wasn't there. She turned and looked across Eglinton and didn't see him on the north side of the street, either. But he was watching her. She could feel the ghostly touch of his gaze on the margins of her awareness, could feel the hair at the nape of her neck lifting as she turned and resumed walking toward the subway station.

Somebody was following her. Earlier, Sandy had dismissed Sergeant Gaine's warnings, figuring they were just a ploy to frighten her into cooperating, but now she wasn't so sure. What if he was right? What if she'd become a target for murder? *Dio,* what if Mr. Vanish himself was stalking her? Just a couple of blocks from Yonge Street, she increased her speed, fighting not to break into a run.

At last, Sandy spotted the maroon-and-gold subway sign ahead of her; and in that instant, the swelling bubble of unease burst inside her head, showering her thoughts with tiny icicles of fear. She bolted for safety, sprinted through the entrance, paused only briefly to fumble in her handbag for her pass. Prancing impatiently, she waited for two other people to pass the ticket-taker's booth ahead of her, hearing the long screeching hiss of a train pulling into the station below and praying it was a northbounder she was missing. At last she was through the turnstile and racing down the wide terrazzoed stairs toward the platform.

Sandy pulled up short. The southbound side of the platform was empty, and a red light showed beside the outbound tunnel. She'd just missed her train. There wouldn't be another one for three minutes. Uneasily, she glanced behind her at the scattered groups of people waiting for the northbound train. They stood chattering amongst themselves, hardly paying any attention to her at all.

A bus had unloaded at the terminal overhead. People began trickling onto the platform in twos and threes, some of them coming to stand on the southbound side of the platform.

Suddenly Sandy noticed a Blue Jays cap bobbing at the far end of the subway platform, and a tentacle of anxiety seemed to wrap itself around her throat, cutting off her next breath. Had he seen her? Her heart pounding, she sidled past a couple of teenaged girls sharing a radio headset and put a heavy tiled post between herself and the man in the Blue Jays cap. If he'd seen her, of course, it was useless to hide. However...

She spent the next half hour ducking around corners, deliberately mingling with crowds and fighting down a swelling wave of panic as her invisible pursuer followed her down stairs and up escalators, through tunnels and turnstiles and revolving doors, onto the railway platforms, into the brocaded satin lobby of the Royal Hotel, down the long corridor to the GO Bus Terminal and back. She merged with groups of travelers, using them as cover while she darted into cross-corridors and public washrooms.

At last, the moment came when Sandy knew he was gone. No elusive shadow tickled the edge of her peripheral vision; no more unseen eyes exerted their phantom pressure from hidden corners of the station. She'd either lost him or regained her grip on reality—she didn't know which, nor at the moment did she care.

Standing at the hub of Union Station, grazed and jostled by the unending stampede of busy people in transit, Sandy drew in a long breath and felt relief and purpose flow like a cool, swift-running stream into every part of her. The best defence was a good offence. If she had become a target, then it was time to catch a northbound train back to the magazine office. Time to locate Bert's file and do some pursuing of her own.

Shortly before eleven o'clock, Sandy hauled open the heavy glass door to Editorial, noting with some satisfaction the three rows of empty desks. She'd been hoping she would be alone here today.

Dropping her purse into her lower desk drawer, she kicked it closed and sat down in front of Frank Leslie's computer terminal.

She had made a couple of phone calls yesterday after lunch. On the pretext of gathering information for a special memorial article for the magazine, she had contacted Bert Waldron's grown daughter, Anne; and then, at Anne's urging, she had phoned an old camping buddy of Bert's and chatted with him for twenty minutes.

Thus armed with a list of her late colleague's achievements and pastimes, Sandy now logged onto the computer and began trying passwords: CESSNA, MUSKIE, YAMAHA, CARIBOU....

This could take her a long, long time, Sandy realized as she got up an hour later to stretch her legs. Bert had been a "man's man," interested in virtually any activity that had an element of danger to it—auto racing, motocross, big-game hunting, skydiving, even private investigating. It boggled the mind to think of all the six-, seven- and eight-letter words from which Bert could have selected his password.

And Sandy now knew, from the research she had done on him, that Bert must have selected one. A man as accustomed as he was to calculated risk-taking would have realized when opening a file on Mr. Vanish that there was a possibility the hit man might get to him first, that a successor might have to conclude the investigation for him. Therefore, he would have ensured that a copy of his file survived him, by hiding it where only another investigative crime reporter, a fellow *Police Digest* staffer, could find it—deep inside the magazine's computer system.

Trying to rub some of the tension out of her neck muscles, Sandy wandered over to the bulletin board beside the glass doors. People who had loaned photographs to the memorial collage had begun reclaiming them, she noticed, leaving spaces, and in some cases revealing details in other pictures that had been covered over before. Suddenly one of those details seemed to leap off the bulletin board at her—a hand-hewn wooden sign in the bottom half of a snapshot of Bert in front of someone's cottage. The sign read Hideaway.

Sandy stared at the photo for a long moment, hardly daring to make the connection. The file was in a sort of hideaway, wasn't it? And here was evidence of one of Bert's personal memories. What passwords might it yield?

Racing back to Frank's terminal, she began word associating. It was a COTTAGE, of course. Where? MUSKOKA, maybe? Or HALIBURTON—no, too many letters. He probably went there on the WEEKEND, or for a month in the SUMMER, to ROUGH IT for a while. The place had a name, HIDEAWAY—too obvious. What kinds of hideaways were there? she wondered.

Immediately, the song from *Damn Yankees* popped into her head, and on impulse she keyed in HERNANDO.

PASSWORD ACCEPTED, said the computer.

For a stunned moment, Sandy just sat and stared at the directory that came up on the screen. Then the enormity of her accomplishment sank in and she had to clap a hand to her mouth to muffle her joyful shriek.

She'd found Bert's file! *She'd found the file on Mr. Vanish!*

And it was huge. She had to scroll upward twice to read all the subfile names. The first batch seemed to be lists: CASE.LST; WEAPON.LST; SCENE.LST; SUSPEC.LST; SOURCE.LST. Then followed at least a dozen more that ended with the extension code .POL—possibly summaries of police investigations. Sandy scanned for a name she might recognize and found it almost immediately: PARMEN.POL. The Parmentier case.

So Bert had suspected a connection between the councilman's slaying and Mr. Vanish? Interesting. The Parmentier case was Ted Gaine's investigation. If Bert had made a nuisance of himself while pursuing the connection with Mr. Vanish, that could explain Gaine's negative attitude toward reporters.

It occurred to Sandy as she stared at the long rows of subfiles that there was an enormous amount of information here, representing years of patient investigation. It would be foolhardy to attempt to digest it all by just reading it off the screen. She needed to print out the entire file and take it home for close study. Perhaps tomorrow, when Production only ran a half shift and she wouldn't have to worry about Paul finding out.

Her attention kept snagging on one subfile, the shortest one on the list, with a name that told her absolutely nothing about its contents. Sandy glanced around the room once more. She was still alone, and there was certainly time for a quick peek, a preview.

Rapidly she typed in the command to display the contents of COMP1.XXX, and the screen cleared itself and showed her:

DAVE RAGUSZ
DRAGNET
DUNDAS AT OSSINGTON
APPROACH WITH CAUTION

Puzzles within puzzles, thought Sandy, bemused, as she exited the subfile and then, reluctantly, exited from HERNANDO. Tomorrow she would read the rest of the file, she promised herself. Tomorrow everything would come clear. For now, she might as well get to work revising her second article for that Monday deadline.

Two hours and five paragraphs later, Sandy leaned back in her chair, groaning with frustration. Her imagination was in overdrive now, and the last thing it wanted to bother with was the properties of the poison Eliza Marchand had bought at the apothecary shop in Brewster's Mill.

If she didn't satisfy at least part of her curiosity about Dragnet, this article would never get written. Reluctantly Sandy exited her file and logged off.

Dio, rose gardening and furniture antiquing had never affected her like this!

DRAGNET TURNED OUT TO BE a smallish store with an opaqued front window on the old but still proud south side of Dundas Street, just east of Ossington Avenue. Whoever ran Dragnet hadn't wanted it to be found easily—the only sign on the weatherbeaten brick building was an unevenly cut rectangle of cardboard, with the single word hastily scribbled on it in felt marker, taped at eye level to the inside of a new aluminum screen door.

More puzzles. She'd come here to satisfy herself that there really was a Dragnet at this intersection; she'd fully intended to turn around and go straight home afterward. But now that she was standing just a few short steps from the door... She had to begin the investigation somewhere, didn't she?

Sandy stood on the sidewalk for a moment, considering how to approach Dragnet. The name Dave Ragusz possibly referred to a contact, whom she might or might not find inside the store. The subfile had advised caution; maybe Dragnet was just a rendezvous point or a message drop, and only Bert and this Ragusz were supposed to know about it.

What would be the best way to find out? she wondered. Probably go inside the store, browse a bit, then engage the clerk in a few minutes of idle chatter, casually dropping the name Ragusz into the conversation to see whether it meant anything to him.

That didn't sound so hard. In and out in a few minutes. Even a totally green rookie ought to be able to handle that, thought Sandy.

She pulled open the screen door, gripped the worn brass knob on the inner door and turned. It was locked.

Frowning, she glanced at her watch. It was just three-thirty, too late for lunch and too early for the store to be closed on a Saturday. Suddenly she realized that there were noises filtering through the door. She stood quietly for a moment and listened. They were electronic sounds, like those at an arcade. And interspersed with the dinging and buzzing was the sound of a man's voice: "C'mon, c'mon, okay, you sucker, now! Gotcha!"

Sandy looked around for a doorbell and, finding none, knocked loudly. The electronic chattering inside stopped. Heavy footsteps approached the door. Not until it swung open, revealing a darkly scowling man built like a bear, did it dawn on her that there might have been other reasons for Bert to warn a successor to "approach with caution."

"Yeah?" growled the man standing in the doorway. He was Sandy's height, maybe an inch or two taller, with dark hair curling around his ears, bulging arm and shoulder muscles beneath a tight, cropped T-shirt, and a well-nourished beer belly. And he looked thoroughly annoyed at having been dragged away from his game.

If Sandy had been holding a sales sample at that moment, she would have thrust it behind her back. She searched her mind for a lie that would excuse both her and the interruption without further angering him, but came up blank. So, she blurted out the truth: "I'm looking for Dave Ragusz."

"I'm Ragusz," he said, pronouncing it Rag-OOSH. Dark eyes scanned her up and down, registering approval. "Come on inside."

Mentally reviewing everything she'd ever learned about self-defense, Sandy followed him hesitantly into the store, only to find herself in the middle of a room that resembled a warehouse. From floor to ceiling and wall to wall, she saw nothing but stacks of cardboard boxes, all stamped with shipping numbers and foreign-sounding brand names. It even smelled like a warehouse—dust mingled with the aromas of sweat and stale coffee.

"What can I do for you today?" he asked, grinning to reveal a mouthful of yellow-stained teeth.

It was too late to plead mistaken identity, but Sandy could still "approach with caution." Her mind racing, she smiled in what she hoped was a disarming manner. "Hi," she began, "I'm a friend of Bert Waldron's. I understand you knew him."

Ragusz frowned. "Knew him? Not really. Why?"

"Why?" she repeated, her nervous confusion only half-feigned. "Oh, I was . . . given a list of people to interview for a memorial article about Bert, and your name was on the list. It must have been a mistake," she added with a helpless shrug, then took a cautious step back toward the door. If he didn't notice, she would take another one. And another one. Through the door and onto the street.

"Wait a minute," barked Ragusz, his pointing finger riveting her to the floor. "A memorial article? That means you've gotta be with *Police Digest*."

Dumbly, she nodded.

"So, you work for *Police Digest*." He strolled around her, slowly sizing her up all over again. "Rudd's never hired a woman before. I guess you must be pretty special."

The leering emphasis he placed on the final word made Sandy's skin crawl. "Look, I'm really sorry I wasted your..." The last word died in her throat. Ragusz was now standing between her and the door, his beefy arms folded across his chest.

Sandy went clammy all over. *Dio,* what had she gotten herself into?

"Did you work with Bert Waldron?" he asked quietly.

"Not with him, exactly," she admitted uncomfortably. "I was hired to replace him."

Ragusz cocked his head, eyeing her narrowly while he evidently considered this. Sandy's pulse grew very loud in her ears. Then, several eternities later, he finally shrugged and dropped his arms to his sides.

"Okay, Miss...?"

"DiGianni," she supplied.

"Miss DiGianni. Let's quit snowing each other. Your editor didn't give you my name for any memorial article. And maybe I did know Bert Waldron a little better than I said. So why are you really here?"

Sandy didn't realize she'd been holding her breath until it hissed out in a long sigh of relief. "I wanted to find out what your connection was to Bert."

A pause, then, "What made you think there was a connection between us?"

"Your name...was on a piece of paper I found in Bert's desk," she lied.

"I see," he said. "Well, Miss DiGianni, Bert and I did a little business occasionally."

"And what kind of business would that be, Mr. Ragusz?"

He impaled her with another long stare. "Show me your press ID," he said at last.

Obediently, she pulled the laminated card out of her handbag for him.

"Okay, I guess you're legit." He gestured toward the dim rear of the warehouse. "Come into the back room and I'll show you."

Sandy followed him between the stacks of cartons and through a doorway into a large, blessedly air-conditioned room lined with electronic equipment, with radios and televisions and video-game systems and computer gear, all out of their cartons, warmed up and ready to be used. She gazed around her, wide-eyed and slack-jawed, at what had to be a half million dollars worth of electronics.

Unless Ragusz had rearranged things to suit a clientele who preferred entering by the back door, Dragnet was clearly not a store.

He dropped into a chair in front of one of the computer screens. "Okay," he said briskly. "I am what large institutions and corporations sneeringly refer to as a hacker. You are familiar with the term?"

"Of course," she retorted. "It means you break into their computer systems and steal or rearrange their data."

"Wrong. Only a kid or a rank amateur would actually tamper with the information. I simply gain access to it as quietly and unobtrusively as possible. Then, for someone like Bert Waldron, who's one of the good guys and has the right amount of cash, I copy certain information that can't be obtained any other way—as long as it isn't government-classified. Hey," he said in answer to her skeptical stare, "I'm a loyal citizen. Even a hacker can have principles, y'know."

"When was the last time you saw Bert?"

"Two, maybe three years ago," he replied with a shrug.

An icy finger began stroking Sandy's spine. *Approach with caution.* Bert had dropped Ragusz in favor of other sources of information, and then had placed that warning in his file for his successor. Obviously Dragnet wasn't the safest place for a reporter on the trail of Mr. Vanish.

"Well, thank you, Mr. Ragusz. I appreciate your talking to me."

"Any time, Miss DiGianni," he said, grinning as he escorted her to the front door. "Any time you need me, you know where I am." He watched her leave, appreciating the graceful sway of her hips. Then he relocked the door, returned to his back room and pulled a cellular phone out of a small cupboard. He punched up a number from memory, counting three and a half rings before a man's voice answered.

"This is Ragusz, down at Dragnet. A girl was just here, wanting to know about Bert Waldron. Yeah, that was her name—DiGianni. I *thought* you'd be interested...."

TRAVELING FROM DUNDAS and Ossington to Sandy's apartment near Eglinton and Bayview should have taken just under three-quarters of an hour by streetcar, subway and bus; today it took her an hour, and she spent the entire sixty minutes brooding over the terrible mistake she had made that afternoon by going to Dragnet.

Well, at least she hadn't said anything about Bert's file, she consoled herself. Perhaps the situation could still be salvaged if she just avoided Ragusz and took every possible precaution.

Preoccupied, she stepped off the Eglinton bus and strode quickly down the street and into her building, one of a row of narrow old stone houses that had been renovated inside and divided into two apartments.

Sandy lived in the upstairs one. As the front door closed behind her, she glanced up automatically toward the landing—and froze.

Sergeant Gaine was standing at the top of the stairs, his hard gray eyes trained disapprovingly on her face.

"I've warned you twice now, Ms. DiGianni," he said.

Sandy relaxed with a faint groan. Wasn't this just what she needed to put the icing on her day?

As she climbed the stairs, digging her key out of her handbag, she noticed that even Sergeant Gaine had shed his impeccable gray suit in favor of blue jeans today, and a baseball cap, white and navy, with a Toronto Police crest sewn onto its front panel. He was probably off duty—but still not off her case, she observed wearily.

"Stop worrying, Sergeant," she sighed as she passed him on her way to the door. "I haven't been playing detective."

"Then what were you doing at Dragnet this afternoon?"

Bending to put her key into the lock, she glanced up, startled. "How did you know I was there?"

"I know when you arrived, I know when you left, and I know what was said in between. Writers aren't the only ones with sources, Ms. DiGianni."

"Obviously not," she agreed, managing to keep her voice low pitched and level as she pushed in the key and gave it a vicious twist. "However, if you really do know what we discussed this afternoon, then you're aware it had nothing to do with the Parmentier case, or any on-going police investigation, or Mr. Vanish. So just what the hell do you want from me, Sergeant?"

Gaine's expression hardened to stone. "I think we'd better continue this conversation inside," he said, nodding curtly toward her door.

Sandy whirled angrily and preceded him into the apartment.

Ted paused in the doorway, sweeping a policeman's trained eye over what he could see from the entrance. The apartment was small, but tidy and cheerful, too. The walls were pale gold, fading to tan in the section of kitchen that was visible from the front door. In the living room, Ted saw no sofa, just a pair of orange wicker love seats facing each other across a wicker-and-glass coffee table on a rust-colored carpet. And everywhere he looked, there was green: potted plants lined the windowsills, decorated the coffee table and lamp stands, even hung from the ceiling in the corners of the room. Thriving, carefully tended plants, he amended on closer inspection. She obviously took a lot of care with them.

Just like Carol. Ted felt something tighten inside his chest as he recalled his ex-wife's singular passion for anything that bloomed. In the two years before their divorce, it had been the only passion he'd seen in her.

Did Alessandra talk to her plants, too? he wondered, yielding momentarily to his personal interest in her. Did she call them her babies? Give them names? Leave the radio on for them during the day when she wasn't home?

Suddenly he realized there were no blossoms on any of Alessandra's plants. All green, the hanging plants overflowed their pots and sprawled in skinny fronds halfway to the floor. A few of the others were succulents—one resembled a prickly pear wrapped in spider silk—but mostly they were tidy arrangements of varicolored leaves.

What had the psychology professor told him? Something about people preferring leaves to flowers because they hated to see petals fall....

Alessandra stood pale and taut on the other side of the living room. "I believe you had some questions for me, Sergeant," she reminded him stiffly, making no move to sit down or offer him a seat.

Ted turned his back on her boisterous greenery and thrust it—and Carol—firmly out of his mind. "What made you decide to visit Dragnet, Ms. DiGianni?"

"The truth is I was curious," she replied. "What made you decide to ask me about it?"

She was on her own turf now and it showed, Ted noted. She met his eyes more directly today, and there was a confidence in her voice he hadn't heard before. For her own good, he would have to toughen his approach to overcome it.

"Because I happen to know that there's only one way you could have found out about Dragnet," he told her, frowning. "But even if it was a coincidence, you gave away your source when you asked Ragusz about his connection with Bert Waldron."

Encouraged by the stunned expression on Alessandra's face, Ted went on, "Bert kept a file on Mr. Vanish. It went missing shortly after he died, but I was certain it would turn up again. So I kept in touch with some of Bert's confidential contacts, in case some bright reporter with a lot of curiosity came calling on them."

"Contacts—like Dave Ragusz," she murmured faintly, comprehension dawning.

"First the Parmentier file and now this. You do have a knack, Alessandra," he said, shaking his head. "And you do have Bert's file, don't you?"

Uneasily, she nodded.

"Does Rudd know?"

Sandy shook her head.

"Have you told anyone else? Spoken to any other of Bert's contacts?"

She took a step backward, disquieted by the intensity she heard in his voice. "No."

"Perfect," he said, half to himself. "I don't suppose you'd be willing to turn the file over to Homicide? Didn't think so," he concluded as her chin reflexively assumed a defiant angle. "In that case, there's only one thing to do, Alessandra."

When had he begun using her first name? she wondered, as he crossed the room, halting only two feet away from her.

"You're not to discuss that file or its contents with anyone but me," he told her sternly.

It took a moment for his words to register. "What?"

"Since you're committed to this investigation, we're going to work on it together," he told her. "Don't fight me on this, Alessandra. Keep in mind that having Bert's file gives you a better than even chance to prove Mr. Vanish exists. And having me for a partner gives you a better than even chance of surviving the experience."

"But yesterday you said—"

"Yesterday I didn't know you had the file," he told her bluntly.

"I see. And if I refuse your kind offer?"

"Then I'll be forced to arrest you for withholding important evidence in the Parmentier case. That I can do. Take your choice, Alessandra."

"That's not a choice—it's an ultimatum," she protested.

His granite gaze didn't waver. "Take it or leave it, Ms. DiGianni."

Her stomach clenching like a fist around three days' worth of swallowed anger, Sandy returned Gaine's unyielding stare. This partnership he was talking about would be anything but equal, she was certain; for she'd met Ted Gaine's type before—had even dated a couple of them. He was a man who wouldn't rest until he had full control—of the situation and of her.

And then common sense cut in with a reminder that Ted Gaine was already in control. He'd given her two choices: let him direct her investigation, or go to jail. With a despairing sigh, Sandy picked the less unacceptable alternative.

"All right, you damned chauvinist," she muttered, turning her back on an unmistakable snort of male laughter.

"You know, we really ought to sit down and discuss how to go about this," he suggested after a moment's silence. "Maybe over dinner. How about it, Alessandra? Are you hungry?"

Discuss how to go about it? Who did he think he was kidding? Sandy pivoted with an angry retort on her lips, but her stomach rumbled a complaint before she could say a word.

"I guess you are," said Gaine, and suddenly Sandy found herself gazing into an open, smiling, incredibly appealing face. This was a Ted Gaine she'd never seen before. He had a dimple in his right cheek, and his mustache tilted rakishly atop a lopsided grin; and all at once her heart seemed to be pounding its way up her throat and she had to swallow hard to force it back down.

"I'm ravenous," she told him, realizing as the words came out that it was the truth. She hadn't bothered eating lunch that day.

They settled on seafood. Forty minutes later, Sergeant Gaine was sitting across a Formica-topped table from Sandy, doing his best to ignore the toddler in the next booth who kept leaning over the back of her high chair to flirt with him. Involuntarily Sandy smiled; and the little girl, encouraged, redoubled her efforts.

"You're sure you don't want anything else?" he asked, for the third time.

Their waitress was visibly impatient now. Sandy just shook her head. He'd already talked her into ordering chowder, salad and three kinds of shrimp, plus a pot of orange pekoe tea. Hungry or not, after a meal like that she would be lucky not to waddle out the door of the restaurant.

As the waitress spun away—busy wasn't the word for the Dockside restaurant on a Saturday night—Gaine glanced around cautiously, then leaned forward on his elbows.

"Bert was a thorough professional," he told Sandy in a voice she had to tilt her head forward to hear, "and I know he was close to wrapping up the case when he died. If you're in possession of all his notes, then you probably have enough leads to conclude the investigation. But I don't want you doing anything by yourself. For your own safety, we're going to follow up those leads together."

Reflexive indignation jerked her erect in her seat. Not do *anything* by herself?

"It'll have to be during my off-duty hours, of course," he went on, completely ignoring her reaction. "Officially Mr. Vanish doesn't exist, and the Department takes a dim view of detectives who chase phantoms while on duty. I'll try to make my free time correspond to yours as much as possible."

It did make a kind of sense, she reluctantly conceded. She had her own full-time job to do, too—and Paul wouldn't exactly be thrilled to discover she was ignoring his edict and pursuing the investigation, after all. But not do *anything*? And just how did he expect to prevent her? she wondered rebelliously.

"There'll be three stages to this investigation," Gaine continued. "Studying the printouts, interviewing possible leads and gathering physical evidence. We'll have to be especially careful after stage one—Bert was conducting interviews when he was killed, so it's a safe bet that one of his leads points directly to Mr. Vanish."

Sandy eyed Gaine narrowly. He seemed to know a great deal about Bert's "secret" investigation. And he'd known about her visit to Dragnet—from Ragusz. And he'd been very pleased when she'd told him that nobody, not even her editor, knew she had the file. As pieces began falling into place, she felt her throat turn into a desert. Was that why Bert had stopped using the hacker, because he'd found out Ragusz was passing information along to Gaine? When she read the printout of Bert's file, would she also find a subfile on Detective Sergeant Ted Gaine, urging that she APPROACH WITH EXTREME CAUTION? *Dio,* it was much too late for that—!

Just then the waitress arrived and set steaming bowls of chowder in front of them. Gaine began stirring bits of clam and potato through the creamy soup; distractedly Sandy did the same. It was odd, she thought, how they called it "cold feet," as though that was the only part that went icy when you suddenly realized you'd made a terrible, possibly fatal, mistake....

"What's the matter, Alessandra?"

Startled, Sandy glanced up into Ted Gaine's concerned face. "Oh...I... Nothing, I just..." Swallowing a dry lump of fear, she decided to plunge ahead. "I was just wondering how you happened to know so much about Bert's investigation."

Gaine paused thoughtfully, then, "No one was supposed to know about this—and it's still just between you and me," he warned, "but Bert consulted with me, unofficially. He was a good investigator, but he realized that Mr. Vanish was going to be...a different kind of case. So he approached me for support, and I helped him out whenever I could."

Wondering just how much Sergeant Gaine knew about Bert's past, Sandy leaned forward tensely. "When you say Bert was an investigator, do you mean...?"

"He was a licensed private investigator before he got into crime writing. That's how we originally met."

The wave of relief that swept through her then was so exhilarating that Sandy almost laughed out loud. "So you were old friends," she said.

"More like old business acquaintances. Bert came to me because he knew he could trust me."

"And did he show you what was in his file?"

Gaine swallowed a mouthful of chowder before replying, "Some of it. I knew that there *was* a file, and that it supposedly disappeared shortly after he was killed. And knowing Bert," he added wryly, "I also knew I could count on its eventually reappearing in the hands of another intrepid reporter. And when it surfaced, wherever it surfaced, I knew I would have to offer my assistance."

Involuntarily Sandy stiffened. "Is that what you were doing back at my apartment when you threatened to throw me in jail if I didn't cooperate? Offering your assistance?"

He paused with his spoon halfway to his mouth, his brows drawing together with displeasure. "Keep your voice down, Alessandra. If you're upset because you think I've arbitrarily taken over your investigation, then let's get something straight right now. Bert was a seasoned veteran, well able to take care of himself. I occasionally rendered assistance to him—I didn't worry about protecting him. I was wrong—he's dead. I'm not going to make that mistake again.

"I happen to think Mr. Vanish does exist and that he poses a threat to anyone attempting to unmask him. Therefore, we are going to retrace Bert's steps—together—and I am going to watch over you the whole time like a mama bear with a cub. With luck, we'll both come out of this alive. Now, if you don't mind, I'd like to finish my chowder before it gets cold."

Her cheeks warming with embarrassment, Sandy turned her attention to her bowl, as well, glad to have something to look at besides Sergeant Gaine's handsome but annoyed face.

When the silence between them had grown too heavy to bear, she broke it. "I'm sorry, Sergeant," she said with a sigh, hating herself for being the one to bend.

Gaine glanced up, his lips quirking at the corners. "Finish your soup, Alessandra. We have a lot more to discuss."

IT WAS TIME TO ASSEMBLE some props. He waited in the shrubbery beside the house, listening as the back door opened and closed, as the garage doors were swung wide, as the doors of a silver-blue BMW clicked twice each and a second later the well-tuned engine purred to life.

Standing in the lengthening shadows, he watched the road in front of the house as the car glided down the laneway, silently made the turn and disappeared down the street.

He pulled on a pair of surgical gloves, counting off thirty seconds in his head. Then he strolled casually toward the rear of the house, one hand searching his pants pocket for the keys he'd made last August.

The back door opened without a sound. He paused in the rear hallway just long enough to slip off his shoes before making for the security alarm switch concealed in the front-hall closet. Then he pocketed the keys and walked through the darkened house to the study.

Here he could switch on a light. The electric typewriter was standing, uncovered, on the huge walnut desktop. Carefully he reached inside the machine and took out the metal sphere with all the letters and numbers in raised relief. He found the letter *a* on the ball, pulled a jeweler's screwdriver from his pocket and pressed a dent into the loop of the letter. Then he replaced the sphere in the typewriter, searched desk drawers until he'd found a piece of paper, and sat down to type, "I'm sorry. I killed Lou and Roger. I shamed my family. Now I can't live with the guilt. May God forgive me."

He reread the note and smiled. He pulled it out of the typewriter and carefully filed the sheet of paper in one of the hanging files in a lower desk drawer—S, for suicide note. A nice touch, he thought.

Then he opened the middle desk drawer and took out the gun he'd seen on an earlier visit. It was a .38 caliber Webley revolver, exactly the same model he'd used on Parmentier, and it was loaded. Perfect. He slipped the gun into his waistband under his jacket and put everything else back the way he'd found it. Then he stepped into his shoes, let himself out the back door and went for a stroll through the park, toward the subway station.

That wasn't the way he usually acquired his murder weapon. Usually he bought it in pieces from pawnbrokers all over the city and put it together himself just before the hit. Then he disposed of the gun the same way he'd gotten it—in pieces, all over the city. It was his standard procedure. He'd assembled, used and gotten rid of guns more times then he cared to remember, and not a single murder weapon had been found, let alone traced back to him.

But this time would be different. This time he wanted the weapon to be clearly traceable, from Lou Parmentier's body to the lifeless hand of a "suicide" with a grafted-on guilty conscience. It was, thought Mr. Vanish with a smile, a ferociously apt solution to an annoying problem.

THE CONVERSATION WAS SPORADIC as they drove back to Sandy's building. All the main streets were clogged with traffic on Saturday nights, so Gaine took an alternate route, along narrow side roads where the light of widely spaced street lamps spilled through oak and maple boughs, dappling the pavement. Away from the hustle and neon of Yonge Street, it was more difficult to make small talk. The darkness was so pristine here, and the silence felt too precious to break with superficial chatter.

Over dinner they had hammered out the details of their partnership. Sandy had never dickered so hard in her life. The printout of the file, it was decided after a harshly whispered battle, would remain with her, as long as she withheld none of its contents from Sergeant Gaine. And he had to be informed immediately of any conclusions she reached independently that were based on the information in the file. They would interview all leads together, examine all evidence together and present their findings to the Chief of Police together, assuming there were findings and they were both alive to present them.

Once everything had been settled, they had toasted the agreement with ice water and sealed it with a solemn but perfunctory handshake. And then they had run out of things to talk about. Things that mattered, anyway, Sandy amended. Things that she was willing to reveal about herself to a man she didn't really know—but was wishing she could get to know better.

At last the dark green sedan pulled to a stop at the curb in front of her duplex.

"Thanks for the dinner, Sergeant," she said, as they both got out of the car.

"My pleasure, Ms. DiGianni," he replied formally, accompanying her inside and up the stairs to her apartment door. As she groped in her handbag for the key, he added with forced casualness, "It will certainly be interesting working together."

Yes, it would be...a brand-new experience, she thought. Just as she was getting used to having him for an adversary, they'd become allies. Sergeant Gaine couldn't have chosen a better strategy for keeping her off balance.

At last she felt her fingers close on metal. She pulled the key out of her purse, then inserted it—and the unlatched door swung open on its own.

Sandy gasped. She had left the living-room lamp turned on for security. The first thing revealed was dirt strewn all over her furniture and carpet.

Instantly she realized where the loamy soil had come from. "*Dio,* my plants!" she wailed. Sandy dropped her purse beside the telephone and rushed to rescue the up-rooted greenery near the windowsill.

"Don't touch those!" barked Sergeant Gaine, stopping her in her tracks. "There'll be fingerprints all over them."

"But they'll die if I don't repot them," she protested indignantly.

He didn't hear her. He was already on the phone to the Burglary Squad, using a handkerchief to protect any fingerprints that might be on the receiver. Fine, that was how she would save her plants, Sandy decided, and she ran to the kitchen to fetch some tissues and paper toweling.

One step into the room, she froze. The kitchen had been ransacked. Every drawer had been pulled out and emptied onto the floor. Cupboards were left open, their contents stirred and scattered as though by miniature tornadoes. Even the fridge had been pulled away from the wall.

"Check all the rooms," growled Sergeant Gaine behind her. "Don't touch anything, just look around to see what's missing."

Grimly, Sandy marched through her apartment from one devastated room to the next, taking mental inventory. Her radio, her jewelry, the money she kept in an empty relish jar in the kitchen—all had been left alone. But in the bedroom she found her photo albums lying open on the bed, their padded covers slit open. All the snapshots had been removed form their mountings and scattered around the room.

The intruder had come through the bedroom window; a pie-shaped piece of glass had been neatly removed from one corner of the pane. Sandy shivered and hugged her shoulders, feeling a sudden chill.

"Well?" Gaine prodded, only a pace or two behind her.

Reluctantly, she shook her head and said in a choked voice, "I can't see anything missing. Maybe a photograph..."

Gaine swore under his breath. "I was afraid this would happen. Whoever broke in here wasn't a thief, Alessandra. He was looking for something. Maybe he was looking for you. Just imagine what would have happened if you'd been home."

The chill seeped into her bones, making her teeth chatter. Gaine reached out for her, but Sandy evaded him and returned to the living room, still hugging her shoulders, not wanting the touch of any hand but her own. She felt violated, and blinked back tears as she surveyed her ruined plants once again.

Gaine had followed her and now stood quietly to one side, watching her. "I've been telling you since Thursday that you were in danger, Alessandra."

"Are you saying Mr. Vanish did this?" she asked dully.

He was silent for a moment. "No, I don't think Mr. Vanish would operate this way. But some other criminal might. Someone who thinks you have evidence against him—Lou Parmentier's killer, maybe. Or whoever murdered Lucas James. You printed enough facts in that article to suggest you did. It'd be a small matter to find out who was actually behind the article, and then get your address."

Sandy's temples began to throb, making her wish she had put some headache tablets into her handbag earlier. She couldn't go looking for them now; her bathroom was part of the scene of a crime and mustn't be disturbed.

Suddenly there was a strong arm around her shoulders, gently urging her toward the door while a honey-smooth voice murmured into her ear, "You look ready to collapse. Let's go wait for the Burglary Squad outside."

Nodding, she relaxed gratefully into the curve of his arm, resting her cheek against the front of his shirt, feeling strong muscles flex and play beneath the fabric as he adjusted his stance to support her. It felt so reassuring to be able to lean against him like this, to share his strength when her own failed her. She hadn't been held this way in so long, she thought with a sigh.

As Alessandra snuggled against his chest, Ted automatically tightened his embrace, smiling as he heard her sigh with pleasure. What a bundle of contradictions she was, he thought wonderingly—fiercely independent one minute, soft and yielding the next. A man could easily fall in love with a woman like Alessandra. Ted looked down at her and found her lush, full lips invitingly close.

For a breath-stopping moment they stood on the landing outside her apartment, locked together, neither one moving a muscle as his awareness of her, of what he had been about to do, grew more acute. Then, slowly, regretfully, Ted shook his head and released her, forcing himself not to react to the troubled expression in her eyes.

He couldn't. Not now. Not yet . . .

Seconds later the front door swung open as two stocky men in business suits entered the building.

"Burglary Squad, ma'am, Sergeant," said the older one, nodding to each of them in turn.

Ted almost sighed with relief.

Chapter Four

Sunday, June 10

As her sleep-fogged mind struggled to identify the persistent noise that had dragged her back to consciousness, Sandy opened one eye in the direction of the digital clock on the nightstand. She squinted hard to bring the numbers into focus, and in that instant realized that the shrill, insistent sound was coming from the telephone right beside the clock. It was 6:20 a.m. Somebody was phoning her at 6:20 a.m. Sandy moaned.

Muttering a crude Italian phrase under her breath, she groped for the receiver and actually managed to bring it to her ear without giving herself a black eye. "H'lo," she breathed.

There was a short click, then a dial tone.

Sandy frowned uneasily as she hung up. Normally she would write the call off as a wrong number, with the caller too embarrassed or thoughtless to say anything. But this, following so soon after the break-in last night, was disquieting.

Suddenly Sandy felt restless. She sat up in bed and hugged her knees, feeling knots of tension gather in her shoulders as her gaze swung to the temporary cardboard patch Ted Gaine had put over the hole in her window last night.

What if he was right about the intruder? What if the guy had broken in expecting to find and silence a writer who knew too much, and had had to settle for ransacking her apartment instead? What if he was planning to try again? A piece of cardboard wouldn't stop him. *Dio,* a new pane of glass and changing the locks wouldn't stop him, either, if he was determined to get in.

No, she told herself firmly, she would make herself crazy if she dwelt on this. Sandy threw back the covers and swung her legs over the side of the bed. She hadn't spoken to Uncle Hugo yesterday about Tommy as she'd intended. At the earliest decent hour, she would have to have a talk with him. But first, she had to reclaim her apartment.

After the detectives had left, Sandy had stayed up past midnight repotting all her plants; and then she had collapsed into bed, exhausted, leaving the rest of the work for morning. Well, she thought, sighing as she surveyed the shambles the intruder had left behind, morning was here and the place was still a mess. Everything looked dirty. Everything she touched felt grimy. She would have to clean every room from top to bottom, so she might as well get started now.

She would have to dust and mop and vacuum and polish and scrub. She would have to launder all her clothes and towels and linens. She would have to wash every dish and every pot and pan and knife and fork she owned. She would have to eradicate every trace of the person who had violated her home and her possessions last night, and every trace of the team of detectives who had followed in his filthy footsteps and added their own to the mess. Her apartment would be hers again, even if she had to clean it to within an inch of its life.

By 10:15 a.m., Sandy had accomplished her objective. She had also answered the phone five times and the caller had hung up on her five times; and each time it happened she threw herself even more energetically into her cleaning, as though the ringing of the phone had materialized on the floors and furniture as additional dust and grime to be scrubbed away.

In the end, her kitchen could have doubled as an operating room. Even her plants sparkled. Wearily she wiped a forearm across her damp brow and headed toward the bathroom, stripping off her T-shirt and shorts as she went. The buses ran every half hour on Sundays. She had time to shower and change and drink a fast cup of tea. Soon she would be knocking at Uncle Hugo's door.

At 10:45, as Sandy was double-checking the contents of her purse, the telephone rang again. For a moment, she froze. Then, forcing down a panicky flutter at the back of her throat, she hurried into the living room and picked up the receiver on the third ring. Before she had even finished saying hello, the caller hung up.

Sandy stared uneasily at the receiver for a moment before replacing it on its cradle. She still had to talk to Uncle Hugo this morning, and she would. Tommy's future was important to her. But the disquieting feeling of danger was back, clinging to her thoughts like a cobweb.

Glancing down, she saw Ted Gaine's business card lying beside the phone. He'd added his home number in ink and made her promise to call him, night or day, if anything untoward or frightening happened. He had refused to leave her alone in the apartment last night until she'd accepted his card and promised to use it. Thoughtfully, Sandy picked it up and fingered it. Had he insisted because he expected further trouble? Like these phone calls? Or because it threatened his control of the situation if she actually handled something herself?

After a moment's hesitation she replaced the card beside the phone, picked up her briefcase and left, closing the door firmly behind her.

ONE HUNDRED AND FIFTY. One hundred and fifty-one. One hundred and fifty-two.

Ted let go of the handles of the rowing machine, removed his sweat-saturated terry headband and dragged his forearm wearily across his stinging eyes. This wasn't going to work. He'd been punishing himself for more than an hour already. If feelings could be measured in drops of water, then he'd already shed a gallon of guilt over his near lapse the previous evening. But the needle-like stabs of his conscience still weren't letting up.

He'd come *that* close to kissing Alessandra DiGianni last night, not because his razor-sharp police instincts told him that it was the best way to break down her resistance to his questioning—interrogating her hadn't even been on his mind at that point—but simply because she was warm and beautiful and already wrapped in his arms.

Ted had always prided himself on being the consummate investigator. His career with the Department had been marked not by reckless heroics but by thoroughness and attention to detail. Those qualities had put him at the top of his class coming out of Aylmer Police College and had ensured his rapid promotion out of uniform and up to the rank of detective sergeant before he'd been assigned to Homicide two years ago.

True, his years on the street had made him wily. Working undercover, he'd learned to think like the criminals he hunted. Sometimes it took a "scam," as Joe referred to it, to secure a confession or flush out a suspect;

but more than anything, police work was cerebral. It was painstaking examination of circumstances and details. It was logic and extrapolation. It was observation and deduction. And it demanded objectivity.

Somehow, in spite of all his training and experience, Ted was finding it impossible to be objective about Alessandra. He kept imagining how it would be to taste the honeyed warmth of her mouth, feel the silk of her hair against his cheek....

It was a wonderful fantasy, but it was still only a fantasy. Ted closed his eyes, gritted his teeth and put the daydream on fast forward: *Standing on the landing outside Alessandra's apartment door, kissing her hungrily—until she pulls back. For a moment she gazes into his face, her eyes troubled.... "I don't need this," she tells him in a voice that could cut glass. "And I certainly don't want it from you. As you can see, I'm perfectly capable of getting myself where I want to be, by myself."*

No, he amended, shaking his head impatiently, that wasn't Alessandra; it was Carol the day she demanded her divorce. Since meeting Alessandra, he'd found himself thinking with disturbing frequency about his ex-wife. Carol, the social climber. Like Alessandra, she was a strong, independent woman, with enough ambition for two. Funny how he still seemed to lean toward that type. After the number Carol had done on him when they divorced, anyone would think he'd be keeping his distance from Ms. Alessandra DiGianni, instead of wanting to grab every opportunity to get closer to her.

Chemistry, that was all it was, he reminded himself savagely. The curse of the male species. A fresh, lovely face came along, and he was gone. How else could he have ended up married to Carol, who called him "a badge on legs''? And why else would he feel so drawn to Alessandra, who, except for one vulnerable moment last night, barely tolerated him?

A good detective ought to be able to control those kinds of feelings—or at least not let them show. Resolutely, Ted gripped the handles of the rowing machine and resumed counting strokes.

One hundred and ninety-five, one hundred and ninety-six... After three hundred, he'd go upstairs and take a shower. Or maybe after four hundred. Or five.

THE FILE ON MR. VANISH was easily three hundred pages long and had taken three hours to print out. Watching the fanfold sheets pile higher and higher in the out basket hanging from the printer in the *Police Digest* composing room had gradually distracted Sandy from her other nagging worry of the moment—the apparently failing health of Uncle Hugo.

She had surprised him at home that morning; and he, in turn, had surprised her. Stunned, Sandy had looked into Hugo's unnaturally flushed face with its dull, weary eyes, and had seriously wondered whether this tired old man was capable of helping anyone. Just the thought of what she had come to say to him had sent a pang of conscience lancing through her; but she had said it anyway, after making Hugo promise to visit his doctor the very next day for a checkup.

All the way to the magazine office, his face had haunted her. And then the printer had begun spewing page after page of margin-to-margin words. Sandy had scanned the printout, lifting a dozen or so sheets at a time to peek between the fanfolds; and she had realized with dismay that studying all this information, in only their spare time, would take the sergeant and her a long while, possibly longer than Mr. Vanish was willing to grant them.

Carefully she tore off the final page, lifted the print-out out of its basket and placed the stack of paper in the briefcase she'd brought from home. So far, so good. Now she just had to get it back to her apartment without alerting anyone.

She had telephoned Ted Gaine from Editorial, asking him to meet her at her apartment to look over the file. He'd offered to drive down and pick her up, but she'd refused, pointing out that a police escort was the surest way to tip off a watcher that there was something valuable inside the briefcase. Reluctantly, he had to agree.

So, tense behind a mask of carefully composed features, Sandy marched rapidly up the back stairs to Editorial, past her desk to the double glass doors, and back down again to the street. She had been seen entering the front door of the building, carrying a briefcase; she would have to leave the same way. And she would have to treat the briefcase as casually as if it held only the uneaten portion of her takeout lunch.

To her relief, the journey home went without a hitch. Sandy was smiling as she carried the briefcase through the front door of her building and up the steps to her apartment. After locking the door behind her, she filled the kettle for tea and opened the briefcase on her kitchen table. Then she gathered writing instruments and paper and arranged them precisely on the table around the printout. This was her all-night study ritual, begun back in college. After Ted Gaine had gone home, she would keep at it until her eyes refused to focus anymore.

He arrived about five minutes later, as Sandy was making the pot of tea.

"All right, let's see what Bert left us," he said, making directly for the stack of paper on the table.

The computer had printed out the subfiles in alphabetical order by filename, which meant that lists, police reports and interviews were all interspersed.

Gaine scanned the first few files impatiently. "Did you print the directory, too?" he asked.

She handed him a separate, much thinner printout.

"That's better. Let's start separating and sorting all these."

Twenty minutes later, their tea looked more like coffee, but they had all the .LST subfiles paper-clipped together, and all the others separated into piles according to category. They were ready to begin studying Bert's file.

"Let's see what the shrinks have to say about our man," said Gaine, reaching for the stack of files ending with .PSY. "We may not have a lot of time, so you take Dr. Philip Hooper, and I'll take Dr. Glendon Prewitt. Read it, summarize verbally, I'll do the same, and we'll see how they compare."

"You've got this down to a science, haven't you?" Sandy remarked as she took the five-page-long printout from his hand.

"It goes with the territory, m'dear," he said, in a fair imitation of W.C. Fields. But she noticed he wasn't smiling.

"Okay, Dr. Hooper is a psychologist with the New York Correctional Services Bureau. He says Mr. Vanish sounds like a sociopath with schizophrenic tendencies—totally remorseless and fading in and out of reality, perhaps hearing voices, like Son of Sam, or else deluded into thinking he has a divine mission to rid the world of evil, wherever and however he perceives it."

His face concealed by the printout in his hand, Gaine asked, "What does he think the killer does between hits? Prewitt thinks he's an actor, or a circus clown."

"Because of the disguises, of course," said Sandy. "Somebody who has ready access to wigs and makeup and knows how to use them to conceal his appearance. I wonder if anyone has ever seen Mr. Vanish's real face," she added thoughtfully, "or if he only appears in disguise."

"Dr. Prewitt says Mr. Vanish is arrogant and has a superiority complex, which is reinforced when he dupes people with his false faces. What does Hooper have to say on that point?"

Sandy scanned the second page of the interview she was holding. "Expediency and survival. He wears the disguises to enable him to make his kills more effectively and to prevent identification, which could lead to capture."

"He's pragmatic and a little stodgy, your Dr. Hooper," remarked Gaine. "Prewitt is more imaginative. He says Mr. Vanish is a performer who lets performing get out of hand. As long as the murder is committed by somebody who doesn't look like him, he can hold himself blameless. In that case, he'd probably pass a lie detector test."

"How about background? Hooper says Mr. Vanish was brought up without values, was probably an only child in a well-to-do or wealthy family in which the parents were too selfish and busy to spend any quality time with him, had a brilliant mind, which went unchallenged and therefore turned to evil. May have killed both parents to inherit so he wouldn't have to work. Stodgy, you say?"

"Okay, I apologize. Prewitt guesses that Mr. Vanish came from a broken lower-class home, was probably abused as a child and sought relief in fantsay. Then, when older, sought employment in the world of fantasy. I've had enough of this guy," declared Gaine. "You?"

"Let's try the next two. Maybe they'll agree on something," sighed Sandy, not holding out much hope. After all, how could these professionals claim to understand a person they'd never met?

Bert had collected six reports from six different psychiatrists and psychologists all over North America, and one reprint of a magazine article by a seventh. The six reports all painted different portraits of the elusive murderer, although they did have several things in common.

"Let's write these down," said Gaine, reaching past her for a sheet of paper and a ballpoint pen. "They all agree he has a brilliant mind, which was probably not stimulated or challenged enough while he was growing up. And he enjoys wearing his disguises and probably takes great pride in making them as realistic as possible. He's meticulous about details, probably a compulsive planner. And he's had theatrical training of some sort and may still be actively involved in stagework or films."

"Or a clown in a circus," sighed Sandy, picking up the reprint and beginning to scan it.

"I wish we had more consensus on why he wears the disguises," muttered the sergeant, still scribbling.

Sandy shrugged. "Maybe he does it because his own face is too recognizable. Maybe he's a rock star or something and would be mobbed by fans wanting autographs if he appeared in public undisguised."

Gaine stopped writing and leaned back thoughtfully in his chair. "That's an interesting notion. He wouldn't have to be a celebrity, either—just a known public figure."

"Dio!" she breathed, as the words she was reading finally registered. "Listen to this, Sergeant: He was an unloved child, not abused but neglected, and filled with unresolved anger... Unable to form normal relationships, he became a user of people, in private a loner with perhaps one or two companions to whom he could feel superior, in public a charming and popular pretender... Disdainful of those who conformed to the rules of a society that to him didn't deserve obedience or respect, he felt the end justified the means... Unquestionably he had extremely high intelligence, but he could not feel remorse for any wrong action, even when confronted with the sometimes tragic results of that action.... This isn't generalization or gobbledygook, Sergeant. It sounds as though she knew him."

"What's her name?"

"Dr. Michaela Liszt. The reprint is almost twenty years old—Case History of a Child Psychopath."

He frowned. Repeating the name to himself under his breath, Gaine snatched up the sheaf of lists and began searching. "Here it is, under case reports," he said at last, and dropping the lists back onto the table, he began sifting through the stack of .POL subfiles. "Got it. Liszt. She died under suspicious circumstances in 1974. The case was never solved."

Sandy inhaled sharply. "And maybe Bert suspected Mr. Vanish?"

Gaine nodded. "If Vanish was the subject of that article, then you've just found the first piece of the puzzle. Congratulations, Alessandra. Now let's see if we can make some sense out of these police reports."

Dinnertime came and went. Sandy fixed sandwiches for them to eat while they continued reading, and another pot of tea, this one deliberately strong. Eventually, however, they were fated to run out of steam.

They were halfway through the eighth .POL subfile when Gaine pushed his chair back, shaking his head. "I'm getting stale," he said. "I think that's going to be all for me tonight. Do you have a safe place to hide all this?"

"Of course," she replied, seeing him to the door.

He paused on the threshold and turned, as though wanting to say something. Taut with anticipation, Sandy watched his expression change three times before he finally sighed and murmured simply, "Good night, Alessandra."

She waited for the sound of the front door closing behind him. Then she quietly locked up and returned to the kitchen table.

Sandy still resented the way he'd forced her into this partnership, but she had to admit, as she surveyed the copious hand-scrawled notes littering the table, that they appeared to be off to a good start. They were getting a handle on Mr. Vanish, at least, beginning to understand him a little.

About to clear Gaine's empty mug and sandwich plate off the table, Sandy changed her mind and sat down in his chair instead. It was nearly eleven o'clock, but her eyes were still focusing, and there was a manageable-looking pile of miscellaneous subfiles that might yield something of interest.

Just then, the telephone rang.

The shrill sound instantly set her nerves on edge, but Sandy was determined not to answer it. She let it ring. And ring. And with each ring, her fingers clenched more and more tightly around her pen and the edges of the printout.

Finally, she couldn't stand it anymore. Hurrying into the living room, she picked up the receiver on the sixth ring. "Hel—" she got out, before the caller hung up. "Hell," she muttered, dropping the receiver back into its cradle.

That made eight times today, including the call that had rudely awakened her early this morning. There was nothing wrong with the telephone—she and her downstairs neighbor had tested the line before Sandy left for Uncle Hugo's that morning. And there hadn't been any calls the whole time Ted Gaine had been with her, she suddenly realized. Somebody was waiting until she was alone and then deliberately harassing her.

To a woman living alone that was frightening enough; but Sandy's apartment had been broken into and searched last night, and her telephone number was visible on the fronts of both her phones. What if this crank was the intruder, letting her know he intended to try again?

Gaine's card hadn't budged from its spot beside the phone. Sandy stared at it for a moment, gnawing her lower lip uncertainly. How long would it take him to get home? She didn't even know where he lived....

Suddenly the telephone rang again. Frozen in place, Sandy watched it ring, twice, three times, four times... Finally, her nerves threatening to unravel permanently if she heard that noise even one more time, she reached out and snatched up the receiver. "Hello?"

"This is Dooley. You Tom's sister?"

Even if he hadn't identified himself, the sound of an answering voice would have startled her. But this particular voice, like a steam valve right next to a gravel chute, lifted the hair at the nape of Sandy's neck.

"Y-yes," she replied uncertainly.

"Listen, I'm gonna hafta make this short. I tried to call you a few times before, but somebody came around the corner every time and I had to hang up"

For a moment, anxiety gave way to a rush of anger. "*You* called me at six-twenty this morning?"

"You crazy? I was asleep at six-twenty," he told her indignantly. "Now listen to me, lady, 'cause when he finds out I'm the one who saw him, I'm dead meat, y'unerstand?"

"When who finds out?"

"The guy who iced Lou Parmentier." Dooley hissed in a breath. "I saw the hit go down," he confided. "It was done by a guy named Mr. Vanish."

Sandy inhaled sharply and began searching the drawer of the telephone table for pen and paper. "Are you sure?" she demanded. The last thing she'd expected to have drop into her lap was an eyewitness to the Parmentier murder who could identify Mr. Vanish as the perpetrator. It was almost too good to be true.

"Sure, I'm sure. I was hangin' out at Sunnyside last August fourteenth, and from behind a bush I see this late-model Dodge pull up and park on Howard Road. A guy gets out of the driver's side, looks around to make sure he's alone, opens the back door, pumps three shots into the back seat. Then he puts away his piece, locks all the doors and walks away real casual, like someone goin' for a late stroll in the park, right?"

Scribbling madly, Sandy prompted him, "And then what did you do?"

"I stayed hidden till he was out of sight, then I snuck over to the car—sure enough, there's a stiff in the back seat who's, like, the twin of the guy who iced him. That's when I figured out the hit was done by Mr. Vanish.''

Sandy was puzzled. "Because they were twins?"

Dooley paused, and she could practically hear him shaking his head in disgust. "Listen up, lady. Nobody has ever seen this dude's actual face—he wears disguises so he always looks like someone else. That night he looked like the stiff. Okay? Anyway, I kept quiet about what I seen. Somebody with lots of juice musta wanted this guy Parmentier out of the way. Mr. Vanish don't work for just anyone, y'know? When he didn't come after me right away, I figured I was safe. But the word on the street is that Vanish is back to take care of a 'loose end.' Ya don't hafta be a genius to figure out who's the loose end, right?''

Sandy gripped the receiver tightly with both hands as a sudden hollow in her stomach began eating away everything else inside her.

Her darting eyes came to rest on the business card beside her telephone. "Look," she said in a choked voice, "if you've witnessed a murder and the killer may be after you, then you should be talking to the police."

"That ain't the kinda help I need, lady," rasped Dooley. "I'm not Honest Joe Public bein' a good citizen here. I'm a street hood with a record longer than your arm, and I happen to know I'm wanted by the uniforms at Dundas Station for . . . somethin' else that went down not long ago, okay? They're not gonna listen to me. They'll prob'ly lock me up and forget about me. And then this Vanish guy will just come and get me, like shopping at a supermarket. They say this dude can walk through walls.''

"You could phone in an anonymous tip," she suggested.

"With this voice? You gotta be kidding! Every cop in the city recognizes this voice. My old man gave it to me for a birthday present—punched me in the throat when I was ten and wrecked my voice box."

"Then get Vito to do it for you."

"No. Listen, don't get me wrong—Vito's my buddy, but he don't keep secrets too well. He likes to talk, y'know? I want you to do it."

Sandy's heart began a slow spiraling descent into her toes. A new crack in the Parmentier case? An eyewitness suddenly coming forward? If ever a lead was too hot to handle, it was this one.

"I can't—"

"Look, lady, please, Tom says you write police stuff, so that means you talk to cops all the time, right? They'll believe you."

No, only one cop would believe her, thought Sandy unhappily—Sergeant Gaine. And he would probably arrest her on the spot for actively investigating the Parmentier case.

"Tell them there'll be another stiff on the street if they don't grab this Mr. Vanish guy, like right now," Dooley urged her. "He's after me. Will ya *please* tell them!"

On the other hand, she suddenly realized, whether or not Dooley was the intended victim, he was genuinely in fear for his life. Maybe there was an opportunity here to free her little brother from the influence of the Knights.

Sandy closed her eyes and heard the metaphorical crash of a conscience being thrown out the window. "Okay, I'll tell them," she said at last, "but only if you'll do something in return."

"Yeah?"

"Yeah. Starting right now, you and Vito have to keep away from my brother. Kick him out of the Knights. Tell him he's too young or too stupid or too anything to hang out with you, I don't care. Just make sure you leave him alone from now on."

There was a brief pause, then, "Okay, but now I want somethin' else. I hear that you writers ain't allowed to tell the name of a source. Is that right?"

"That's right."

"Well, I want you to treat me like a source. I don't want them connecting me with the Parmentier hit, you understand? I wasn't there and I didn't see anything."

Sandy swallowed hard, remembering the legend about the young Spartan soldier who concealed a wild fox under his tunic and then stood silently at attention as the panicky creature clawed him to death. She had already taken one street-rat under her protection this week. Charlie. Was there room inside her tunic for a second one?

There would have to be, for Tommy's sake. She took a steadying breath. "Okay. But I'm warning you, if you and Vito don't stay away from my brother, I'm giving your name to the Homicide Squad."

"You're tough, ain'tcha?" said Dooley after a beat. "Okay, deal."

When Sandy hung up the phone a moment later, her heart was pounding and her conscience was screaming. She had just struck a bargain with a confessed criminal, protecting him from the most persistent investigator on the Homicide Squad while simultaneously passing on a message guaranteed to put her back on an adversarial basis with that same investigator. At this rate, she thought dispiritedly, she and Ted Gaine would probably be at loggerheads for the rest of the century.

Sandy returned with a sigh to Bert's file, noticing that the first printout on the miscellaneous pile had to do with the mythology of masks. Evidently, the hows and whys of Mr. Vanish's disguises had bothered Bert just as much as it did Gaine and herself. And then, suddenly, a tickle at the back of her mind became an itch. Something was not quite right about Dooley's account of the Parmentier murder.

With growing suspicion, she leafed through the police reports to Bert's notes on the Parmentier case and discovered two things: first, they were virtually identical to the material Charlie had sold her back in May—no wonder he'd been so willing to give her a "bargoon"!; second, they did not jibe with what Dooley had told her just now over the phone.

Victim: Lou Parmentier, born July 12, 1939, in Montreal, died August 14 last year of multiple gunshot wounds. Found August 15, lying on back seat of rented Dodge sedan, abandoned at foot of Howard Road, near Sunnyside Beach. No witnesses to car being parked. Victim's Occupation: professional entrepreneur. For last six years, partner with Nicholas Vermeyer in clothing business, wholesale and retail: Duds 'n' Dudes, Unity Sportswear. Both companies showed profit every year of operation. Partners were not cross-insured, never argued about business....

There was more. Sandy skimmed past the car rental details and election results to the pathologist's report, which gave the time of death as somewhere between 9:00

p.m. and 12:30 a.m. Here she paused, frowning at the discrepancy: according to Dooley, there had still been enough daylight to make out the killer's face from a distance when the murder took place; but according to Charlie's notes, and the witnesses she'd contacted to corroborate them, the victim had been seen alive around midnight, at an election victory party at the Vermeyer home.

Sandy's breath caught in her throat. *Dio,* what if...! Riding a wave of excitement that swept every other feeling out of its path, she rushed to the telephone and punched in Ted Gaine's home number.

He picked up the receiver on the second ring, sounding a little out of breath as he said, "Hello."

"Sergeant, it's—"

"Alessandra! Is something wrong?"

She shook her head emphatically, then realized he couldn't see her and blurted, "No! Listen to me, Sergeant. What if he doesn't choose his disguises randomly? What if he deliberately poses as his victims?"

"We shouldn't be discussing this over the phone."

"But I just did. I just had a phone call from a witness." And as Gaine listened intently at the other end of the line, Sandy described her conversation with Dooley.

"You're going to have to come in," he said when she was done. "We'll need a formal statement for the Parmentier case file."

She swallowed hard. "Wait a minute—you mean you're putting this on record?"

"If we're ever going to convince the Department that this guy exists, I'm afraid we have to. Come in tomorrow morning."

She sighed, thinking of the article she still had to write, and the fit her editor would throw if she spent the morning anywhere but at her desk. "I can't. Tomorrow's my deadline."

"Tuesday morning, then," he said after a beat. "Nine o'clock. Don't be late," he added sternly. "And make sure you get that window repaired."

Chapter Five

Sandy arrived at the *Police Digest* offices shortly before nine the next morning and found a meeting taking place around her desk. Instantly her heart sank. *Dio,* what now?

"She just came in," said Paul's voice from the center of the huddle. "DiGianni, get over here!" And the several staff members he'd been conferring with immediately dispersed, revealing a strange man sitting in Sandy's chair.

He was fair and slight and wore a tie with his short-sleeved white shirt. He stared at her through thick glasses as she approached, obviously sizing her up, as well. "Are you the user of this terminal?" he demanded.

Frowning, Sandy halted a yard from her desk and drew herself erect. But she smothered her indignation when she saw Paul clamp his teeth firmly around his cigar and raise both bushy eyebrows in silent ultimatum.

"Mr. Blass works for the company that maintains and repairs our computer system," he told her.

Blass? Why did that name sound familiar? Sandy wondered.

"I've had to replace the keyboard," Blass explained in a now-see-what-you've-done voice that set her teeth on edge. "This is a brand-new keyboard, Ms. DiGianni. I've already tested it and it works fine. As long as you don't spill anything on it, it shouldn't give you any trouble."

As long as *she* didn't spill anything?

Paul was still watching her. Reminding herself that this Blass fellow was simply doing his job—never mind that he'd just leaped to an insulting and completely erroneous conclusion—Sandy managed a tight little smile. Her hands, meanwhile, had clenched into fists at her sides. She could feel her fingernails gouging her palms.

Suddenly Paul was shaking Mr. Blass's hand and thanking him for coming by first thing on a Monday morning.

"Paul . . . !"

"My office, DiGianni," he growled. And Sandy snapped her mouth closed and followed him into his cubicle.

"Why do I get the feeling I'm being blamed for what happened to that keyboard?" she demanded.

"Shut the door," he sighed, and sank down on his chair. When they had privacy, Paul continued in a voice almost as stern as the repairman's, "Your keyboard had a dozen shorts in it, kid. Blass says they were caused by liquid spilling over the keys and down onto the circuitry. Logic says you must have knocked over a cup of coffee—"

"I don't drink coffee."

"Some kind of drink, then, by accident while you were working."

She shook her head stubbornly. "It wasn't me, Paul."

Gazing steadily into her face, he took the cigar out of his mouth and rolled it slowly between his thumb and forefinger. "Nobody else uses your terminal," he pointed out. "Nobody else even sits at your desk. And I've seen you on occasion sipping club soda from a tin while working through your lunch break. Maybe this was one of those fluky accidents. Maybe you weren't even aware it happened. But in any case, I don't want it happening again. Is that clear?''

Sandy swallowed a huge lump of outrage. Evidently Paul had made up his mind and wouldn't be swayed by the facts. Or a display of emotion, she realized. She took a calming breath before replying stiffly, ''Perfectly clear, Paul.''

''You've got a 5:00 p.m. deadline,'' he muttered, stuffing the cigar back into his mouth. ''So get to work.''

Sandy nodded once, curtly, and returned to her desk, muttering darkly to herself in Italian.

Blass was gone, and all the other staffers were concentrating on their own screens and keyboards, pretending they'd been deaf and blind to the scene at her desk. Sandy sat down and positioned her fingers on the keys, then removed them again. The keyboard was at the wrong angle—the little retractable legs hadn't been pulled down to tilt it forward for typing.

She lifted the keyboard to adjust the legs. There was a white envelope taped to its underside.

Cautiously, Sandy glanced around at her fellow staffers. Everyone was busily working at his own terminal, seemingly oblivious to her discovery. She tugged the envelope free and turned it over in her fingers. The name DiGianni had been printed on it in large, precisely formed block letters. And it was sealed.

Part of her wanted to believe that this was nothing more than an extra copy of the operator's manual, left as a preventive measure by a repairman who didn't want to make too many repeat calls. But her name was on the envelope, and it had been deliberately concealed so that only she would find it—and considering everything else that had been happening to her lately, Sandy had begun to doubt whether anything as innocuous as a tech manual would ever come her way again.

Trying to be inconspicuous, she tore the envelope open. It contained a single sheet of paper, a green-tinted page ruled off in columns that looked as though it had been torn out of some kind of accounting ledger. The block lettering at the top of the page spelled out the name Unity Sportswear, and in the space marked Supplier she saw only a handwritten nine-digit number. There were dates down the lefthand side, and in one of the columns a list of large dollar figures corresponding to the dates— seven entries in all, ending with the previous August fourteenth.

Sandy shifted uneasily in her chair and let her gaze sweep Editorial once more. Unity Sportswear. Her memory was tingling, as it had done when Paul had introduced Mr. Blass... Of course! Suddenly she knew where she had seen both names: in Bert's file, last night. Unity Sportswear was one of the companies owned by Lou Parmentier and Nick Vermeyer. And Blass had to be Roger Blass, listed in one of the subfiles as a source.

Clearly, Blass had left this envelope for her to find. Sandy paused to consider the implications of that. One of Bert's sources had sought her out with information. Either Blass knew she'd found Bert's file, or he was hoping she had.

She replaced the page inside the envelope and slid it into her purse. She would need time to review this message, to figure out its significance. Meanwhile, a few more nagging questions had taken root in her mind. How many other people knew she had that file? How had they found out? Was one of them Mr. Vanish?

"I UNDERSTAND YOU HAD quite a weekend, partner," observed Joe Wegner as he dropped into the chair behind his desk. "Aidman told me about the break-and-enter at DiGianni's place—said you were a pillar of support for the devastated victim. That was great timing, I've got to tell you. So did it work?"

Ted kept his head down and continued flipping the pages of the bound report in front of him. He didn't really feel like discussing his unprofessional lapses of the past few days in his and Joe's work space, which sat cheek by jowl with all the other detectives' cramped work spaces, separated from them only by a shoulder-high partition.

"Did you scam her source out of her?" Joe persisted, undeterred by Ted's silence.

"Nope." Ted slammed the report shut and dropped it noisily into a desk drawer.

"Did you get her to say anything at all?"

"Last night she informed me that Mr. Vanish killed Parmentier. I told her to come in and give us a formal statement to that effect."

There was a moment of stunned silence before Joe burst into laughter. "You're kidding."

Ted shook his head.

"You're not," said Joe incredulously. "Well, I hope she had this on damned good authority, because Nielsen's going to want both our badges when he reads about this imaginary killer in our report."

"Alessandra's pretty sure he exists, Joe."

Wegner studied his face for a moment. "So it's Alessandra now? Why do I get the feeling that your waters have become slightly muddied, partner?"

"They're not muddied," Ted assured him. "She thinks she can prove this guy is real, and I believe her."

Joe shook his head indulgently. "You should hear yourself." He laughed. "Listen, if all the cops in North America have been trying for ten years to nail him down, without success, what makes you think your girlfriend can do it?"

"First of all, she isn't my girlfriend," Ted corrected him mildly. "Second, what she told me last night was that she'd been contacted by an eyewitness to the Parmentier murder."

Joe's smile froze on his face and then slowly melted into a frown. "What? An eyewitness? Coming forward after all this time?"

"He knew the killer was Mr. Vanish and he was scared. Now he thinks Vanish intends to silence him and he's twice as scared—so he's talking."

Wegner's expression became skeptical. "Yeah, to a reporter."

"Who's talking directly to us. This guy saw the car being parked on Howard Road, Joe. He saw the shots being fired and the killer walking away, and he saw it by the natural light of the setting sun. I told you there were things about this case that didn't add up, and that was one of them."

"But all those witnesses we interviewed, who saw Parmentier at the victory party just before midnight . . . ?"

" . . . could have been celebrating with a master of disguise. Who were they, anyway? Envelope stuffers, canvassers, campaign workers giddy with their success. They were probably half-sloshed on champagne before he ever showed up."

Joe heaved a martyred sigh. "So we're back to that? What about the Vermeyers? Neither of them can drink because of their various medications, and they both gave us sworn statements to the effect that Lou Parmentier was alive and partying at their home until 11:55 p.m. the night of the murder. Parmentier was a close personal friend, as well as a business associate of theirs, Ted. The campaign workers might have been fooled, but nobody could have slipped a ringer past the Vermeyers."

"All right," said Ted, changing tack, "what about the other car, the Mercedes?"

"Parmentier's car?" Joe frowned. "It was found abandoned in the parking lot of an all-night convenience store."

"And the only prints on it were Parmentier's."

"That's right. So he must have left the party, remembered he had to pick up some milk or something on the way home and stopped off at the store, and that was when the killer must have kidnapped him," Joe recited impatiently. "Get to the point."

"How did the killer know he was going to stop at the store?"

"Maybe he followed him from the party."

"Doesn't that strike you as a little chancy? Consider—this wasn't an impulse killing. Whoever murdered Parmentier planned ahead and pulled off a slick, professional job. He picked the ideal spot to abandon the rental car. No witnesses—he thought. He left no fingerprints anywhere, not even latent prints on the car rental contract. Forensics has now put that car through every test known to man and come up blank. The murder weapon has apparently disappeared into thin air. Why would someone that careful about details adlib an important step like the kidnapping of the victim? It makes no sense—unless Parmentier was kidnapped and killed long before that car pulled into the parking lot."

Joe slowly shook his head. "The Vermeyers would have spotted an impostor a mile away," he said flatly. "Parmentier was alive until midnight."

"There's a witness who saw him die before dark."

"Only according to your Alessandra."

"Would you quit calling her that? She isn't *my* anything," Ted snapped, his annoyance increasing as a rush of heat suffused his neck and began to rise into his cheeks.

And that was something else she had in common with Carol, he thought as Joe raised both hands in a gesture of surrender and retreated, chuckling, a little farther behind his desk.

FIRST SHE'D HAD THAT CALL from Dooley, and now Blass had left her a sheet torn out of a Unity Sportswear accounts payable ledger, showing a transfer of $25,000 to a nine-digit account on the day Lou Parmentier was killed.

It was eerie how all this new information had begun falling into her lap, even eerier that it related to the Parmentier case. Maybe she'd found Bert's ghost along with his file, Sandy mused as she picked up her cup and took it and the ledger page into the living room.

Evening sunlight poured through her front windows like molten gold and the air was just beginning to cool. She eased herself onto one of the love seats with a sigh, feeling the freshening breeze and the warmth of the tea unwind her at last. Even for a Monday, the afternoon had been rough. She'd made her deadline with moments to spare, and then had been summoned to an editorial meeting about the remaining articles in her series, during which Paul had chewed his cigar to ribbons and rubbed his bald spot to a dazzling shine before finally letting her keep both the articles and the byline.

Sandy sipped slowly and scanned the piece of paper Blass had left under her keyboard that morning. The nine digits designating the supplier could be some kind of retrieval code—it was difficult to believe that a company the size of Unity Sportswear wouldn't have computerized bookkeeping. This page probably came from the manual records used for data entry.

Perhaps the numbers referred to a bank account. Roger Blass could probably tell her, since according to Bert's information, Blass had supervised the accounting department of Duds 'n' Dudes, Parmentier and Vermeyer's retail fashion outlet, until the previous December, when he'd suddenly quit to become a service representative for Global Data. Interesting career move, thought Sandy, and added one more to the list of questions she intended to ask him.

She let her eyes wander down the left side of the page, noting that there had been seven transfers of money in all, made over a period of three years. Somebody had to have authorized these payments. What if it had been Parmentier himself, paying off a blackmailer, or buying political support?

Dio, what if she was holding in her hands the very reason for his murder?

Setting down her teacup, Sandy hurried back into the kitchen, where her pens and clipboard still lay on the table. She would have to copy down all the information on this sheet and give the original to Ted Gaine first thing tomorrow morning, for the Parmentier investigation. The detectives would have to talk to Roger Blass—

No, wait, she thought suddenly. If Blass had wanted to talk to the police about what he knew, he would have given them the page instead of her. Sandy would have to make the contact herself, preferably as soon as possible.

Fighting to keep her hands steady, she leafed through the printout of the SOURCES subfile and found his name above an address on Glen Manor Road. No phone number. Sandy ran back to the living room and pulled the thick Toronto directory out of its slot in the telephone table, hurriedly finding the page and running her finger down the column of names. No number was listed.

She would have to travel to his home to talk to him. But Glen Manor Road was in the Beaches area of the city, and there had been assaults lately on lone women after dark in the Beaches. Perhaps it would be wiser to wait until Ted Gaine could accompany her there. He wouldn't object to that, as long as it was part of the Mr. Vanish investigation.

She would be seeing Gaine tomorrow morning. She could ask him then, make the date for that evening. No, date was the wrong word, especially for time spent with Sergeant Gaine, she thought with a sigh, replacing the phone book in its slot. Conference, maybe, or field excursion, but regrettably not a date.

As she straightened, she noticed Gaine's card still sitting by her telephone. He'd insisted on patching her bedroom window that night, with a square cut from a corrugated cardboard carton and about half a roll of duct tape. He'd pressed his card into her hand, felt it still trembling and refused to leave unless she promised to call him, at any hour, if there was any further trouble or if she was frightened...and he'd held her, at precisely the moment she needed to feel strong arms around her, tightening his embrace, letting her know she was safe and secure as long as he was with her.

Sandy smiled softly as she lost herself in the memory of that embrace, refusing to think about what it might mean, afraid it might mean something else altogether. As long as Ted Gaine was with her tomorrow night, she told herself, she had nothing to worry about. Not a thing.

THE GUN CAME APART like a child's toy, but he was only interested in one component—the barrel. That was where the rifling was, the grooves that spun the fired bullet to give it flight stability. Each barrel had slightly different rifling. Each put slightly different markings on a slug, making it possible for a ballistics expert to match a bullet with the gun that had fired it—provided it wasn't a .38 Webley with a switched barrel.

He smiled to himself. What he was doing right now went so completely against his usual procedure—against all logic, in fact. But he knew it was brilliant, because he had foreseen and planned for this moment ten months ago, when he had chosen another .38 caliber Webley to use on Lou Parmentier, and then had disposed of every part of it except the barrel.

A single screw, acting as a fulcrum, held the barrel of the Webley in place. With deft movements, he removed the screw and the barrel and set them aside. Then he reached for his camera, popped it open, and took out the small, tissue-wrapped package concealed inside it—the barrel of the Parmentier murder weapon.

Some day, he thought, he would have to put some film inside that camera.

Moments later the switch had been made. He was in possession of a traceable and very dirty gun.

Tonight he would take care of the first part of his contract—the sooner the better, since the prey had evidently sensed the hunter. He hadn't expected to have quite so many problems to solve all at once; if his client wasn't paying him so well, he might consider letting them go. But he'd taken his fee in advance this time, and earning it was a point of honor with him. He would make both the hits. Then he would turn his attention to solving his own nagging problem, hopefully eliminating it before it got too much closer.

Mr. Vanish cocked the Webley and sighted down its long, smooth barrel. It was terrible, being torn in two directions like this....

Chapter Six

The vacuum cleaner was huge and gray and upright and, ironically, dusty. It was the institutional model, weighing a short ton, better than barbells for developing the upper arms. It made a devilish racket when it was turned on and tended to squat sullenly when it was off. Yesterday it had squatted in Andover and Zosky's working space, the day before that in Coolidge and Singh's working space, and this morning it was squatting in a corner of Joe and Ted's working space, reducing it by nearly a quarter.

Ted paused at the entrance to their office and glared at the monster machine for a moment. Then he turned his attention to the short stack of files he'd brought from home.

He had been up half the night running a paperwork maze—statements thirty pages long, reports from pathology and ballistics and forensics, sketches and photographs and lists and warrants... And this was just the interim report for the Chief of Police. After the arrest had been made, he and Joe would have to prepare the brief for the prosecutor, a bound document that could run to more than 1000 pages.

And they would have to do all that for each case in their current load of eight confirmed homicides, not to mention the three suspicious deaths they'd investigated the previous week, two of which were probable homicides.

It was a wonder his eyes could still focus.

Joe strode into the office and dropped his own stack of files onto the middle of his desk. "I see Byron was here last night," he remarked, nodding in the direction of the vacuum cleaner.

"We've got to have a talk with that kid," growled Ted, but even as he said it, he knew he could never bring himself to do it. None of the detectives could, in spite of their grousing; for they all recognized that Byron was special.

Byron was the youngest member of the cleaning staff, hired six months earlier as part of an affirmative-action program providing employment opportunities for the disadvantaged. Against all expectations, Byron was working out well, meeting and even surpassing his job objectives. His supervisor's unstinting praise made him fairly glow with pride when he donned his khaki coveralls. Now, if they could just get him to remember to put away all the cleaning supplies when he was done, particularly that behemoth of a vacuum cleaner....

Ted's ruminations were interrupted by the buzzing of the intercom phone.

Joe picked up the receiver and spoke briefly to the receptionist. A moment later he hung up the phone, a bemused expression on his face.

"She's here, partner. Alessandra DiGianni."

"JUST TELL SERGEANT WEGNER what you told me on the phone Sunday evening."

Sitting across the wooden desk from her, Wegner finished writing a few preliminary lines on his legal-size pad of paper and glanced up expectantly.

Sandy nodded and tightened her fist around a crumpled tissue, reminding herself for the fifth time that she wasn't a criminal. She hadn't been apprehended and brought here for questioning. There was no reason to be nervous. None at all.

This interview room was smaller than the classroom where she had waited for Gaine before, but it was far from cozy. The furnishings consisted only of a desk and two chairs, and the cold fluorescent lightbulb overhead. The walls, the floor, even the two detectives preparing to take her statement presented a solid, neutral surface—Wegner seated behind the desk with his pen poised, Gaine standing beside the door, his gray eyes surveying her stonily from the impartial mask of his face. Sandy swallowed hard, feeling the familiar flutter at the back of her throat.

"I'm ready to take your statement now, Miss," prompted Sergeant Wegner.

"Yes, of course. I was at home Sunday night at about eleven o'clock when the phone rang. It was . . . a person who would prefer to remain anonymous."

As she repeated what Dooley had told her about the murder, Sandy glanced back and forth between the two detectives. Ted Gaine was prowling the little room like a stalking jungle cat, occasionally pausing to nod agreement with a remembered detail. Sergeant Wegner had his head down and was grimly capturing on paper every word she uttered, scribbling so furiously his pen seemed to fly across each line.

The moment she stopped speaking, the jungle cat cast a triumphant glance at his partner. "So the murderer was a Parmentier lookalike?"

Sandy nodded. "That's how my caller knew it was Mr. Vanish."

"And did your informant say what time he'd seen the murder take place?"

"He didn't specify a time, but it was before dark."

His brow furrowed with concentration, Ted Gaine turned away from her. "Is this the same informant as before, Alessandra?" he asked, in a much gentler, more persuasive voice.

A frisson ran down Sandy's spine. She straightened. This must be the real reason he'd insisted she come in to make a formal statement—he wanted to grill her once more about her confidential source. Obviously when he'd said they could only be allies during his off-duty hours, he'd meant they would otherwise continue as adversaries.

Why had she expected anything different from tough, smart Sergeant Gaine? Just because he'd put his arms around her once, at a moment when she desperately needed it? As soon as she'd let on that she was enjoying the embrace, he'd pulled away, shaking his head as though to say, "Nothing personal, ma'am." Maybe she'd been deluding herself, thinking that he cared about her when reassuring crime victims was just another part of his job.

"No, Sergeant," she sighed, "it was a different informant this time."

Sergeant Wegner turned another page and continued scribbling furiously. Sandy resisted the urge to lean forward and read what he'd written, upside down.

"Did he say why he'd chosen to contact you instead of us?" asked Sergeant Gaine.

Sandy moistened her lips with her tongue. "Yes. He wanted me to be his go-between because he thought you would take me more seriously than you would him."

The triumphant glance now passed the other way.

"And where is he now, Alessandra?"

She shrugged, feeling the tissue in her hand begin to dissolve. "I don't know."

Sergeant Gaine bent down, placing his face close to hers. "Let's hope Mr. Vanish doesn't know, either," he said quietly. "If your informant is right about being the 'loose end,' then he's in grave danger, Alessandra. But we can't protect him without knowing who he is."

Doggedly she shook her head. "I gave him my word, Sergeant."

"You're a target, too, Ms. DiGianni," said Sergeant Wegner. Sandy turned to him and found him staring at her.

Then Ted Gaine spoke again, dragging her attention back to his forbidding face. "Both your lives are at stake, Alessandra," he insisted.

"Mr. Vanish won't stop with silencing the witness."

"You may be withholding our only chance to nail the killer."

"Are you sure you want to obstruct this investigation, Ms. DiGianni?" Wegner concluded in an icy calm voice.

Sandy repressed a shiver. They were using fear and guilt to batter at her defenses, not realizing that she'd erected them around her brother. "Like a mama bear with a cub," Gaine had said. Well, he wasn't the only one with a duty to protect the innocent.

Struggling to remain calm, she stared directly into his eyes and said, "I'm well aware of the risks, gentlemen, and also of the fact that as a private citizen I'm entitled by law to take them if I choose."

Exhaling a sharp, annoyed breath, Sergeant Gaine straightened up and returned to the door of the interview room.

"If you have nothing else to tell us, ma'am...?" prodded Wegner.

"There is something else. I don't know how relevant it is, but—" Sandy reached into her handbag and pulled out the folded ledger page "—I found this under my keyboard at work yesterday morning." Paper rattled as she unfolded the sheet and laid it on the desktop in front of Sergeant Wegner.

Both his eyebrows rose for an instant. Then his face resumed its official police expression. "Unity Sportswear," was all he said. A half second later Ted Gaine was scanning the page over his partner's shoulder and frowning darkly.

"Do you know who left this for you?" Sergeant Gaine asked softly, his eyes hard as granite on Sandy's startled face.

She opened her mouth to tell him, then changed her mind, for although Bert's file had given her a fairly good idea of who might have left the envelope, Sandy hadn't actually seen Blass tape it to her keyboard. And if the way she'd been treated today was any indication of what awaited him at police hands, she decided she'd rather not share any speculations about Roger Blass with these detectives.

"No, I just found it there," she replied.

"Has anyone else handled this note besides you and the person who left it?" Gaine demanded.

She shook her head.

They were carefully not touching the piece of paper, she noticed. Wegner opened a desk drawer and pulled out a clear plastic bag. In a second drawer he found a surgical glove, which he put on before picking up the ledger sheet to insert it into the bag.

Now began another grilling. Who sat near her desk at work? Who had been around her computer that day? Had she noticed anything strange about this computer repairman? How long had she been in her editor's office before coming out and finding the envelope? Did she know if any of her coworkers had any connection with Unity Sportswear?

At last, Sergeant Wegner closed his writing pad and told her, "That will be all for now, Ms. DiGianni. If we have any further questions, we know how to contact you." With a sigh of relief, Sandy got to her feet.

"I'll walk you to the elevator," said Sergeant Gaine, his tone of voice suggesting he wouldn't take no for an answer.

Lips pressed tightly together, she let him escort her out of the room.

"Alessandra, I'm sorry we had to be so rough on you."

"You were doing your job, Sergeant. I understand."

"Alessandra—"

"Tell me, Sergeant, have I seen your real face yet or are you saving it for some special occasion?" she asked bitterly.

The elevator doors slid open then, and Gaine thrust his arm across the opening, stopping her from entering.

"Meet me for dinner," he said in a low voice. "I want to hear what else you've learned about Mr. Vanish." When she hesitated he added, "Partners don't keep information from each other, Alessandra, no matter how they feel about their partnership. I'm sure you spent most of last night immersed in that file. And we made an agreement, remember?"

"All right," she said reluctantly.

"Meet me at the corner of Front and John Streets around five o'clock," he told her, an instant before the elevator doors closed between them.

He found Joe waiting for him back in their work space, rereading the handwritten transcript of the interview. "I'm still not convinced, partner," Joe sighed. "How do we know she didn't make it all up? How do we know this source of hers is reliable? He told her himself that he didn't think we would take him seriously. All we've got here is hearsay, some ramblings about the mythical Mr. Vanish. If Nielsen reads this in the report, we're both going to be bulletin-board material. People are going to be chuckling about us around the water cooler for a long time."

Ted shook his head stubbornly. "I believe her, Joe."

"Of course you do—she's feeding your pet theory. But is it the truth?"

That was a good question. Could Ted trust his instincts, knowing that just being around Alessandra DiGianni blew his professional objectivity all to hell?

Grimly, he thought about the workout equipment in his basement. At this rate, he was going to be the fittest detective on the force.

FIRST THE COMPUTER ATE her article—then it went berserk.

Sandy stared in angry amazement at the splatter of nonsense characters the computer had tossed onto her screen.

Punching the keys with unnecessary vigor, she instructed the processor to return her file to the terminal.

FILE NOT FOUND, said her screen.

"What are you talking about?" she muttered to herself, and called up the directory listing all the articles she had filed on the system. There it was, in the directory—the third instalment of her series. If she could find it, why couldn't the damned computer?

Once again, she asked for the file.

FILE NOT FOUND, insisted the computer.

"Stop lying to me," she warned it.

Frank Leslie, polishing his column at the terminal two desks away, swiveled his chair toward her and sighed. "What are you grumbling about?"

By now Sandy was fuming. "It won't let me work on my article," she replied through gritted teeth. "The file name is right there, in the directory, but the computer refuses to call it up for me."

"Here, let me try," said Frank, and Sandy made room for him at her desk.

Frank's instruction elicited a different message from the computer: FILE DELETED.

Her heart plummeting, Sandy cursed softly in Italian.

"Don't panic yet," Frank advised her. "It's on the fritz. Maybe it only *thinks* it's deleted a file."

But when he called up her directory, the article was gone.

"I don't understand this. It was working just fine before lunch," she complained.

Frank shrugged helplessly. "Tell you what—my terminal is still user-friendly. Once I've finished filing my piece, you can log on at my desk and access your backup file—again."

"We've got to stop meeting like this, Frank."

"Sure," he said with a grin, and returned to his station. Fifteen minutes later, Frank leaned back in his chair and stretched his arms lazily over his head. "Your turn, kid," he announced. "I'm done for the day."

Sandy took Frank's place and logged onto his terminal with no problems. Then she called up the directory of her backup files. There should have been three, one for each of her articles. Instead there was only one, and it was impossibly small.

A sudden chill settled in her bones. Sandy drew in a long, steadying breath and called up her remaining backup file. As the screen cleared and repainted itself, she stared in numb confusion at the three letters it thrust at her: RIP.

Rest in peace. Sandy's skin began to crawl. This was a message from someone who knew her I.D. code and password. Whoever had broken into her files was letting her know that virtually any part of her life could be accessed. Who was sending her such a message?

Suddenly the screen cleared itself again, and the computer informed her: FILE DELETED.

Muttering in Italian, she yanked her hands away from the keyboard as though it were growing hands of its own. He was there right now, tampering with the system. Destroying the ominous message so she couldn't prove what she had seen.

Damn him! But she knew where he was now. And she wasn't going to let him get away with this.

Suffocating with rage, Sandy leapt to her feet and raced downstairs, straight-arming every door she encountered and a couple of startled people, as well. One of them was the security guard stationed just inside the entrance to the computer room.

"I'm sorry, you can't come in he—Hey, lady!" he protested, grabbing her arm as she pushed past him. "Are you blind? There's a sign on that door says No Admittance."

"Where is he?" she demanded coldly.

"Who? There's nobody here but me."

"If you're protecting him . . . !"

"Protecting who?" he exclaimed. "I don't understand."

"Whoever was down here a minute ago deleting all my files."

"There's nobody down here. There hasn't been anybody in this room since I came on duty at two-thirty. Honest! If you don't believe me, just have a look around."

Sandy looked around. Except for the guard, and the walls and desks covered with humming machines, the room was empty. There was nobody to confront. Swallowing her frustration, Sandy apologized to the guard and returned upstairs, trembling with unvented fury.

But by the time she'd returned to her desk, she was trembling for a much different reason. Somebody had evidently reached into the computer from a distance and tampered with the files, somebody to whom access codes and passwords presented very little difficulty. She could think of only two people with the necessary expertise: Roger Blass . . . and Dave Ragusz. Ragusz was the likelier possibility.

APPROACH WITH CAUTION.

Anxiously, she glanced at the wall clock. Only one more hour until Ted Gaine was off duty. Realizing that the minutes would pass agonizingly slowly if she didn't at least try to fill them, she made a halfhearted effort to locate her notes for the third article in her lower desk drawer. But her mind wasn't on rebuilding her file. It was working hard to get comfortable with the fact that an infuriating detective named Sergeant Gaine had somehow become the single most important man in her life.

When at last the clock read four-thirty, Sandy shut down Frank's terminal with an almost tangible sense of relief. She snatched up her handbag and set out for the subway, visualizing dinner with Ted Gaine at one of the restaurants in the convention corridor of the city. Front and John was directly opposite the Skydome and the CN Tower, and a stone's throw from the Toronto Convention Center, Harborfront, and the city's three major theaters. All the eating establishments in the vicinity tended to cater to people who had been on the go all day and needed a private corner, with or without atmosphere, in which to unwind.

And, *Dio,* how she needed to unwind!

Sergeant Gaine was waiting for her on the sidewalk, in shirt sleeves, beside a street vendor's hot-dog stand. No, he wouldn't, she told herself, feeling her stomach twist with apprehension as he turned and spoke to the vendor. No fast food, eaten standing up. Not today. Today she needed to sit in a quiet corner with him and feel his protective aura surround her as they talked.

To her immense relief, Gaine turned away from the hot-dog vendor and strode across John Street to meet her.

"How about the Rose Garden Café?" he suggested, continuing to walk with her along Front Street to the next traffic light.

She gave him a grateful smile.

Over iced tea and a fruit-salad plate, in a booth at the rear of the café, Sandy told him about her disappearing files, and about the threatening message that had been left in their place, and watched his expression grow darker and darker.

"It might have been a warning, rather than a threat," Gaine pointed out grimly. "Either way, somebody with access to the magazine's computer system is trying to scare you off. Possibly the same somebody who erased Bert's case file on Mr. Vanish.''

Sandy's next breath was a gasp. "Could it have been Mr. Vanish?''

"Pray that it wasn't," Gaine advised, gazing steadily across the table at her. "But whoever it was, he obviously knows that you're pursuing Bert's investigation. Do you have any idea who that might be, Alessandra?''

She shrugged uncomfortably. "Besides you, there's Dave Ragusz.''

As she'd expected, Gaine shook his head vehemently. "It wasn't Ragusz. I'd stake my badge on it.''

Not feeling up to an argument with him, Sandy decided to change tack. "Then how about Roger Blass? I'm sure he was the one who left me that ledger page yesterday morning—''

"Blass couldn't have tampered with your files this afternoon, either," said Gaine.

"Why not? He certainly knows his way around computers. And he's listed as a source in Bert's case file. Maybe we ought to go out to the Beaches after dinner and ask him a few pointed questions.''

Gaine exhaled wearily. "Alessandra, after you left Homicide this morning, Sergeant Wegner and I decided to track down your computer repairman. He wasn't at his office or out on a call, so we went to his house to look for him.''

"And?''

Gaine reached across the table and gathered her suddenly clammy hands into his large, warm ones. "We found him dead, Alessandra.''

"Dead?'' The word came out a horrified whisper.

"He was shot to death sometime last night.''

Icy fingers began dancing across her shoulders, making her shiver. "He was one of Bert's sources and he came to me with information. If he was killed because he gave me that piece of paper...!"

"We don't know that."

"Mr. Vanish won't settle for just silencing a witness. You told me that yourself. He'll go after anyone the witness may have spoken to."

The air was becoming too thick to breathe. Sandy glanced down at the table, startled to find the plate of untouched food in front of her. She felt her hands being squeezed and looked up again into Ted Gaine's determined face.

"I also told you I would protect you, Alessandra, and I will," he told her fiercely.

Yes, she thought, feeling the heat of his hands warm her all the way to her soul—and beyond, if she let it—if anyone could find a way to keep her safe from Mr. Vanish, it was Sergeant Ted Gaine.

"Thank you," she whispered.

"It's the least I can do for my partner. Now, how about those subfiles? Did you learn anything new last night?"

Sandy sighed. They were back to business. And he still hadn't smiled at her. "Two things. First, I began thinking about the idea of a killer posing as the victim to confuse the investigation, and I went through the case reports for instances where the pathologist had set the time of death within a three-hour range but the victim had been seen alive close to the end of the range."

"And?"

"I found five cases where that happened, including the Parmentier murder."

Gaine nodded thoughtfully. "We may have the beginnings of something here. Go on."

"I tagged them and put them back into the pile. Then I began reading through the miscellaneous subfiles. One of them describes all the possible ways that a client might contact Mr. Vanish, and appended to it I found a list of ten retrieval codes for the newspaper morgue at the *Toronto Daily News*. I became friendly with the librarian down there while I was researching my articles, so I called her up to ask which pages the codes referred to."

Gaine's eyes widened with alarm. "You did *what?* Alessandra, I thought we'd agreed not to interview any leads until we'd gathered all the information we could from the file."

She frowned, puzzled. "I wasn't interviewing a lead. And in case you're interested, Sergeant, each of those pages was from the classified section, and each from a different edition of the paper."

Slowly, his cheeks began to flush as he scolded in a whispered voice, "Listen, it's one thing to sit at your kitchen table and make notes. It's quite another to discuss them with an outside contact. What if the person who placed those ads also bribed the librarian to let him know if anybody expressed an interest in them? What if he would kill to prevent you from learning his identity?"

"I hadn't thought of that," she murmured, shamefaced.

"All right, maybe we lucked out and your librarian isn't the pipeline to Mr. Vanish." He sighed. "Just don't talk to anyone else until we've wrung everything we can out of Bert's file, okay? There's no sense alerting Mr. Vanish before we're ready for him."

Paranoid, she thought bleakly. The only way to be ready for Mr. Vanish was to be completely and utterly paranoid.

ONE DOWN, ONE TO GO. Smiling faintly to himself, he withdrew the parcel from his well-traveled Samsonite suitcase and unfolded the tissue paper. He wanted to be tall for tomorrow's meeting.

He had ordered both the lifts and the shoes they fit into while disguised as a well-known Lebanese entertainer. It was the one and only time Mr. Vanish had knowingly impersonated someone he didn't intend to kill.

Setting the shoes side by side in the closet, he took a large leather briefcase down from the shelf. This, too, he'd had specially modified. Slowly, he unlocked and opened the case. Then he lifted out the two removable trays, shook each one gently to level out the contents of their many small compartments, and placed them on either side of the briefcase. The trays had clear plastic lids, permitting him to see everything with one sweeping glance.

He'd spent years collecting these. The first tray held noses and chins, one per cubbyhole; the second displayed various scars and wrinkles, as well as an assortment of appliances for changing the slope of his cheeks or forehead, the angle of his ears, the shape of his eyes. At the bottom of the case, in fixed, larger compartments, lay a kit for applying facial hair, a selection of tinted contact lenses, and a complete range of masking foundations and shading pencils.

Unhurriedly, he selected the pieces of his disguise and placed them inside a second, smaller case, which already held a short-handled brush and a bottle of spirit gum. Then he closed and locked both cases.

Smiling to himself, he extracted the minicassette player from the special pocket he'd built for it inside his suitcase. Then he reached into his shirt pocket for the book of matches and placed it beside the telephone.

The number written inside the matchbook connected with an answering machine. "Hello," said a woman's prerecorded voice. "We can't talk right now, but you may leave a message at the sound of the tone, and we'll get back to you...."

Mr. Vanish had once attempted, unsuccessfully, to locate Charlie's answering machine. All he'd been able to determine was that it wasn't attached to a stationary telephone. Charlie was obviously a careful man. It was a trait Mr. Vanish couldn't help but admire, because he, too, was careful. When the prerecorded message had ended, he brought the cassette player close to the mouthpiece of the receiver and pressed Play; and someone else's voice, a voice surreptitiously recorded while Mr. Vanish had been studying an earlier problem, spoke into the telephone. "This is L'Estrange. You will meet my representative tomorrow morning at the usual time and place...."

Mr. Vanish permitted himself another brief smile at the irony of one machine talking to another with the voice of a dead man. Then he hung up the phone.

NO RISK, NO OBLIGATION TO BUY...NOW OR EVER!

GUARANTEED

PLAY "ROLL A DOUBLE" AND GET AS MANY AS SIX GIFTS!

HERE'S HOW TO PLAY:

1. Peel off label from front cover. Place it in space provided at right.With a coin, carefully scratch off the silver dice.This makes you eligible to receive one or more free books, and possibly other gifts, depending on what is revealed beneath the scratch-off area.

2. You'll receive brand-new Harlequin Intrigue® novels. When you return this card, we'll rush you the books and gifts you qualify for ABSOLUTELY FREE!

3. Then, if we don't hear from you, every other month we'll send you 4 additional novels to read and enjoy. You can return them and owe nothing, but if you decide to keep them, you'll pay only $2.24* per book-a savings of 26¢ each off the cover price.And, we'll send you the entire shipment for only 49¢ delivery.

4. When you subscribe to the Harlequin Reader Service®, you'll also get our newsletter, as well as additional free gifts from time to time.

5. You must be completely satisfied.You may cancel at any time simply by sending us a note or a shipping statement marked "cancel" or by returning any shipment to us at our expense.

You'll love your elegant 20K gold electroplated chain! The necklace is finely crafted with 160 double-soldered links, and is electroplate finished in genuine 20K gold. And it's yours FREE as an added thanks for giving our Reader Service a try!

"ROLL A DOUBLE!"

PLACE LABEL HERE

SCRATCH HERE

SEE CLAIM CHART BELOW

380 CIH RD53
(C-H-I-10/90)

DETACH AND MAIL CARD TODAY!

YES! I have placed my label from the front cover into the space provided above and scratched off the silver dice. Please rush me the free book(s) and gift(s) that I am entitled to. I understand that I am under no obligation to purchase any books, as explained on the opposite page.

NAME

ADDRESS   APT.

CITY   PROVINCE   POSTAL CODE

CLAIM CHART

⚅ ⚅	**4 FREE BOOKS PLUS FREE 20k ELECTROPLATED GOLD CHAIN PLUS MYSTERY BONUS GIFT**	
⚅ ⚅	**3 FREE BOOKS PLUS BONUS GIFT**	
⚅ ⚅	**2 FREE BOOKS**	

CLAIM NO.37-829

All orders subject to approval.
© 1990 Harlequin Enterprises Limited.

Offer limited to one per household and not valid to current Intrigue subscribers.
PRINTED IN U.S.A.

HARLEQUIN "NO RISK" GUARANTEE

- You're not required to buy a single book - ever!
- You must be completely satisfied or you may cancel at any time simply by sending us a note or a shipping statement marked "cancel" or by returning any shipment to us at our cost. Either way, you will receive no more books; you'll have no further obligation.
- The free book(s) and gift(s) you claimed on this "Roll A Double" offer remain yours to keep no matter what you decide.

If offer card is missing, please write to: Harlequin Reader Service®, P.O. Box 609, Fort Erie, Ontario L2A 5X3

Chapter Seven

Sandy had ordered a sandwich and a club soda to eat in, but it was a mistake. The snack bar was right across the road from the magazine office. As she sat toying with a lunch for which she had no appetite, she had a clear view of the *Police Digest* logo, reproducing itself across the bottle-glass windows on the second floor of the adjacent building.

This morning had been the final straw.

First, there had been the police interrogation yesterday. Then her computer files had been sabotaged. Then Ted Gaine had told her about Blass's death, and it had taken the rest of the evening for her to shake off the feeling that there was a murderer lurking around every corner. Gaine had no sooner delivered her to her front door than her mother had phoned, frantic because Tommy had yelled at her for driving away all his friends and then had packed his gym bag and run away from home. Sandy's darkly churning thoughts had kept her awake most of the night, and she'd slept through her alarm and not arrived at work until nearly eleven o'clock this morning. When she'd stepped into Paul's office to explain her lateness, he had lambasted her for carelessly shorting out her keyboard again, waving in her face an empty soft-drink tin he'd scavenged out of her waste-basket as evidence.

And then something inside Sandy had snapped. She wasn't sure whether she'd exploded then or simply caved in under all the pressure of the past few days. But somewhere inside her a dam had burst, releasing a torrent of resentment and fear. She couldn't remember all the things she'd yelled at him, only that at the end of her tirade she had quit her job.

Or tried to. Paul hadn't accepted her resignation. He had told her to go cool off and come back later. Maybe he would believe she was serious when she sent him a postcard from Hawaii....

"Didn't your mother ever tell you not to play with your food?" Sandy's heart leapt as the familiar soft voice floated over her shoulder.

She glanced up just as Ted Gaine, wearing a charcoal-blue business suit, dropped into the chair opposite her. "Are you still upset about Blass, or is this something new?" he asked.

Sandy tried a smile and found her lips wouldn't co-operate. With a sigh, she told him about the stormy scene in Paul's office that morning. Life, she concluded, had become incredibly complicated in the past week.

Gaine nodded agreement. "I did try to warn you, Alessandra," he pointed out. "But never mind that. How would you like to hear some good news for a change?"

She leaned forward expectantly.

"It's possible that Blass was responsible for your dis-appearing files, after all."

"What? But I thought he—"

"We found out that he called in a lot of favors to get assigned to repair your keyboard on Monday. While testing the newly installed gear, he could have gained access to the system through a back door and installed a worm program.''

Sandy was lost. ''A what? A where?''

''It's like a little bomb ticking away inside the computer. Come on,'' he said, pulling her to her feet and urging her out the door. ''Ragusz is setting up a demonstration for us right now.''

Ragusz?

Instinctively, she dug in her heels. ''Sergeant, wait a minute. Are you really sure about this guy Ragusz? I mean, breaking into large systems and tampering with files is what he does best. What if you're wrong and he was the one...?''

''Absolutely not,'' Gaine declared.

Sandy glanced up just in time to see him nod to someone or something down the street before he turned his attention back to her. She tried to follow the direction of his nod, but saw only the usual lunchtime crowd milling randomly along the sidewalk. Then the traffic light changed and Gaine hurried her across the street to where he'd parked his car.

''How do you know he didn't do it?'' she persisted. ''Bert suspected him, you know. There was a warning in one of the subfiles to approach Ragusz with caution.''

As they pulled out into traffic, she heard Gaine's exasperated sigh. ''Alessandra, do you know the meaning of the term dragnet?''

''Of course.''

''Think about it, and that will be your answer. Meanwhile, please trust me on this—Ragusz did not leave that threatening message in your file.''

Sandy opened her mouth to protest, thought better of it, and sank uneasily into the car seat.

A dragnet was a police roundup operation. Unlike a sting, in which police baited a trap and waited for the criminals to come to them, a dragnet involved going out and gathering up a group of suspects, to be sorted out afterward by the process of elimination. Gathering up and sorting out, just like trawling for fish. Or like the research she'd had to do for her series of articles, Sandy thought.

Suddenly she made the connection, and she sat up with a gasp. "He's a cop?" she exclaimed.

"I didn't say that," said Gaine, poker-faced.

"If he's a cop, then Dragnet is a front," she mused, "probably for digging up information about suspects. Which proves nothing, Sergeant."

"Oh?"

"You may be incorruptible, but others aren't necessarily. Ragusz's position of power—"

"Alessandra," said Gaine, sighing, "who do you think taught Bert how to hide things inside the magazine computer? If Raggie were tapping into the *Police Digest* system—"

"He certainly wouldn't let *you* know about it," she pointed out sharply.

Gaine fell silent, his features contracting in a scowl. Fifteen minutes later, wearing his official police face, he formally introduced Sandy to Dave Ragusz, "the D. Rag in Dragnet."

Ragusz grabbed her hand in his huge fist and declared heartily, "Well, I'm glad to see that two of you have gotten together at least. Come into the back room—we're all ready to start."

The demo lasted half an hour. At the end of it, Sandy's head was swimming with more information about modems, worm programs and back doors than she'd ever thought she wanted to know—but they were no closer to determining who might have been responsible for the computer tampering that had so unnerved her Tuesday afternoon. Ragusz's explanations had actually widened the field of suspects.

"According to Ragusz, anybody with a telephone and a keyboard could have installed that worm program by remote control," she said as they got back into Gaine's car.

"Anybody with a telephone, a keyboard, access to the system, *and* sufficient knowledge to create the program in the first place," Gaine corrected her. "But I hasten to point out that because of the timing delay, Roger Blass could have installed the program on Monday, setting it to run a day or even a week later, depending on when you called up the file that would trigger it."

Sandy shook her head slowly. "Blass gave me the ledger page. That means he wanted to help the investigation. Why would he immediately turn around and try to frighten me into dropping it?"

"I only said it was possible, Alessandra."

Abruptly, he fell silent. Sandy turned and saw him staring darkly through the windshield, and she immediately felt her heart give an odd little twist. She sensed pain behind the stubborn set of his features. What was he thinking about now? If only she knew more about him!

Say something, she commanded herself. *He's comforted you often enough, after all.*

But words wouldn't come, and she didn't dare try to put a hand on him. Tough, smart Sergeant Gaine would rebuff her immediately, making her feel small and foolish for even thinking he needed reassurance. If only they could have met in a different way. Bumped carts at the supermarket, been introduced by a mutual friend at a party...

He sighed and shook his head.

"I'm sorry," she murmured.

He looked up, startled. "For what?"

"You went out of your way today to try to lift my spirits, and instead of thanking you I picked holes in your arguments."

"You used your investigative skills, Alessandra, as I should have expected you to do. Please don't apologize for that."

He said this in such a calm, reasonable voice that for an instant she had the urge to smack him. Why had she bothered to say anything? she wondered. How was it that nothing she did seemed to be able to touch him inside, and virtually everything he did sent her into emotional paroxysms?

The car was sitting in the sun. Even with the windows rolled down, it was as hot as the desert inside. As she impatiently shifted position, Sandy could feel her blouse clinging damply to her back.

"All right, here's the situation," Gaine went on. "So far we have evidence that you've been targeted by two individuals. The second one, in spite of my wishful conjecturing just now, is probably Mr. Vanish. As for the first one, offhand I'd guess that you must have ruffled some feathers when you wrote about the James and Parmentier murders—although I don't really see how you could have, since you didn't go digging for your information. You told me you got your facts from a source who sought you out, right?"

Reluctantly, she shook her head. "I didn't have to dig, but I did have to corroborate, Sergeant. Paul is a stickler for that—two independent sources per published fact. I talked to a number of people who were mentioned as witnesses in each case."

"You spoke to *witnesses*?" Gaine straightened in his seat as though a puppeteer had yanked a string attached to the back of his neck. Pulling a spiral notepad out of his shirt pocket, he flipped to a blank page and demanded, "Who were they, Alessandra? I want names. The Parmentier case first, then the James case."

Sandy hesitated a moment, then came to a decision. They were partners in an investigation. If they were to make any progress at all, she would have to cooperate to the fullest extent permitted by her professional code.

"I'll give you more than that, Sergeant," she told him. "I'll make you a copy of all the information my source gave me and deliver it to Investigative Services as soon as I can. Bert saw a connection between the Parmentier case and Mr. Vanish, and that phone call I received Sunday night seems to confirm it. So whether you want me to be or not, I guess I'm involved in your murder investigation. Why are you staring at me like that?"

His lips quirked briefly upward and his eyes glinted with amusement as he said, "I'm trying to decide whether you're incredibly brave or incredibly foolish. What we're doing now represents quite a stretch for someone whose most dangerous story of the past six years concerned the hazards of inhaling fumes from certain kinds of furniture polishes."

Her eyes widened. "You've been checking up on me," she exclaimed.

"Just curious about my new partner. I've been wondering what quirk in your character to blame for the spot you're in right now. Is there a gene for risk-taking? Was Evel Knievel your natural father, by some chance?"

Involuntarily, she smiled. "I could ask you the same question," she pointed out. "What makes a man want to put his life on the line tracking down killers?"

"Homicide isn't that dangerous, Alessandra. By the time they call us in, the excitement is usually over. Believe it or not, I'm more at risk of getting a hernia from carrying around all the paperwork than I am of getting shot or stabbed," he said.

"I'll bet your family is happy about that."

He shrugged uncomfortably inside his suit jacket. "I don't have a family. My wife and I were divorced a couple of years ago."

Sandy immediately felt foolish. "I'm sorry, Sergeant. I didn't mean to stir up unpleas—"

Suddenly there was a hiss of static as a radio that Sandy hadn't noticed before came on. "Sergeant Gaine, call Dispatch," said a woman's flat, nasal voice, slicing through their privacy like a dull knife. At the same instant, an insistent beeping sound began emanating from one of Gaine's pockets. With a muttered curse, he pulled the paging device out and silenced it.

"I'll have to call in," he told her. "Buckle up. There's a pay phone at the gas station on the next block."

It had to be an urgent call for them to be summoning him on both the radio and the pager, Sandy thought, and the grim expression on Gaine's face as he hung up the receiver and returned to the car confirmed her suspicion.

"There's been a murder," she said softly.

He nodded. "Someone found a body behind the Lucky Shot Video Arcade."

Sandy could feel the color drain out of her face. "Do they know who it is?"

"Not yet. We just got the call. I'll drop you off at the magazine first—or would you rather go home?"

"What? No, I'm staying with you."

He made an exasperated sound. "Alessandra, it's the Parmentier case you're helping with, remember?"

"Sergeant, please! My Uncle Hugo manages the Lucky Shot Video Arcade. He's old and he's not well. He could even be—" Unable to bring herself to say the word, she turned beseeching eyes toward him.

Gaine had gone a little pale himself. "Your uncle? Good grief, maybe there *is* a gene that attracts trouble. All right, Alessandra, by all means. Accompany me. I'll get a constable to drive you back to work later. Or home. Wherever."

IT WAS JUST HALF-PAST NOON, but the alley behind the Lucky Shot was dim and, without the canned rock music blaring through all the doors of the arcade, eerily quiet.

Gaine's car pulled to a stop across the south end of the alleyway. As Sandy swung herself out of the front seat, she saw two other police cars, both marked, their lights flashing, and a dozen or more curious onlookers—none of them her uncle—crowding the waist-high police barriers that blocked off the scene of the crime. Quickly she glanced around, fear for Hugo lodging in her chest like a heavy stone.

"This officer will drive you back," said Gaine, as a grave-faced young constable separated himself from the others and came to stand quietly at Sandy's right elbow. Then, with scarcely a glance at either of them, the sergeant stepped through to join his partner.

Altogether, Sandy saw three uniformed officers and the two plainclothes detectives inside the restricted area.

They were conducting a close search of the alley, poking around in the tall weeds that hugged the chain-link fence on the east side, carefully examining the area behind and around the large green dumpster, and apparently ignoring the murder victim, who lay sprawled against a thicket of weeds at the far end of the alley and had—*dio grazie!*—dark hair instead of white.

Sandy shivered with relief as her worst fear was laid to rest. Uncle Hugo wasn't the murder victim. But he also wasn't among the spectators hanging over the police barriers. Where could he be?

Turning, she uttered a startled gasp as she bumped into the young constable who had been standing silently just behind her. "Do you have to shadow me like that?" she asked impatiently.

"I'm afraid so, Miss," he replied.

"Once I've found my uncle, I'll let you drive me to work, honest," she assured him. "I'm not going to sneak away and take the subway instead."

"I'm sorry, Miss, but I have orders from Sergeant Gaine."

Sandy shot an exasperated look in the sergeant's direction. Suddenly her eyes were drawn back to the murder victim. There was something familiar about that hair, about the shape of the head... She leaned sideways a little, for a better look.

It was Vito. Somebody had murdered Vito.

And Tommy had run away from home. *Dio,* she'd been so wrapped up in her own problems that it hadn't even occurred to her...! Sandy whirled blindly and pushed her way past the startled constable, through the crowd and onto the street. Hugo had to be inside the arcade. He had to. He wasn't a well man. He was probably lying down. As she ran toward the nearest doorway, she finally caught sight of Hugo's shock of white hair—in the back seat of an idling patrol car parked on the side street.

It was even worse than she'd feared—he was under arrest!

Feeling as though a large cold fist were closing around her heart, Sandy dodged the young constable and the uniformed officer who was apparently guarding the prisoner, and slid into the back seat of the patrol car to comfort her uncle.

Immediately there was a commotion.

"Wait a minute, Miss—you can't get in there," protested the officer, and he reached in to pull her out of the car.

But Sandy wouldn't let him. She warded off his hands with stinging slaps and yelled at him to leave her alone. Couldn't he see that Hugo needed her?

"My orders are to drive Mr. Savarini, *alone,* to the Dundas Street Station. Ow! Stop that, Miss, or I'll have to arrest you."

"Sandra, stop fighting," said Hugo weakly. "The man is just doing his job. I'll be fine, *cara.*"

Sandy turned and studied her uncle's face. It was flushed and weary-looking, but no worse than she'd seen on Sunday. "Are you sure?" she insisted.

He nodded and patted her hand. "Go, please, before you get in trouble."

It took a moment before she calmed down, but finally Sandy got out of the car. "I demand to know what you're charging him with," she said coldly.

"He's not being charged with anything," came Sergeant Gaine's disgruntled voice over her shoulder.

The detective looked tired and rumpled rather than angry. He'd been down on one knee in the alleyway, evidenced by the dusty patch on his trouser leg.

"He's not being charged?" she repeated uncertainly.

"Mr. Savarini was the one who found the body, Miss," the officer explained. "We just have to take him to the station to get his statement. It's standard procedure."

Flanked by Ted Gaine and the young constable, Sandy watched the other officer get behind the wheel and drive away with her uncle.

"He'll be home in a couple of hours," Gaine reassured her. "Now let's talk about you. Constable Browne here says you bolted when you saw the body. What's the story, Alessandra? Did you know that kid?"

"Well, no, not exactly," she replied, and shifted her weight uneasily from one foot to the other. "I knew who he was."

As she watched with growing anxiety, Sergeant Gaine assumed his official police expression, pulled his pen and spiral notebook out of his shirt pocket, and turned to a clean page.

"Victim's full name?"

"I don't know. I just heard him being called Vito."

He paused, then jotted the single word in his notebook. "And how do you happen to know Vito?"

Sandy shrugged, searching her mind for a safe version of the truth. "I've been at the arcade when Vito and Dooley were there. I got a look at them."

Gaine muttered to himself as he scribbled rapidly in his notebook. "Dooley. Is that a first or a last name?"

"I . . . Last name, I think."

"Can you describe him?"

Sandy struggled to separate what she'd seen and heard that one Saturday morning at the arcade from what Tommy had told her earlier about Dooley, and what Dooley had told her about himself later on. "Uh, about my height, curly blond hair, blue eyes. His voice was very strained and raspy.''

''Did they speak to you?''

''No, to someone else. I didn't hear exactly what was said,'' she explained.

''Then how did you know who you were looking at?''

He was watching her carefully, watching her teeter on the brink of his trap. Too late, she realized there was no safe version of the truth.

Sandy tried to swallow and nearly choked. ''By the jackets they were wearing,'' she managed.

''Describe the jackets,'' he commanded sternly.

''Black leather, windbreaker style, with lettering on the back. Knights of the Night, they said.''

''Alessandra, how did you know they would be wearing those jackets?''

Sandy's heart dropped. ''My brother told me about them,'' she murmured, feeling sick inside. She had to force herself not to glance over Sergeant Gaine's shoulder toward the body. According to Tommy, Vito always wore his jacket, winter or summer. But there was no jacket on the murder victim in the alley.

''And how did your brother know Vito?'' persisted the detective.

She sighed. ''Vito was some guy Tommy brought home after school one day. My mother took one look at him and threw him out of the apartment. Tommy rebelled, began spending more time with Vito instead of less, and ... that's it. I only saw him once, at the arcade.''

''What kinds of things did they do together, Vito and your brother?''

''I don't know exactly,'' said Sandy, licking her lips nervously. ''They hung out.''

"I see. Any connections with organized crime that you know of?"

"No."

"Any drugs? Extortion? Blackmail?"

While Gaine waited patiently for her answer, Sandy shifted her weight back and forth and struggled to collect her scattered thoughts.

"I don't know. He could have been doing any of those things," she said at last.

"Okay, how do I get in touch with your brother, Alessandra?"

Sandy's breath turned to dust in her throat. The whole point of her bargain with Dooley had been to protect Tommy from the fallout of a situation like this. And now, not only was her brother involved, but Sandy herself had betrayed him.

"You want to question Tommy?" she said brokenly.

"That's right. You said he lives with your mother?"

Automatically Sandy gave Sergeant Gaine her mother's address. Then, as he closed his spiral notebook with a snap, she suddenly realized what she'd done. Her mother was going to have a fit when the police came banging on her door, wanting to question Tommy about a murder.

"All right, Alessandra, you've found your uncle and I've got work to do," said Gaine. "Constable Browne will drive you back to your office. After work, go straight home and stay there. I'm going to want to speak to you later."

Ted watched Alessandra follow the young officer to his patrol car. She looked numb, practically in shock, and for a moment he hated himself for taking advantage of her obvious emotional distress to pull information out of her. He'd had to do it, he told himself. This was a murder investigation, and drawing facts out of upset witnesses was just part of his job. Nobody had ever faulted him for doing his job—except Carol.

Her biggest complaint was that he had stopped doing his job and simply become it. Was she right? Was this the sort of thing Carol had meant when she told him he was a cop right down to his bone marrow, that he was incapable of relating to anyone who didn't fall neatly under the heading of suspect, witness or victim?

If that was true, then he couldn't help wondering... had he just turned Alessandra into a victim?

SHORTLY BEFORE EIGHT that evening, Sandy dragged herself up the stairs to her apartment, fumbled her key into the lock, and dropped wearily into the love seat facing her still-open front door.

It had been, by all accounts, a very full and stressful day. She shouldn't have let Paul talk her out of resigning, she thought with a moan. There would have been no way to back up and cancel out what had happened earlier in any event, but at least she wouldn't have had to spend the entire afternoon on the phone with the reference librarian, trying to replace the three recent crimes in her third article with three equally ghastly historical ones. She'd finally had to settle for an arson-murder, an armed bank robbery and a lynching. By the time she was done, Sandy, sure she had a cauliflower ear, felt like doing some lynching herself.

Of course, her common sense cut in, because she'd been so busy she'd had no time to dwell on the scene that had taken place beside the arcade that afternoon. She'd had no time to nurture her feeling of guilt over having betrayed Tommy, or her dislike of the tough, smart cop who had badgered her into doing it. Ted Gaine would say that he'd just been conducting a thorough investigation, no doubt.

Dio, how she hated that little spiral notepad of his!

"Oh, good, you're finally home," said a perky voice from the doorway. Sandy glanced up and saw her downstairs neighbor standing there in a flowered housedress. "You wouldn't believe how busy it's been around here today," she said with a forced laugh. "First I had to let the telephone repairman into your apartment—"

Sandy jerked upright in her seat. "You let someone in here?"

The shocked expression on her face gave the other woman pause. "Well, yes," she replied uncertainly. "He had a work order with your name on it, and I knew you'd been having a little trouble with your phone. Didn't you put in a service call?"

"No, I didn't."

Nervously the neighbor combed her short bleached-blond hair with her fingers. "Maybe that's why the police officers wanted to look around. Although it did seem rather strange the way they followed right on this fellow's heels."

Sandy's jaw dropped even farther. Misinterpreting her reaction, the neighbor hastened to assure her, "I saw both their badges before I opened your door for them, Sandy. And nobody touched a thing. I was watching them like a hawk the whole time."

Sandy was dumbfounded. First a telephone repairman who knew her name and address but hadn't been summoned, then two police officers—or, more likely, two men claiming to be police officers—who "wanted to look around"?

Holding on to her fragile composure with both hands, Sandy asked, "What did the phone repairman do?"

"He checked out your phones and phone lines. Their computer indicated some problems. There was a power outage, and a few residences were affected. He looked at mine, too."

"That still wouldn't account for the other two men," Sandy pointed out, frowning. Suddenly her apartment was full of strange footprints again, setting her stomach writhing like a trapped animal. "What did they tell you? Did they have a warrant?"

"They... asked about the phone repairman. When I told them that he'd only touched the phones, they asked if they could have a look at them too. Their ID looked genuine, so I let them in. Showed them mine, too."

Sandy bit back a sarcastic comment about cereal box prizes. "And?"

She shrugged. "They took our phones apart and put them back together again. Then they thanked me and left."

Sandy's head was beginning to throb. "And that's all they did?"

"That's all," replied the other woman in a tiny, contrite voice. "Do you want your spare key back?"

"No, it's all right," she sighed, rubbing her temples with aching fingers.

"Well, I've left dishes soaking downstairs," said the woman, her voice almost hysterically bright, "so if you'll excuse me...?"

Sandy waved her away and got up to close the door. Then she dug into her handbag for a couple of headache tablets, her mind foaming and churning with unpleasant possibilities.

The phone man could have been for real, of course, in which case Sandy was upsetting herself unnecessarily.

But if the phone man was an impostor, or if the two police officers were impostors, they could have been casing the apartment for a future break-in. Or else they could have been looking for something.

The printout.

Fear and anger knotted together into a cold lump and nested at the back of her throat. Sandy raced into the bedroom and flung open the closet door. None of the clothes looked disturbed, but that didn't mean anything. She swept them aside with one arm and shoved her chair into the closet with the other. Standing on the seat of the chair, she pushed open the little trapdoor to the attic.

Dio, please, let it still be there!

Sandy reached blindly through the opening, sighing with relief when her fingers touched the molded plastic handle of her briefcase. Then it occurred to her that that didn't mean anything, either, and she pulled the case down and opened it on her bed to make sure the printout was still safely inside. *Dio grazie,* it was, all five pounds of it.

Nonetheless, Sergeant Gaine ought to know about these three visitors, she decided. Sandy locked the briefcase again and replaced it in its hiding place. Then she hurried into the living room, snatched up the telephone receiver and punched in the home phone number on Gaine's card. No answer.

Muttering to herself, she tried his office number. After seven rings, the phone was picked up by a Detective Sergeant Andover. No, Sergeant Gaine wasn't in the office right now. He was out investigating a case. If she cared to leave a message, Sergeant Andover would be happy to pass it along. Or, if it was an emergency, Sergeant Gaine could be reached on his pager. Was this an emergency?

Sandy glanced around her apartment. Everything was in its place. Nothing looked touched. If her neighbor hadn't made a point of running upstairs to tell her about it, she wouldn't even have known that anyone had been here during her absence. That was the truly frightening part, she thought with a shiver. That was the way Mr. Vanish would operate. However, as long as there weren't any bodies littering her living-room floor . . . And Gaine had promised—threatened, actually—to call her later this evening anyway.

No, this probably wasn't an emergency, she told the sergeant reluctantly before hanging up.

Hugging herself, Sandy walked through the apartment, trembling to think how easy it was for an intruder to get into a place like this. And she was all alone here, and plenty of people knew it—including, no doubt, Mr. Vanish. She looked around and could practically see the footprints of the three men who had tricked her neighbor into letting them in that afternoon.

She would have to scrub her apartment down again. And maybe, while she was at it, she ought to get herself a gun.

Chapter Eight

"Sergeant Gaine is out on a case right now," apologized the receptionist. "Perhaps one of the other detectives could help you?"

Sandy uttered a small, frustrated moan. "No, thank you. I really only want to talk to Sergeant Gaine."

That was an understatement. Sandy had awakened at five that morning, coiled tight as a spring with tense anticipation. She had logged on the magazine computer at seven and worked nonstop until one-thirty, when Frank Leslie had come to reclaim his terminal. And as she worked, pieces had begun falling into place in her mind, and she'd realized with a start that she must have been put under police surveillance. That was how Gaine could promise so confidently to watch over her twenty-four hours a day.

Now she understood whom he had nodded to on the street, and why Constable Browne had shadowed her so closely at the scene of Vito's murder. How long had they been watching her? she wondered. Since the discovery of Blass's body? Since she'd turned over the ledger page Tuesday morning? Or had the surveillance begun even earlier than that, for a different reason? Had the eyes she'd felt boring into her at the subway station last Saturday belonged to a plainclothes police officer with orders to make her feel vulnerable and in danger?

The more she'd thought about it, the angrier Sandy had become. That Gaine had put her under surveillance was wonderful; that he'd done it without letting her know was, well, was peeping. It made her skin crawl.

So, no, Sandy didn't want to talk to another detective. She'd come here at two o'clock on an empty stomach specifically to straighten out Ted Gaine.

"Then can I give him a message for you, or at least tell him that you stopped by?" suggested the receptionist, flashing a sympathetic smile.

Sandy considered for a moment. "Yes, you can," she said, handing over the sealed manila envelope containing the photocopies of Charlie's notes. "Please tell him that Alessandra was here, and give him this, and say 'I told you so.'"

The receptionist looked momentarily puzzled. "That's it? 'I told you so'?"

"That's all of it."

She shrugged and copied down the message on a pad of printed yellow forms. "He'll get this as soon as he returns," she promised, tearing off the slip of paper and taping it onto the envelope.

Finally feeling pangs of hunger, Sandy stopped at a fast-food place for a chicken sandwich and some salad before going home. While on the subway platform, however, she changed her mind and took a southbound instead of a northbound train. She hadn't spoken to Uncle Hugo since yesterday noon.

She had lectured him about family obligations; she was a fine one to be doing that, Sandy scolded herself now. She'd watched him being driven off, sick and weak, in a police car, and then hadn't even thought about him for over twenty-four hours. *Dio,* what was the matter with her?

The video arcade had been temporarily shut down because of the murder investigation. All the doorways but one had been sealed, and the interior of the building was filled with a dark, eerie silence. Sandy took a cautious step inside, waiting a moment for her eyesight to adjust. As the dim outlines of the game machines became discernible, they reminded her of a troop of camouflaged soldiers waiting in ambush.

"Can I help you?" came a stern voice from behind her. Sandy spun around and found herself face-to-face with Barney Bruce, arms folded and wearing a carved expression.

"Oh, it's you," he said, and relaxed. "Looking for Hugo, I guess."

"Yes, I am." Her voice sounded unnaturally loud in the unnatural silence of the arcade.

"He isn't here. He phoned me early this morning and said he was feeling sick."

After yesterday's ordeal, Sandy wasn't surprised to hear that. She marched double time to Queen Street and rode the streetcar directly to Uncle Hugo's place.

But Hugo wasn't there. The building superintendent let her into an apartment that was as neat as a pin—and empty.

Not sure yet just how worried to be, Sandy thanked the woman and went directly home. She would phone her mother right away; maybe she'd heard something and hadn't been able to reach Sandy earlier. And against her better judgment she would contact Charlie, as well.

Things had really begun to come together in her mind as she'd worked on the computer early that morning. She had developed a theory that tied in Blass and the ledger page with Mr. Vanish; now all she needed to do was test it. To accomplish that, she would need information from a variety of police files, and since the confidentiality of the Mr. Vanish investigation would be blown if Gaine officially delved into Department records, it appeared she had no choice but to hire Charlie.

Sandy sighed. Hire Charlie and conspire to commit a theft from police records. Obviously it would be wiser to do this without Ted Gaine's knowledge. There was no way the magazine would back her up, either, if she got caught knowingly purchasing stolen information. But she wasn't buying it for a *Police Digest* article, she reminded herself. It would be used to assist the police in nailing Mr. Vanish. It might even solve the Parmentier case.

As she stepped through the door of her apartment, Sandy glanced at her watch. It was nearly 3:45 p.m. She had time to make her phone calls and then put in a couple of hours researching her next article before dinner.

Her mother's line was busy. And when Sandy dialed the number scrawled inside the matchbook cover, she got an answering machine. Reluctantly, she left a message and hung up.

TED UTTERED A LOW WHISTLE of surprise. "Will you look at this?" he murmured.

"Look at what?" said Joe, crossing their office space to scan the photocopied pages spread across his partner's desk. "Armed robbery, kidnapping..." he read. "Why did you pull all these files?"

"I didn't. Alessandra has very kindly provided us a copy of the information she got from her first source back in May."

Joe glanced up, his blue eyes widening. "I think we've found a leak, partner. Only I don't understand how he could have broken into that many files without being detected. Look, he even makes reference to a photograph in the evidence vault—''

"A photograph? Let me see that."

As Ted read the summary of the five-year-old Haltford kidnapping, his thoughts and his pulse began to race together. Alessandra told him she'd had to contact some of the people named as witnesses to corroborate the facts in each case. He had only questioned her about the two murders, but what if she'd corroborated the kidnapping as well? What if she'd discussed the existence of that photograph with someone who'd rather it was destroyed?

His mind flashed the image of her ransacked bedroom, the window left ajar, the photo albums sliced open, their contents scattered all over the room. And all at once Ted knew, without a shred of doubt, that the intruder had been looking for the Haltford photograph in Alessandra's apartment Saturday night.

He cast a worried eye over the other eleven cases on his desk. How many more nervous perpetrators had her in their sights? he wondered.

Just then the phone rang. Preoccupied with Alessandra's twelve cases, Ted was vaguely aware of Joe picking up the receiver, having a brief conversation, and hanging up again.

"That was Ballistics, partner," said Joe, then loudly a second time to get Ted's attention. "They confirm that Roger Blass was killed by a bullet from the same gun used on Parmentier back in August. I don't know where you got that hunch from, but it was right. Let's pull the files and get to work."

But Ted's thoughts were heading in a slightly different direction. So Blass and Parmentier had been killed by the same gun? And if Alessandra's mystery witness was right and Mr. Vanish was responsible for both murders, then he had to be closing in on her, as well. Ted felt a chill ripple across his shoulders. He'd kept the surveillance on Alessandra informal until now to avoid frightening her; but informal surveillance would no longer be enough. Tonight he would have to frighten her to get her to go along with the next stage of his plan to protect her. And judging by what little he knew about Alessandra, that wouldn't be easy.

SANDY MADE A HERCULEAN EFFORT to immerse herself in the research for her next article; but a darkening cloud of guilt and fear and anger kept fragmenting her concentration and sending her thoughts off on frightening tangents.

When the telephone rang, rescuing her from what had become a hopeless task, Sandy virtually pounced on the receiver.

"Hello!"

It was Dooley. "Vito's dead," he rasped, wasting no time on preamble.

"I know. I was there with the police just after he was found."

"Have the cops got anything? I mean, do they think they know . . . ?"

"It's a murder investigation, Dooley. The police aren't about to share sensitive information with a crime journalist."

"So you talk to them, but they don't talk to you? That means you can't tell me if they're out lookin' for Mr. Vanish, neither, huh?"

"No, I can't. I'm sorry." Sandy sighed with genuine regret. She would have liked to reassure him that there was an investigation going on, but she and Gaine had agreed to keep it secret.

Silence gaped like a chasm between them for a moment. Then, hesitantly, Dooley said, "Mr. Vanish got Vito, y'know. He thought it was me but he got Vito instead. Shot him in the chest and left him in that alley."

Sandy nearly dropped the phone. "Wait a minute—you witnessed the killing? You're going to have to tell the police—"

"Tell them what?" cut in Dooley. "That Mr. Vanish thought Vito was me? Not even the cops are that dumb, lady. They'll put two and two together. They'll figure out that I was the one told you about seeing the Parmentier hit go down. He's really gettin' close now. I'm gonna disappear until they get him. So long."

"But where will you—?" She was talking to a dial tone. Slowly Sandy hung up the receiver, torn between relief and anxiety. She had an awful feeling about this, a premonition that wherever Dooley went to ground, Tommy would be with him. And if Mr. Vanish realized he'd made a mistake and went after Dooley...!

There was a knock at her door. *Now what?* she thought as she wrenched it open.

Ted Gaine was standing in the hall, wearing blue jeans and a denim jacket, and holding a fistful of wilting chrysanthemums.

"I got your message," he said with an ingratiating smile, "and I've come to pick you up for dinner."

The day had been too much for her. "Dinner?" she echoed, staring at the tired bouquet.

Belatedly he remembered them and held them out to her like a schoolboy handing his teacher an apple with a bite taken out of it. "These are for you. They're a little thirsty...."

"Dinner," she repeated impatiently, brushing away the flowers. "Okay, Sergeant Gaine, how long have I been under police surveillance?"

"Since you left Investigative Services Tuesday morning. And we've had this building staked out since Tuesday noon. Can we discuss this after dinner, please?"

He tried to give her the flowers again, and once again she brushed them away.

"Have a heart, Alessandra," he pleaded. "These poor mums need water."

With an exasperated sigh, she snatched the bouquet out of his hand and carried it over to the sink. "You're a chauvinist," she said from the kitchen. "There's a problem between us and you're going to try to solve it by giving me flowers, feeding me and patting me on the head."

"Not at all," he replied from the doorway. "The flowers and the food and the pat on the head are to calm you down so we can discuss our problem and work things out like reasonable people. I'm sure I'd rather do this on a full stomach than an empty one. So how about dinner?"

Sandy stared at him for a long moment. He was right, she realized with a sigh. And he was regarding her with a warmly amused expression that seemed to call forth an answering smile, making it very difficult for her to remain annoyed with him.

"Dinner sounds fine," she said at last, putting the vase down on the telephone table. "I'll go change my clothes."

"Don't bother. Casual is just fine for the place we're going to."

The place turned out to be Ted Gaine's house in the suburbs, a small town house on a crescent, three doors away from a neighborhood playground swarming with

children. And dinner, she discovered, would be a backyard barbecue for two, a sampling of suburbia for the
deprived city dweller.

Sandy surveyed the smallish backyard and saw a sap-
ling supported by stakes and loops of rope, anchors that
had once held a swing set, and a tiny garden sprouting
little green shoots in impossibly straight rows.

"Is this really your house?" she asked.

He flashed an unexpected grin. "Did I borrow it to
impress you, you mean? I didn't. One-third of it is all
mine."

"Oh, you share it with two other people?"

"Nope. I share it with the Police Credit Union."

Sandy shook her head wonderingly. "I'm sorry. It's
just so hard to believe—"

"What? That I have a home and a life away from
Investigative Services?" he reproved her gently. "Well, I
do. I just don't get to enjoy them very much—especially
right now."

This reminder of the investigation that had brought
them together effectively killed the conversation until at
last the charcoal caught fire. While they waited for the
heat to steady, Gaine went into the kitchen to assemble
the rest of their meal, and Sandy followed curiously.

"This isn't your house," she insisted with a shake of
her head. "It's too clean. Everyone knows that men living alone are supposed to have a sinkful of pots and pans,
dust bunnies in every corner, and—" Gaine took some
salad vegetables out of the refrigerator and she glanced
inside "—green fur growing in the fridge," she concluded.

"No, that was Carol's place before we got married—I
was always the tidy one. She only cleaned as a conces-
sion to me." As he placed the lettuce, tomatoes and cu-

cumber around the cutting board on the counter, he sighed and added thoughtfully, "She . . . desperately wanted to have better things to do than keep house."

An uncomfortable silence fell between them then. "I'm sorry," Sandy murmured. "I seem to have a knack for stirring up—"

"It's not your fault, Alessandra. Look, how would you like to cut up these vegetables for our salad?"

His eyes settled softly on her face, the same shifting gray as the smoke billowing off the barbecue outside the kitchen window. In the quiet that suddenly filled the kitchen, the fridge came on with an importunate growl. Sandy swallowed hard and replied, "Sure. Just point me at your knives."

As she chopped cucumber into submission with Ted Gaine's sharpest knife, she couldn't help wondering just what his relationship with his ex-wife was. Did he still love her? Was that the problem? Or was it hatred that kept tripping up his relationship with Sandy?

Out on the patio, turning hamburgers on the grill, Ted glanced up at the screened kitchen window and saw Alessandra bustling around inside. She was checking the contents of his fridge and taking things down from the cupboard above the stove. He had no idea what she was doing, but she certainly seemed to have made herself at home. More at home after twenty minutes than Carol had been after three years.

He sighed philosophically. Carol had wanted nothing to do with this house or the suburbs. She'd wanted him to finish his law studies and set up a practice, and a few years later run for Parliament. She wanted to live in the style to which she longed to become accustomed. Even if Ted had worked his way up to Chief of Police, she would never have been happy being married to a cop. He knew that now.

And what did he know about Alessandra, besides the fact that she was constantly on his mind? Unfortunately, circumstances hadn't exactly been conducive to long, intimate conversations. There was a small matter of professional ethics to consider, as well.

Ted flipped one of the hamburgers, pressing it with unnecessary force onto the grill. It was considered unprofessional for a detective to become emotionally involved with a witness in an ongoing investigation. It impaired his objectivity, hampered his judgment, twisted what ought to have been a straightforward working relationship, and ultimately delayed the solving of the case. All the textbooks agreed.

And unless he wanted to be officially removed from the Parmentier investigation, which was an important link in the Mr. Vanish investigation, Ted knew he had better appear to agree, as well. No matter how he longed to hold her close, smell the fragrance of her, taste the sweetness of her, he would have to be careful. Love was a dangerous emotion under any circumstances, but especially now, with Alessandra. He mustn't let on too soon how he felt about her. He would have to keep her at arm's length until the case was closed, and pray that she would still feel something for him when it was over . . . assuming she felt anything for him now, he reminded himself with an inward sigh.

All done in the kitchen, Alessandra strolled out onto the patio, sipping from a tin of no-name cream soda. She sat down on one of the canvas lawn chairs, crossed her beautiful legs, inhaled the aroma of cooking beef and sighed with pleasure. She was obviously looking forward to a meal that would have made Carol's lip curl with disdain. For the first time in days, Ted actually felt like smiling.

Half an hour later, they had finished off two hamburgers apiece and most of a bowl of salad, with Sandy's improvised Italian dressing. As she popped the last bite of her hamburger into her mouth, washing it down with the final mouthful of cream soda, Sandy had to admit that this meal had really hit the spot. The conversation had been a little awkward, with both of them carefully avoiding any discussion that might lead to mention of Carol or Mr. Vanish. But the food had been delicious, and the vivid oranges and pinks of the sunset had been an unexpected treat for a city girl used to seeing the sun disappear behind a row of buildings long before it had touched the horizon.

All at once Gaine's telephone was ringing. He excused himself and went inside to answer it, leaving Sandy alone on the tiny patio. The freshening air stroked her skin as she nestled lazily into the lawn chair, determined to absorb as much of this blissfully simple moment as she could.

Behind her, there was the sudden slam of the screen door, and Gaine dropped into the other lawn chair, frowning.

"I'm sorry, Alessandra, but the meal is over. It's time to talk," he said. "That phone call was from the electronic-surveillance unit. They just swept your apartment—"

Instantly her anger reignited. "They *what*?"

"Yesterday afternoon you had a visit from a telephone repairman. Right after he left, two of my men went in there and found listening devices planted in both your phones. I immediately ordered a full electronic sweep of every room, just in case there were other devices hidden."

More strangers' footprints in her apartment. Sandy's stomach began to clench. "You should have told me about this," she said, thrusting each word at him.

"Listen to me, Alessandra. The phony repairman left two listening devices in your telephones. And the electronic-surveillance team, using a bug detector, found three more, all much smaller and more sophisticated than the other two, and all in places your neighbor swears the repairman never even went near."

Her thoughts suddenly racing, she drew in a long, steadying breath. "So you figure two different people bugged my apartment, and one of them obviously did it before your stakeout was set up on Tuesday. And it couldn't have been the same person who broke in Saturday night?"

Gaine shook his head. "Someone who wanted to conceal a bug wouldn't advertise his visit by tearing the place apart first. My guess is that you had a visit from Mr. Vanish. He wants to know how much you know and who you've spoken to, so he'll know who else needs to be killed."

Sandy felt her stomach do a slow cartwheel as she found herself staring into Ted Gaine's official police face.

"And that's not all, Alessandra. I looked at the information you got from your source. It was quite a revelation. All those confidential cases ... all those ruffled feathers when you'd finished corroborating facts that some of the witnesses—and suspects—were hearing for the first time...."

Sandy's eyes widened as it dawned on her what he was saying. "So they're nervous because they think I was investigating them? Nervous enough—"

"—to want to know how much more you know about them, yes," he supplied grimly. "In one particular case, nervous enough to want to find out whether you're in possession of a certain incriminating photograph. And if you've unsettled any more perpetrators with your questions, possibly nervous enough to want to terrorize or kill you," he concluded, over her sharp intake of breath.

Suddenly she became aware that Gaine was watching her with eyes like molten lead. She forced herself to stare back at him, awaiting his next move.

"At this point, we don't know for sure how many people may be stalking you, Alessandra. We just know that Mr. Vanish is among them. Things have become very dangerous, too dangerous for a civilian. I'm taking you to a safe house, north of the city, and putting a policewoman in your apartment as a decoy. We'll go tonight, directly from here."

Being shunted out of the way and locked up for her own good was not at all what Sandy had in mind. "No, you can't," she told him. "Mr. Vanish isn't stupid. He'll spot the substitution."

"That'll be my problem, Alessandra."

"And what about *my* problems? I have to work. I have stories to file, deadlines coming up, and a very nervous mother who would drive the entire Department crazy if her daughter just dropped out of sight."

Gaine made an exasperated sound. "I admire your courage, but you're being very foolish, Alessandra. We're up against a brilliant, cold-blooded killer. You're an untrained civilian and we have to protect you."

"But you're already protecting me," she exclaimed. "I'm under twenty-four-hour surveillance, remember?"

He shook his head impatiently. "The point is, that surveillance is no longer enough to guarantee your safety."

"The point is, the trap is already baited, Sergeant," she insisted. "If Mr. Vanish sees you messing with it, he'll be warned off and all your wonderful precautions will have been for nothing because you'll lose him."

Sergeant Gaine stared at the toes of his running shoes for a moment, visibly embroiled in internal debate. He shook his head with annoyance, glanced at the cooling barbecue, then finally turned to meet her steady gaze, a frown of concern creasing his brow. "Do you realize what you're proposing? I don't know why I'm even entertaining it—the answer is no," he said, deciding abruptly. "The inspector would have my badge and probably press criminal charges if I let you go through with this, Alessandra. You could be killed."

"Would the inspector believe that if you told him?" she asked. "He probably thinks Mr. Vanish is a figment of your imagination. But if we're right about this killer, my life is in danger no matter what we do, Sergeant, and no matter where I go."

Sandy gulped hard as the meaning of her own words hit home. *Dio,* as long as Mr. Vanish was out there she didn't stand a chance anywhere! But she still believed that the best defence was a good offence, and Ted Gaine offered the best offence that she could see. So Sandy stubbornly held his steely gaze and said, in as calm and firm a voice as she could manage, "If I have to risk my life, I'd rather be fighting on the front lines than hiding out somewhere. Wouldn't you?"

She felt extreme fear, but she didn't know how else to deal with the situation. If Mr. Vanish existed, she didn't stand a chance—anywhere.

Gaine stared at her wordlessly for a moment. Then he leapt up and raced inside the house. A couple of minutes later he was back, pocketing his wallet and keys and grumbling to himself, "It's got to be a gene. I don't believe I'm doing this. All right, Alessandra, get your purse," he said grimly. "You're going to meet the rest of the team."

CHARLIE CALLED HER BACK at 1:00 a.m. Normally, Sandy would have been angry at receiving a phone call that late at night, but with all the warnings and instructions from the police surveillance team still ringing in her head, she hadn't been able to sleep, anyway. Being the bait in a trap, it turned out, wasn't much better than being locked up in a safe house.

"So you need some research done?" said Charlie casually. "It's fifty bucks for custom jobs."

Sandy jackknifed into a sitting position in bed, instantly grabbing the piece of paper she kept beside the phone in case he called. "I'll pay it. This is important."

"In that case, it's seventy-five."

She sighed impatiently. "Goodbye, Charlie..."

"Okay, okay—fifty! What d'ya want to know about?"

"I'm going to give you six dates. I need to know whether any unsolved murders or suspicious deaths took place on those dates, in or out of town. And I need to know whether any of the victims had any connection with either Duds 'n' Dudes or Unity Sportswear. Can you do it?"

"Sure," he said. "Give me the dates."

Sandy read them off the paper. When she was done she heard a low whistle at the other end of the line.

"That's a lot of digging," he remarked after a pause. "Why d'ya need to know all that?"

In spite of her weariness Sandy smiled. "It'll cost you fifty bucks to find out."

He chuckled softly. "I'm going to enjoy doing business with you, lady. I'll be in touch."

Slowly Sandy replaced the receiver on its cradle and settled back against her pillow, willing sleep to come but knowing she was too keyed up to succumb to it. Sitting in the dark, listening to the breeze whisper in the branches of the maple tree outside her window, feeling small and alone in spite of the three pairs of eyes she knew were trained on the outside of her building, she found herself wishing Sergeant Gaine were there. She liked his company. She liked him.

He made a good protector, she decided, yawning. In another era, he would have been a knight in armor, wandering the countryside, doing good deeds and rescuing damsels in distress. And holding them, to make them feel safe and secure once more.

It had been a long time since she had last felt that way in a man's arms—over a year now. No, she recalled as the shadowy contours of her room began to melt into a greater darkness, taking her spinning thoughts with them, it had been eight years. The various men she'd dated since moving away from home had aroused many feelings in her, from adoration to impatience, but the only other man . . . she'd felt she could . . . completely trust . . . had . . . been . . . Papa. . . .

Chapter Nine

Sandy shifted in her chair, uncomfortably aware that Detective Feeney was sitting just outside the door in the reception area, pretending to read a magazine while he screened everybody who walked into Editorial.

Sergeant Gaine had advised her to ignore Feeney, to act as though he wasn't there. Maybe one day Sandy *would* be able to disregard the hovering presence of a grim-faced ex-linebacker armed with a small cannon. For the moment, however, it was damnably difficult to do.

After thoroughly checking her desk for explosive devices—bombs weren't Mr. Vanish's style, but it was best to be safe—Feeney had taken up his post in the reception area. He hadn't moved from there all day, but his presence seemed to throw an unnerving pall over the entire office.

The receptionist sat only five feet away from him. She had spilled her coffee twice that morning, the first time when he unbuttoned his jacket to reveal the dark leather strap of his shoulder holster, the second time when he asked her whether there was a back door to Editorial. Feeney's voice sounded like Sylvester Stallone talking through a megaphone.

Feeney was Sandy's "shadow."

For Sandy, the word shadow had always conjured up images of wraithlike insubstantiality, of stealth, of silence. Being shadowed by Detective Feeney was like getting a little hug from an anaconda. In the Old West, he would have been an overeager deputy riding shotgun for the new schoolmarm. In the offices of *Police Digest* magazine, he was an embarrassing distraction.

That was probably why Gaine had sicked him on her, she reflected with some annoyance. The sergeant had wanted her to call in sick and she had refused. She would definitely have to have a word with him about this.

With difficulty, Sandy forced herself to focus on the text scrolling upward on her computer screen. She was very close to finishing this article, a full working day ahead of schedule.

"DiGianni, a word with you please?" bawled her editor from the door of his office.

Hastily Sandy saved her article and logged off.

As she stepped into Paul's glass-walled cubicle, he thoughtfully pulled the extra chair into position beside his desk for her. "Please, sit down," he invited politely.

Something was up. Paul Rudd didn't normally waste good manners on his employees. Uneasily Sandy sat down in the visitor's chair.

Paul set his cigar carefully on the cheap foil ashtray. "I've been on the phone with Sergeant Gaine," he began stiffly. "He tells me there may be a contract killer after you...that he offered to put you in a safe house but you refused because you had stories to file and deadlines to meet...?"

"And family obligations," she added quietly.

Instantly Paul's eyes lit up with understanding. "Ah! You know, I was going to castigate you for being reckless with your life, for having a secret wish to be a war correspondent, and maybe also for being stupidly un-realistic. But since you're doing all this for the sake of your family... How close are you to finishing your third article?"

She shrugged. "Another hour or two."

"Excellent! As soon as you've filed that article, you're on vacation, DiGianni."

"For how long?"

"Until your safety is no longer a police matter. Finish the piece and go home. And, please," he added, pop-ping the cigar back into his mouth, "take Rambo with you."

HE WAS RUNNING the damned maze again, only this time it was leading him in circles. Ted sat reading and re-reading the file on the Vito Taglia murder, and shaking his head in frustration.

According to Alessandra's second source, Mr. Vanish had killed Vito; but even a cursory glance at his and Joe's notes showed that Mr. Vanish couldn't have done it.

The Sunnyside job had been slick and professional—obviously the work of a skilled assassin. By comparison, Vito's murder had all the earmarks of an impulse killing by a sloppy amateur with incredible good luck—done in broad daylight, near a crowd of potential witnesses, and the body left where it was sure to be discovered almost immediately, giving the murderer no getaway time.

"Here, this ought to help sort a few things out." Joe Wegner stepped into their work space and handed Ted a one-page computer printout. "It's Mr. Vanish's modus operandi."

Frowning, Ted scanned the information in front of him. "Nobody but me even thinks this guy exists. How did you get the computer to cough up an M.O.?"

"I used unsolved cases where Mr. Vanish was suspected of being the perpetrator. You'll notice that no two of these murders were committed with the same weapon, and no weapon was ever found."

"But Ballistics says Parmentier and Blass were killed with the same gun."

Joe shrugged. "Draw your own conclusion, partner. What have we got on the Taglia case so far?"

"Not much." Ted sighed. "There are still too many ifs in the equation—and too many people with reason to want the victim dead. And I'm sure Mr. Vanish didn't make this hit."

"Well, I'm glad of that," said Joe emphatically.

"And if Mr. Vanish didn't kill Parmentier, Blass or Taglia, then we've planned a surprise party for someone who isn't going to show up, and that isn't going to sit well with Inspector Nielsen."

"Well, you've done one thing right," said Joe. Grinning, he leaned back against the edge of his desk and crossed his arms. "You ordered complete electronic monitoring of DiGianni's apartment."

"Yeah." Ted grunted unhappily. He wasn't looking forward to telling her that her place had been rebugged. It hadn't been an easy or pleasant decision, but the alternative had been much worse.

"Don't look so glum," urged Joe. "Thanks to those bugs, we got a line on her first source late last night."

Ted glanced up, startled. "Definite make?" he demanded.

"Yep." Joe's grin broadened. "He returned a phone call and quoted her a price on some additional 'research.' Taylor's got the whole conversation on tape. And Forensics is preparing a voiceprint for us."

"Bingo," breathed Ted.

Sandy was reaching into her desk drawer for her handbag when the phone rang. It was Charlie.

"You gotta meet me tomorrow night," he told her, his normally cocksure voice tight and jumpy.

Frowning, Sandy glanced toward the reception area where Feeney was waiting to drive her home. "I don't know if I can," she said, lowering her voice. "I'm being watched."

"Yeah, I know about the police surveillance. They listened to us on the phone last night."

Sandy snapped erect in her chair. "They what?" she exclaimed, then, remembering Feeney, added in an incredulous whisper, "Are you telling me my apartment is still bugged?"

"Not still bugged," he corrected her impatiently, "bugged *again*, by the cops."

Her knuckles whitening around the receiver, Sandy forced her voice to remain calm as she asked, "How do you know?"

"I got my ways. Anyhow, I'll be calling you at work from now on, assuming we're still doing business after tomorrow night. Meet me at the back door of the Shamrock at nine sharp. Make sure you're not followed and don't be late."

Sandy stared at the humming receiver for a long, thoughtful moment before she hung it back up.

Sandy arrived at her mother's place for dinner shortly before seven, parking her shadow outside the door. Uncle Hugo arrived a minute or so later, looking pale but not as pinched as before. He'd spent the previous day at the hospital undergoing tests, and had finally been diagnosed as having high blood pressure. With proper diet and medication, the doctor had told him, Hugo would soon be back to his old self.

Well, thought Sandy uneasily, that accounted for her uncle's absence on Thursday, at least. What about Tommy?

Just after seven, Sandy, Angela and Hugo sat down to eat at a table set for four. Sandy glanced across at the empty chair and felt a sudden chill. Tommy still hadn't come home.

Swallowing with difficulty, she laid down her fork. "Mama, I'm sorry—" she began. But she was cut off by the sudden opening of the front door.

Tommy sauntered past them, pausing a moment to stare at the three dumbfounded people around the table before walking into his bedroom and slamming the door.

Sandy felt as though she'd just been kicked in the stomach. He was wearing a jacket—a black leather jacket, with Knights of the Night emblazoned across the back. And Feeney and who knew how many more officers were out there, watching all the entrances to this building. Watching her brother stroll inside wearing that jacket. Dooley's or Vito's jacket. Any second now there was going to be a knock at the door....

She tried to lift her fork again but had to put it back down because her hand was shaking. Sandy didn't want her mother to see that she was trembling, didn't want to have to deal with the questions that would raise. So she stared bleakly at the food on her plate and waited.

A few minutes later, Tommy emerged from his room and took his place at the table with such casual unconcern that Sandy wanted to grab him and shake him until his teeth rattled. She grabbed the edge of the table instead. "You were with Dooley," she accused him quietly. "And he gave you that jacket. Didn't he?"

Tommy shrugged elaborately. "What if I was? And what if he did? Vito has no use for it anymore."

Dooley had turned her brother into a target for both Mr. Vanish and the police. A decoy. A patsy. Trembling with rage, she glared hotly across the table at Tommy.

"Don't you understand what this is going to look like to the police?" she cried. "Vito is killed and you disappear, and then you suddenly reappear wearing the dead boy's jacket?"

Suddenly there was an authoritative knock at the door. As Sandy's heart began spiraling coldly down into her stomach, Angela drew herself up, slid back her chair and went to see who was there.

"I'm Sergeant Gaine and this is Sergeant Wegner of the Homicide Squad," said a polite, familiar voice that froze Sandy in her seat. "May we come in, please?"

Wordlessly, Angela opened the door wide and let them in.

Ted Gaine seemed to fill the doorway as he stepped through it. His cold gray eyes swept the tiny apartment like a searchlight, taking in the half-eaten meal on the dining-room table and then moving impersonally from face to face. Bypassing Sandy without even a flicker of recognition, he finally settled his attention on Tommy.

"Mr. DiGianni? We'd like to ask you some questions about your friend, Vito Taglia."

Tommy sucked in a breath and leapt to his feet, startling everybody at the table and almost overturning his chair. The detectives drew themselves up, seeming to grow half a foot before Sandy's shocked eyes.

"You were wearing a jacket when you entered the building," said Sergeant Wegner blandly. "Would you bring it out here, please?"

Tommy's eyes narrowed momentarily, and Sandy recalled that there was a fire escape outside his bedroom window. She leaned toward her brother with a warning shake of her head. "Don't run, Tommy," she told him softly. "If you run now, you'll be running the rest of your life. We love you. Please!"

He hesitated briefly, then pivoted and stalked into his room. A moment later he came out with the jacket and made as if to toss it at Sergeant Wegner.

"Just put it down on that chair," said the detective, gesturing toward the easy chair. Sergeant Wegner was pulling on a surgical glove. They were treating the jacket as evidence, and he didn't want to spoil any fingerprints that might be on it. Sandy repressed a groan. Tommy's prints would be all over that jacket now.

Tommy dropped the jacket unceremoniously on the seat of the easy chair and stepped back. As the whole family held their breaths, Sergeant Wegner picked up the jacket with his gloved hand and turned the garment to and fro, gently spreading or lifting parts of it with the capped end of a ballpoint pen. Suddenly he stopped and pointed at something. When Sergeant Gaine saw what he'd found, he frowned and nodded his head.

"I'm sorry, Mr. DiGianni," he said politely, "but we'll have to take you down to the station for questioning."

Tommy swayed as though a punch had been thrown at him. Casting a look of horrified disbelief at his sister, he began slowly backing away from the two detectives, shaking his head. "I—I haven't done anything," he insisted in a strained voice.

As Sergeant Wegner carefully folded the jacket, Ted Gaine reached behind his back and produced a pair of handcuffs. "We'd prefer it if you came willingly, son," he warned softly.

Tommy froze, swallowing hard, his eyes wide and helpless and riveted on the shiny metal cuffs. Seeing the terror on his face made Sandy's heart writhe in her chest.

For a moment nobody moved. Then Uncle Hugo stepped forward and addressed the two detectives in the resonant voice Sandy remembered from her childhood. "My nephew will come peacefully. And I will come with him, since he's just a boy."

Sergeants Gaine and Wegner exchanged an eloquent look. Then Gaine nodded and replied, "Very well, Mr. Savarini. Shall we go now?"

Helplessly, as though it were happening on a movie screen, Sandy watched Hugo place a reassuring arm around Tommy's rigid shoulders and direct him gently out the door, one step ahead of the police.

Chapter Ten

Saturday, June 16

She was in some kind of maze, a labyrinth, full of twistings and turnings and cold dark corners, and she was running, running, out of breath but forcing her burning legs to keep pumping because she didn't dare stand still again. Suddenly a brick wall blocked her path. A dead end. She was trapped!

And she could hear him coming for her, his footsteps growing louder and louder until she had to cover her ears against the deafening sound—

Sandy bolted upright in bed, a scream quivering at the back of her throat as she stared, transfixed, at the walls of the labyrinth that seemed still to enclose her. Then gradually, her senses returned to normal, and the high stone wall resolved itself into a dappling of shadows cast by the tall maple tree outside her bedroom window. A dream, she thought, letting out a long, relieved breath. It had just been a horrible dream.

Now, if she could only awaken from the *other* nightmare.

Willing her hands to stop shaking, she pulled the summer-weight blanket up to her chin and settled back against her pillow. It made no difference where she looked, all she could see was tough-as-nails Sergeant

Gaine pulling out his handcuffs and threatening a terrified teenage boy. Her mother had stood silently by the whole time, a mannequin with tears in her eyes. And Sandy, too, had been unable to move or cry out. It was as though Ted Gaine's cold gray eyes had turned both women to stone.

Tommy and Uncle Hugo had returned from the police station shortly after midnight, Tommy looking pale and shaken, Hugo pale and weary. The detectives had found the bullet hole in Vito's jacket. They'd wanted to hold Tommy on suspicion of murder, but Uncle Hugo had argued them out of it—for now. For now, Tommy was free. But that didn't mean he was off the hook. He could still end up paying a terrible price for his impulsiveness, and he knew it. Sandy had never seen her little brother this frightened.

And now Dooley had gone deep underground and left Tommy high and dry, a prime suspect in a murder; and Sandy had never felt so frustrated. Dooley was the only way Tommy could be cleared, and Dooley was not to be found.

Or was he? Suddenly the light dawned, and she wanted to kick herself for being so dense. Of course, Dooley could be found—by Charlie, the man who knew absolutely everything that was happening on the streets. The man who wanted her to meet him tonight behind the Shamrock tavern.

With renewed determination, Sandy stripped off her nightgown and headed for the shower. Between now and this evening there were a hundred things to do. And she'd better not mention any of them aloud, she reminded herself. Sergeant Taylor was probably hunched over a tape machine across the road, listening to every sound she made.

Sandy hatched her plan under the stinging hot spray of the shower, and inspected it for holes as she toweled off and dusted herself with talcum. By the time she'd slipped into a halter-top sundress and tied on her leather thong sandals, she was utterly convinced it would work. But as she stepped in front of the mirror to brush her hair, she saw a worried face staring back at her.

The bait was plotting to sneak away from the trap. Ted Gaine would see it as a betrayal. He would be furious. He might even arrest her, as he had wanted to do to Tommy last night. Or perhaps he would simply turn his back sadly and walk away, and quietly hate her for the rest of his life.

Suddenly tears were stinging her eyes.

No, she mustn't cry, she scolded herself, impatiently wiping the moisture away with her fingertips. She mustn't give in to such feelings. Now, especially, she had to be strong, for Tommy's sake.

YAWNING, TED GLANCED at the clock on his nightstand. Nearly half-past seven. The sun had been up for an hour, and he still hadn't got to sleep. Like a dog chasing its tail, his mind had followed the same maddening thoughts around and around all night, refusing to let him rest.

What if Alessandra was right, and Dave Ragusz had gone bad? He'd informed Ted of her visit to Dragnet last Saturday; he could equally well have informed Mr. Vanish about Bert. And Ragusz certainly had had both the opportunity and the ability to tamper with Alessandra's files Tuesday afternoon—and a strong motive for diverting suspicion from himself by demonstrating that virtually anyone could have done it.

Could Dave Ragusz be Mr. Vanish?

And what about that speculative M.O. for Mr. Vanish that Joe had worked up on the computer? Joe was pretty good with computers, but that analysis had to be wrong. All of Ted's police instincts were telling him that the Parmentier case had been a Mr. Vanish hit. It was the only conclusion that made all the inconsistencies make sense.

There had to be a pivotal clue, a key they could insert and twist to unlock the entire investigation. Maybe it was the classified ads Alessandra had found in that subfile of Bert's. Maybe instead of scolding her for checking them out with the librarian, he should have helped her to find out who had placed them. But he'd been so worried about her safety at that point that nothing else had seemed to matter.

Muttering unhappily to himself, Ted swung his long legs out of bed, pulled on a pair of undershorts and padded downstairs to the kitchen to make some instant coffee.

His objectivity was shot to hell and he knew it. That was why he'd bent over backward to compensate last night. Although Joe Wegner hadn't commented on it, Ted realized he'd come on unusually strong with Tommy DiGianni. Initially, it had been a reaction to Alessandra's presence in the room. Then he'd felt he had to maintain that persona throughout the interrogation. If Joe hadn't been there to balance him off, and if the uncle hadn't stood up to them both, Tommy would probably be in a holding cell right now, charged with murder, on the strength of one damning piece of circumstantial evidence. And Ted would be kicking himself even harder this morning than he already was.

Alessandra must think he was an ogre.

But not for long, he promised himself grimly, sipping at his mug of coffee. He would get to the bottom of the Taglia case, and he would do it this weekend. Sean Dooley was hiding out, but Ted hadn't spent all those years on the street for nothing. He wouldn't rest until he'd flushed out one king-size sewer rat and shaken the necessary information out of him.

And then he would go to work on the Parmentier case—that ledger page from Roger Blass had proved to be most informative—and make Mr. Vanish vanish once and for all.

And then there would be only Ted and Alessandra, finding out whether they had anything left to build a relationship on. God, he hoped so....

CAUTIOUSLY, SANDY SHIFTED the edge of her bedroom curtain an inch and peered out through the crack. The golden sunlight of late afternoon was beginning to fade to the silver of dusk. Gaine had assured her there was a detective watching the back of her building at all times, but the tiny, carefully landscaped yard was empty, as was the paved laneway that bisected the block and connected the rear gates of all the homes that lined it.

Maybe the unseen watcher was stationed at one of the windows that faced hers across the laneway, training a telescope or binoculars on the rear windows of her apartment, just as Sergeant Ishito was doing at the front.

Sandy glanced at the clock on her nightstand and did some rapid mental calculation. It was 7:55 p.m., time to begin getting ready.

Forcing herself to walk, not run, she fetched the radio out of the kitchen and brought it back to the bedroom. Then she tuned it to her favorite rock station and turned up the volume, praying that the music would absorb any sounds she made while changing her clothes.

That afternoon, Sandy had coaxed the detectives into letting her go shopping for an hour at a department store of their choosing. She had come back with a disguise of sorts, praying that Detective Feeney had been too busy watching the other people in the store to notice the individual items she'd purchased.

First, Sandy put on a regular outfit from her closet— a short lime-green cotton skirt, matching oversize shirt, and lemon-yellow tank top.

Then she put on her brand new "sensible shoes" and slipped the too-large, flower-printed cotton dress over her other clothes, belting it loosely to give the impression of greater body mass. Finally, she stood at the bathroom mirror and put on the short, platinum-blond wig—a pity it couldn't have had brown roots—that completed Sandy's impersonation of her downstairs neighbor.

Not bad for a cheap wig, she thought as she tucked in a stray tendril of dark hair. From a distance, she ought to be able to fool Sergeant Ishito. Ten minutes was all she needed, just long enough to get on a subway train.

Sandy tied a gauzy scarf around her head, carefully pulling the front edges forward a little to partly conceal her profile. She picked up a tote bag, borrowed from her neighbor earlier that day for this specific purpose. She placed the radio, still blaring, on the coffee table in the living room to cover the sound of her apartment door opening and closing. Then she stepped out into the hall, locking the door behind her—and in that instant knew the panic a high diver must feel at the moment of losing her balance.

Dio, this was never going to work. Her downstairs neighbor was ten years older than Sandy, and two inches shorter. She had a different posture, a different gait. Ishito would stop her before she got half a block away from the building. Charlie would think she'd stood him up. She wouldn't find Dooley. Tommy would go to prison. And Ted Gaine would never look at her again except with his official police eyes.

No, forget Ted Gaine! Forget everyone except Tommy....

A moment later, Sandy was breathing normally again. If Ishito stopped her, he stopped her. At least she would have the satisfaction of knowing that she'd tried to clear her brother. Slowly, she negotiated the wooden stairs in her sensible shoes and pulled open the street door.

The nearest bus stop was a short block away. Keeping her head lowered to help the scarf conceal her features, Sandy walked toward the corner. Her heart was sledge-hammering her ribs. Every breath became a silent gasp. She didn't know why she'd worried about breaking into a run; even if she had the wind for a sprint to the corner, her legs were slowly turning to marshmallow beneath her.

Ten minutes, she told herself again. *Just long enough to lose myself in the subway system...*

The bus pulled up just as she reached the corner. As she climbed on and took her seat, Sandy glanced out the window, half expecting to see plainclothes detectives racing down the street, waving their badges at the bus driver. The pavement was empty.

But she wasn't in the clear yet, she reminded herself. *Five more minutes...*

Every time the bus pulled over to take on passengers, Sandy held her breath. Not until they'd all walked indifferently past her could she release it. *Two more minutes...*

At last the bus turned into the loop at the subway station. Sandy joined the swelling tide of the crowd rushing down the stairs to the platform. She heard the sweet burring sound of a train on the tracks and saw the flash of a headlamp bouncing off the tiled wall of the tunnel seconds before a southbound train roared into the station and screeched to a stop.

The doors slid open. Sandy stepped aboard, and as the doors closed again she heaved a sigh of relief.

She rode the subway to the Bloor station, made her way up to street level, and emerged on Bloor Street, half a block from the Shamrock, into the midst of the casually chattering Saturday-night throng. She let the crowd carry her along Bloor to the entrance of the laneway that ran behind the tavern. Then, with a glance over her shoulder, she darted into the darkening alley, made the left turn, and backtracked the length of the block, counting buildings, until she was standing nervously beside a steel door with an oversize handle and the word Shamrock stenciled onto it in green paint.

In her disguise, she felt like a child rushing Halloween. Should she knock? Anxiously, Sandy glanced around. She'd better do something soon, because the alley was swiftly turning into a place of sinister, scurrying shadows, bringing a lump of fear to her throat that refused to be swallowed. Charlie had insisted she meet him here. Where was he? Was this another of his damned tests to see whether she had the guts to do business with him?

All at once the steel door flew open, and Sandy's heart tried to leap out of her mouth.

"What're you standing out here for?" demanded Charlie from the doorway. "You wanna get mugged?"

Weak-kneed with a mixture of relief and indignation, she replied, "All you told me was to meet you at the back door!"

"Yeah, sorry, next time I'll spell out which side of the door. Jeezus," he exclaimed as she stepped into the rear hallway of the tavern. "What kind of a getup is that?"

"Well, you told me to make sure I wouldn't be followed."

Charlie looked her up and down once more, nodding wryly. "Yeah, that'd do it," he said. "Come on in here and we'll talk."

The tavern was busy at this hour—Sandy could hear voices and laughter and smell the sharp nutty aroma of draft beer right through the door at the far end of the hall. But the door Charlie had opened for her led to a cleaning closet with a cracked porcelain basin and barely enough room for two people to stand in.

"It's not bugged, honest," he said nervously, prodding her as she hesitated on the threshold.

She waited until he had closed the door behind them, then asked, "Do you have the information I requested?"

"D'you have the fifty?"

Nervous or not, Charlie was all business. Sandy fished the money out of her wallet and handed it to him.

"Okay," he said, stuffing the bills into the pocket of his windbreaker. "Every one of those dates corresponds to a death, but none of them was a murder. One was a heart attack, one was a skiing accident, one was a diabetic who OD'd on insulin, one was a car smashup, one was a guy who got drunk and fell off his balcony, and the last one was an accidental drowning."

She groaned inwardly. Accidents. Her theory would only work with unsolved murders.

"But that's not all," Charlie went on. "You mentioned a connection with those two clothing places, remember? Duds 'n' Dudes and Unity Sportswear? The interesting thing about these accidents is that every one of the victims was either leaving them or competing with them."

Sandy did a double take. "What?"

"The heart attack was a competitor with a flashy new line of sportswear. When he died his business fell apart, so no more competition. The car crash was a clothing designer who'd just bought out his contract with Duds 'n' Dudes so he could go to work for another company. And so on, and so on. Every last one."

Her eyes widened. "What are their names?"

Charlie shook his head. "Names'll cost you another fifty," he said. "You just wanted to know if there'd been any deaths connected with those companies on those dates, and I've told you."

"You've told me enough to explain why Roger Blass was killed, anyway," she said thoughtfully. "It's beginning to look as though somebody at Unity Sportswear has put Mr. Vanish on the payroll."

"Mr. Vanish? Oh, jeez," he moaned, looking pained.

"That was great work, Charlie."

"Well, I'm glad you liked it so much, because it's the last job I'm going to do for you, lady. We're through."

"What do you mean?"

"We're finished. I want you to forget you ever heard of me."

Charlie looked nervous enough to jump out of his skin if anything touched it.

"Bert was on the trail of Mr. Vanish, too, you know," she pointed out.

"Yeah, but Bert was careful not to get too involved with the cops. Vanish may have been the one who iced him, but nobody had any reason to connect Bert with me, so I was safe. You've got a police bodyguard and bugs in your apartment, for chrissakes. They recorded our phone conversation, so now they're on to me. And once Vanish has killed you, he'll make the connection and come after me, too. So goodbye, lady. It's been interesting, but this kind of business I do not need."

"I need your help," she concluded simply.

"You've got to be kidding!"

"I'll give you another fifty and then I won't bother you again, I promise. Think of it as a going-away present. I won't bother you again if you'll just do me this one favor. Please?"

He considered for a moment. "Have you got a plan?"

Sandy told him what she had in mind. Charlie resisted the idea at first, but he had to admit there wasn't a hiding place in Toronto that couldn't be reached by a well-placed message, and nobody else could place them the way Charlie could. Accepting the other fifty, Charlie took her to the streets.

Sandy sweltered under her disguise, but would tolerate any condition to get her word to Dooley.

They strolled down Yonge Street to the beginning of the strip, then walked up and down between College and Queen Streets, talking to everyone Charlie recognized as a regular. He was a regular, too, so people talked back. On each street corner, Sandy and Charlie found runaways who had heard of Sean Dooley, who might have seen him lately, who might be seeing him later; on each street corner they left urgent messages and hoped he would get at least one.

On the margins of the strip and on the nearby parallel streets, the streetlights were farther apart, the buildings were dingy and covered with crude graffiti, and the kids Charlie could trust to carry messages were older and more hard-boiled, with bold, calculating eyes that made Sandy almost as nervous as the prospect that Mr. Vanish might be out there, too, watching her perspire beneath too many layers of clothing.

Near a liquor store on Jarvis, Charlie left Sandy standing on the corner while he ducked into a doorway to talk to two girls. It was nearly 11:00 p.m. and the darkness felt like a heavy blanket, kept from smothering her by the light of the nearby street lamp. All around her she heard hushed whispers as people faded in and out of her peripheral vision like malevolent ghosts. As a vagrant breeze raised gooseflesh all over Sandy's arms and legs, she decided that she'd had enough for one night. This would be her last street corner. Charlie could tour the entire Track if he wanted to. She just wanted to go home and wash this evening's adventure off her skin, and try to sleep without dreaming.

Just then a dark green car turned the corner and pulled up at the curb beside her. A large hand reached across the front seat and rolled down the passenger-side window. Then the hand beckoned to her.

Now Sandy's skin was crawling for a different reason. Licking her lips nervously, she leaned toward the passenger side of the car. The wedge of light from the street that angled through the window showed her only an empty seat, with a right hand resting palm down on the upholstery. The rest of the driver remained anonymously in the shadows.

Sandy glanced toward the doorway and found it empty. Charlie had gone inside the second the car had pulled up. She was alone out here, alone in the seediest part of town and already targeted by someone who made her feel cold all over—

Suddenly the hand turned over and flashed a shiny police badge in her face.

A dry, empty feeling spread down her throat and into her stomach as she frantically searched for words. Placating words. Humorous words. *Dio,* any kind of words at all.

"You're making a mistake," she finally croaked.

"Not like the one you've made, Alessandra," growled a blessedly familiar voice. "Get in the car!"

She was in big trouble with Sergeant Gaine and she knew it. But a surfer could have ridden the wave of relief that crashed over her as she got into the passenger seat and buckled up.

He drove in stony silence along a maze of side streets that Sandy didn't recognize except by name.

"Where are you taking me?" she asked meekly.

"Home."

That single word silenced her. In the dark, his profile looked chiseled out of granite; and the tone of his voice was almost as hard. Clearly, Sergeant Gaine wasn't interested in hearing any arguments or explanations, not now, possibly never.

When they arrived in front of her duplex, he pulled over to the curb and turned off the ignition. "Go on upstairs," he told her.

With a sigh, Sandy got out of the car and headed for the front door. Hearing Gaine's footsteps behind her, she ran up the stairs to her apartment, fitted the key into the lock with shaking hands and let herself in. Before she could slam the door in his face, however, he followed her inside and double-locked it.

Sandy fled to the bedroom. Ten minutes later she re-emerged wearing beige slacks and a loose orange top, and marshaling her forces for the inevitable confrontation with Sergeant Gaine. Yes, she had stolen away from his surveillance for purposes of her own; and yes, that had been a very foolhardy and dangerous thing to do. But she would do it again if Tommy's life hung in the balance, and it was time Ted Gaine knew that.

He was standing with his back to her, studying the row of plants on the windowsill.

"How did you find me tonight?" she challenged him.

He turned at the sound of her voice. "I used my sources on the street," he said, frowning. "Once we knew what had happened I put out the word. But I was expecting to find you with *your* source—Charlie, isn't it?"

Sandy stood motionless, staring at him in wounded horror, feeling her own breathing fan the heat in her cheeks. Charlie had been right. There were police bugs in her apartment.

Gaine stepped over to the phone and picked up the receiver.

"Calling up Sergeant Taylor?" she asked, putting a cold edge on her voice. "Why don't you simply talk in the direction of that framed print on the wall? I'm sure he'll be able to hear you just fine."

Gaine stiffened for a moment; then, with a heavy sigh, he hung up the phone and faced her. "I guess we'd better have a talk," he said. "Got any coffee?"

"Tea."

"Okay, tea."

As she went to the kitchen and filled the kettle, Gaine sat down on one of the love seats, stretching his long legs out to either side of her small coffee table. Surrounding it. It was, she observed bitterly, a typical Ted Gaine position.

"What were you doing out there tonight, Alessandra?"

She returned to the living room, wiping her hands on a piece of paper toweling. "I was looking for Dooley."

"Looking for Dooley?" he repeated, shocked disbelief stamped on his darkening features. "What the hell is the matter with you? Aren't you in enough jeopardy already that you have to go out at night looking for more? Or maybe you think you're some kind of superwoman. Yeah, that's it—Alessandra DiGianni, by day a mild-mannered crime writer, by night an intrepid and very short-lived crime fighter."

Savagely crumpling the paper toweling in her fist, Sandy replied, "I'm a big girl, Sergeant. And in any case, you're not my father."

Before she could move to avoid him, Gaine exploded out of his seat, crossed the room in two strides and grasped her tightly by the shoulders, making her gasp with fright.

"Damn right I'm not your father," he said through gritted teeth. "I'm just the cop who's been busting his tail to keep you alive, while you play hide-and-seek with the officers assigned to protect you. After everything that's happened, how can you even think of this as a game, Alessandra? Doesn't it matter to you that people care about what happens to you? That people worry about you?"

Confused, she stared into his face, seeing the raw emotion there, feeling an answering emotion swell at the back of her throat, choking off her voice. His hands were burning her skin, kindling wildfires deep in the core of her that danced and sparked along every nerve.

And then, as if on cue, the kettle began to whistle. "I'd...better get our tea," she whispered, and reluctantly he let her go.

Dishes clattered loudly in the sudden silence as Sandy filled her small earthenware teapot and loaded up a tray with cups and spoons and napkins. Meanwhile, Gaine paced the living room.

Carefully, she set the tray down on the coffee table and began pouring their tea. "Tommy is innocent, you know," she said unsteadily.

"Oh?"

"It was Dooley who gave Tommy the jacket. He must have removed it from Vito's body after Mr. Vanish shot him. Dooley witnessed the murder. He was the one who called me up about the Parmentier case, as well. I agreed to protect his identity if he and Vito would stay away from Tommy."

"And when he gave Tommy the jacket, all bets were off?"

She nodded. "I would have told you earlier if you'd been a little less efficient and a little more receptive last night."

"I'm sorry," he said, scowling into his teacup before he sipped from it. "There is a problem with Dooley's story, Alessandra. Mr. Vanish didn't kill Vito. The M.O. was all wrong."

"But he said...the jackets were identical, and Mr. Vanish thought Vito was Dooley."

"If Sean Dooley saw Mr. Vanish kill Parmentier, he must have realized what a slick professional Vanish was. There's only one reason for him to try to finger Vanish for a slipshod murder like Vito's, and that's to protect the real killer."

Sandy nearly gagged on a mouthful of tea. "Tommy didn't do it!" she exclaimed when she could talk again.

"We know. And that leaves only one person. Think, Alessandra. Who would a scumbag like Dooley be most interested in saving?"

Dio, he was right. Dooley wouldn't care about anyone but himself. A terrible numbness settled around her heart, sending chilling fingers of fear into every part of her body. Slowly, she put her teacup back onto the tray, watching her hand tremble as she withdrew it.

"Charlie left messages for him all up and down the Strip," she said, her voice a hoarse whisper. "If he gets one and decides to come here . . ."

Staring miserably at her half-empty cup, she didn't see Gaine cross to sit beside her, only felt his arms surround her and tighten in a fierce hug. "You'll be safe, Alessandra, I promise," he whispered. "There are detectives watching the building, and listening devices so we can hear everything that goes on inside the apartment. Nothing will happen to you. And just to make sure, I'll be staying right here in your living room—all night."

Wrapped in his embrace, feeling it all around her like a protective shield, Sandy closed her eyes and relaxed against him. There was no danger as long as he was near. If only she could remain in his arms . . .

Chapter Eleven

Sunday, June 17, 12:20 a.m.

"Well, good night, then." There was no further reason for her to stay up. The dishes had been washed and put away. The top of the coffee table had been cleaned off. She had given Sergeant Gaine a sheet and the spare pillow, in case he wanted to try dozing on one of the love seats. Reluctant to put even that much distance between them, Sandy turned and walked the few steps down the hallway to her bedroom.

After slipping into a short cotton nightgown, she locked her bedroom window, then changed her mind. It was a sultry night. If she intended to breathe in that little back room, she would have to leave the sash open at least partway. Reluctantly, she reopened the window. There was a detective watching the back of her building, but the night was so black....

Dio, please, give him eyes like a cat, she prayed, before sliding under the covers and switching off the lamp.

But sleep would not come. She dozed fitfully, snapping alert each time an insect thrummed against the screen.

Then the phone rang just once, startling her fully awake. Gaine had picked it up in the living room. She could hear the buzz of his voice as he spoke quietly into the receiver.

Quickly, she slid out of bed, shrugged into her robe, and padded barefoot into the hall, just in time to hear the apartment door close.

"Sergeant?" she ventured timidly. There was no answer.

Sergeant Gaine had obviously been called away on a more urgent matter, leaving her alone now, in the dark, silent apartment. No, she reminded herself, she wasn't completely alone. Sergeant Ishito was watching the front of her building, Detective Jabry was watching the back, and Sergeant Taylor could hear every sound she made. If only those hidden microphones worked both ways. Resisting the urge to turn on every light in the place, Sandy stepped gingerly into the living room.

At least it wasn't completely dark here. Gaine had raised the blinds, letting in a faint glow from the streetlights outside. It sketched the outlines of the two love seats and the table, and gave a pale aura to the leaves of her many plants.

Sandy glanced uneasily behind her, down the hall toward her bedroom door. Lying in a small dark room, listening to every creak and groan of this old building, would only increase her anxiety. She might as well turn on a light, make herself a cup of tea, and wait for Sergeant Gaine to return.

The floor lamp beside the window gave off the strongest illumination. Sandy crossed the living room and switched it on. And then she froze, listening intently for the noise she thought she had heard coming from the bedroom.

There it was again! Somebody must be climbing into the apartment, through the half-open back window!

"Sergeant Taylor, can you hear me?" she whispered frantically. "There's an intruder. Get someone up here!"

Just then Sandy heard the soft creak of her bedroom door opening and nearly leapt out of her skin. She raced blindly around the love seats toward the front door, grasped the knob and turned it. It was double-locked.

"Goin' somewhere, lady?"

As her mind put a face to that death-rattle voice, Sandy's heart nearly stopped.

"Dooley!" she cried, and spun around to face him.

"Turn the light off," he rasped.

Obediently Sandy went back to the floor lamp and darkened the room again.

"Now, what's this big emergency?" he demanded. As he took a step toward her, she caught her breath. He looked much larger in the dark. "It better be good," he warned. "I don't like games."

She swallowed hard, forcing herself to stay calm and think. Sergeant Taylor was listening to every word of this, and there was no mistaking what was happening here. That meant help was on its way. All she had to do was keep Dooley talking, stall him until the police arrived. She could do that, she told herself anxiously. If she wanted to survive, she must.

Sandy fought to keep her voice steady as she replied, "I don't like games, either, Dooley. The police took Tommy away for questioning Friday night. Because you gave him Vito's jacket with the bullet hole in it, they think he committed the murder."

An ominous pause, then, "Maybe he did."

"You know he didn't."

Dooley was staring at her. Even though she couldn't see his eyes, she could feel them on her, like the crawling feet of an insect, making her skin tighten, making her limbs want to twitch.

The butterflies were stampeding in her stomach again. How long did it take for two police detectives to run across the road and pound on a door, anyway? They should have been here by now. Where were they?

Had she been left alone, after all, in spite of Gaine's promise? Had that phone call been an order from his superior to end the surveillance? Wasn't there anyone out there listening to this and able to end it?

Oh, please, Ted, come back....

Caught in a sudden, icy shower of fear, Sandy gasped as Dooley's harsh voice tore her away from her thoughts. "This whole thing was a setup, wasn't it?" he grated. "The messages from the street, the cops all around this place. It's a trap, right? You been workin' with them all along, just to reel me in."

"No!"

"And I bet you told them that I was the one saw Parmentier get hit, huh? Right?"

"You're the one who broke our bargain," she reminded him. Her throat was closing up now—if she didn't spit the words out quickly she would choke on them. "When you gave Tommy the jacket, I gave your name to Homicide, just as I said I would do."

"Just as you said you would do," he repeated contemptuously. "Get away from that light!" His outline shifted momentarily, and when he gestured at her with his left hand, something in it briefly caught the moonlight—a gun!

Desperately trying to swallow a cold lump of fear, Sandy sidled cautiously to the other side of the window—the window with the sill lined with plants in heavy terra-cotta pots. Maybe, just maybe, if she could get him talking again, put him a little off guard... After all, they were still in the dark.

"Is that the gun you used to kill Vito?" she asked unsteadily. "Why, Dooley? I thought you two were friends."

"I didn't mean to," he said after a beat. "He just got me so mad I didn't know what I was doin'. I figured I better leave town, y'know? To get away from Mr. Vanish. So I wanted to take my half of our stash with me, but Vito didn't want to split it up. We had a fight, out back of the Lucky Shot...and I won. The stash didn't get split up, after all." Dooley chuckled. The sound made Sandy's skin crawl.

"And you blamed Mr. Vanish?" she persisted. "Why?"

"Why not? He's always killin' people with guns. What's one more gonna matter to him? Or two?" As Sandy watched in speechless horror, he raised the gun and aimed it at her. "So long, lady—"

Suddenly the telephone rang. Dooley wheeled and shot it instead. In that moment of distraction, Sandy snatched a large plant off the windowsill and hurled it at him.

All at once, a searing pain exploded deep in her left arm, spinning her helplessly backward to crash against the window frame, and then down, down, into soft, still darkness. And in the distance, she heard, thought she heard...corn popping. Yes, that was what it must be. Popcorn.

FORCING HIS THOUGHTS AWAY from the pale, still form being loaded into the ambulance, Ted strode across the lawn to the curb, where a yellow patrol car sat idling. A front door had been left open, and in the dome light he could see a man fidgeting uncomfortably in the back seat.

Ted ducked his head slightly to reassure himself that this was the same fellow they'd caught lurking in the bushes earlier.

The suspect had just begun to stammer out his story when Sergeant Taylor had buzzed them on the radio to let them know Dooley was inside the apartment.

Cursing himself for leaving his post, Ted had split up his men for a two-pronged approach. There hadn't been time to call for backup. They had to act quickly to prevent a hostage situation from developing. So they'd been forced to handcuff the suspect and lock him inside the patrol car until the more urgent matter could be taken care of. Now that the situation was under control, they could resume questioning him.

At Sergeant Gaine's signal, a uniformed constable helped the suspect out of the car. The man was a head shorter than Ted, with a stocky build, dressed all in black and wearing his curly dark hair long in the back.

"Well, now, Mr.—" Ted glanced at the identification he'd stuffed in his pocket earlier "—Arthur Freiling, of the Lucky Ace Detective Agency. Would you care to tell us again just what you were doing in the bushes over there?"

At that moment, the doors of the ambulance slammed shut and it pulled away in a wide U-turn, lights flashing and siren shrieking. Ted's mind recoiled from the noise— it sounded too much like a scream of pain—and suddenly, he found that interrogating Arthur Freiling was the last thing in the world he wanted to do. Just the thought of being in the same place as this man made his throat tighten with revulsion.

Brusquely, he handed Freiling's ID over to the senior constable.

"Take him in, Muller. We'll get his statement at the station. Meanwhile, I want him thoroughly checked out. I want every scrap of identification in his wallet verified with two separate sources. I want to know whether that's his own hair or a wig. I want to know where the lint in his pocket came from. And I want to know where he was last August fourteenth, from 9 p.m. until 1 a.m. Everything. Do it on my authority," he directed. Then he turned on his heel and stalked away.

"So, Freiling checked out?" said Joe.

"Yeah," Ted growled disgustedly. "His ID checked out, his hair is his own, and he's exactly what he claims to be: Arthur Freiling, the most junior operative at Lucky Ace Detective Agency. He won't be getting a promotion for this, either. His boss is not pleased he got caught, and even less pleased that he broke under questioning and admitted to breaking and entering and planting illegal listening devices. Anyway, Freiling was after the Haltford photograph, so the investigators of record are on his case now."

Bemused, Joe cocked his head and observed, "And you're teed off."

Ted snapped the file folder shut and dropped it with a grudging 'thanks' into the hands of the desk sergeant. Then he strode down the tunnellike side corridor of the Eglinton Avenue Station, past the weapons storage and the officers' locker rooms, back toward the parking lot. Joe caught up with him halfway to the door.

"Hey, partner," he admonished gently, "the guy was fixing to break in again and maybe twist her arm. The trap was sprung by a real perpetrator. It isn't as though we've failed."

But Ted shook his head stubbornly. "We didn't catch Mr. Vanish," he pointed out, giving the fire door an extra hard shove.

Joe breathed a martyred sigh. "Look, I know that what Dooley told her about Mr. Vanish fit in with your own pet theory about the Parmentier case but, dammit, he lied about Vito's murder. He's just not a credible witness."

"Obviously he was lying to cover up his own guilt. But he had no reason to lie about the Parmentier case, Joe. Dooley couldn't have pulled off that hit in a thousand years."

"Even if I believe that, Inspector Nielsen doesn't," Joe reminded him.

Scowling darkly, Ted stopped and whirled on his partner, declaring, "Inspector Nielsen isn't—"

"—in love with Alessandra DiGianni?" Joe cut in. "You talked around it last night, because you knew Taylor had his ears on, but he didn't earn his rank by being obtuse, and neither did Nielsen. You didn't really think you could keep it a secret, did you?" he chided.

Ted nodded thoughtfully and resumed walking toward Joe's car. "So you figure Nielsen suspects that I'm...involved with her, and that everything I told him today was an emotional reaction? That to compensate for leaving her unprotected this morning I'm trying to overprotect her now?"

"Aren't you?" Joe asked quietly.

Ted sighed. "Dammit, I've got to keep her alive."

His partner made an exasperated noise. "Will you lighten up? We nailed a murderer last night, and a second-story man who may hold the key to solving a kidnapping. And with what Taylor got on tape Thursday night, it won't be long before we have this Charlie character in custody—"

"But we don't have Mr. Vanish!" exclaimed Ted. "And nobody will believe that he's still a real threat."

"And with good reason," Joe pointed out sharply, "since you can't show any proof."

Ted glared at him across the roof of the car for a moment. "Yes, I can," he said. He dropped angrily into the passenger seat of Joe's car and slammed the door shut. Ted waited until Joe was sitting behind the wheel, watching his keys dangle from the ignition, to explain, "Alessandra found Bert's file. We've been working on it together for the past week. There's some powerful evidence in that file, Joe. Bert was close to unmasking Vanish when he was killed. With the new evidence that's come up since then, I think we'll have enough to nail him. But until we're ready to make the case, I can't show any of it to Nielsen. And until he's convinced Mr. Vanish is real, he won't approve any further surveillance. And that means Alessandra is a sitting target," he concluded with a disgusted sigh.

"So what's the scam, partner? Do we borrow some whites and spend all our off-duty hours at the hospital, or what?"

Ted eyed him uncertainly. "You believe me?"

"I believe that you believe, and that's good enough for me."

A slow, grateful smile spread across Ted's face. "Thanks, partner," he said softly.

As Joe turned his key in the ignition, he observed casually, "You know, we ought to drop in on Dooley—see if he's awake enough to sign a confession. We could even stop at my sister's place and pick up some fresh-cut flowers for you-know-who."

Ted gaped in mock horror. "What's this? A scam?"

"I guess it's just the company I've been keeping," sighed Joe.

SHE LOOKED SO FRAGILE, so overwhelmed by her injury, so...beyond his reach, as she lay unmoving on the bulky hospital bed, securely wrapped in crisp, hospital-cornered sheets. Ted stood quietly just inside the door of Alessandra's room and watched her sleep. Her left arm looked grotesquely large in its plaster cast. No, he thought with a sigh, the arm was now the right size for the bed, making the rest of her appear disproportionately small. He looked at her face and noticed that she was frowning even in her sleep; and he wondered whether it was the weight of the cast on her chest making her uncomfortable, or simply the pain of having a bullet removed and a badly broken arm surgically reset.

Ted winced at the thought of what she'd had to endure—the terror of finding herself alone with a murderer, the shock of being wounded, the suffering that had followed. Taylor had been impressed with the way she'd handled herself. She'd let him know exactly what was going on by what she said to Dooley, and she'd even drawn a confession out of him. Taylor had delayed signaling the go-ahead to Ted and the officers outside the door until he had Dooley's confession on tape, but he'd cut things perilously close. Another second and Alessandra would have been dead.

And to lose her that way, after promising her over and over that she would be safe, that he would protect her...!

Over and over, the events of that night replayed themselves in his head, as though by reliving his mistake a thousand times he could somehow atone for it. Or diminish it. He knew he would never be able to excuse it.

For Ted had promised to stay in the apartment with her. And then Taylor had called with the news that an intruder had been spotted and apprehended by Detective Jabry—an intruder who wasn't Dooley. And Sergeant Gaine had seen himself as the dispensable member of the surveillance team, the one Alessandra could do without for ten minutes while he went downstairs and made Mr. Vanish. And none of them had realized that in the ninety seconds that Jabry had been distracted from his surveillance, a second intruder had got through.

No matter what the official report might say, Ted Gaine was the reason Alessandra DiGianni was in that hospital bed. If she hated him for the rest of her life, that would make two of them.

As the room swam back into focus, Sandy was first of all aware that she couldn't move her left arm. Then she found and felt the persistent sharp throbbing pain beneath the plaster cast. The ache came and went, came and went, like waves on a beach, each one washing a few more memories up on the fine sand of her thoughts. She was in a hospital. They'd brought her here in an ambulance, a long time ago, after the corn had stopped popping. She'd suffered a severe compound fracture, caused by a bullet, the surgeon had told her. It was a miracle that none of the bone fragments had severed any major blood vessels.

Her family had been here for a while. Then they'd gone home so she could rest. Sandy had been dozing off and on all afternoon, but it wasn't very restful, she'd found, not being able to move her arms. The one not in the cast was impaled on an intravenous needle attached to a transparent tube, attached to a bottle that hung upside down on a tall coatrack affair, and she could tell just by looking that it wasn't going to fit through the door to the bathroom.

Between dozes, Sandy had thought about herself and Sergeant Gaine, about saving Tommy, and about what might have happened last night if Gaine hadn't left her alone. And each time her thoughts began to scatter and melt, she'd concluded that she was pretty damned lucky all around.

Suddenly there was a loud clatter in the hall. Sandy turned involuntarily toward the sound, and saw Ted Gaine, clutching a huge bouquet of marigolds, chrysanthemums and shasta daisies in his hand and staring so mournfully at her that she just had to ask, "Did somebody die?"

He looked confused. "What?"

"Never mind. Let's get those flowers into some water," she suggested, and reached awkwardly for the call buzzer, which, naturally, had been placed on the left side of the bed. It was hospital logic, she decided wearily, like waking someone up to administer a sleeping pill.

"I'll get that," he offered, stepping closer.

But just then the nurse came in, carrying a small tray with a hypodermic syringe on it. "I thought you might be needing something right about now," she said. Then, as she noticed the flowers, "Oh, what a lovely bouquet!"

Gaine stood quietly by while the painkiller was injected into Sandy's IV tube. The shot began to take effect almost immediately.

"Bless you," breathed Sandy. "You read my mind."

"Visitors right after surgery can be a bit of a strain, dear. You rest now," advised the smiling nurse. "And I'll get a vase for those beautiful flowers," she promised Gaine on her way out.

Cautiously, he approached the side of the bed. "How do you feel?"

"Better now," she told him with a weak grin. "The doctor told me he had to hammer a stainless steel pin into my arm. Sometimes I'd swear he's still hammering."

Sergeant Gaine swallowed so hard she could hear him. His gray eyes were misty with undisguised misery, and Sandy's heart ached for him as she heard him say brokenly, "Alessandra, I'm so sorry. If I'd been there when Dooley arrived—"

"Don't blame yourself, Sergeant," she begged him. "It's really my fault. If I hadn't been stupid enough to sneak away and leave those messages for him, he wouldn't even have come."

"But that wasn't stupid," he protested. "Those messages flushed a killer out of hiding. If I'd been thinking like a cop instead of a worried hus— Instead of...letting my feelings get in the way...I'd have realized what might happen and called for backup sooner."

Sandy couldn't contain a smile. "So you have feelings for me, Sergeant?"

His frown melted into a lopsided grin. "As long as half of Investigative Services knows, I guess you ought to know too," he told her. "I tried so valiantly to suppress them, Alessandra."

"But why?"

He reached out and held the hand at the end of the cast. "I was attracted to you—" he said softly, "But I didn't want to fall in love with you because I knew what that would do to my professional objectivity..." He bent and kissed her fingertips, sending a ripple of pleasure halfway up her arm. "And as long as you were involved with the Parmentier case, ethics forbade a relationship between us, anyway. So I fought it as hard as I could."

"And I thought you were so stern and brusque because you disliked me." She sighed.

"I was stern and brusque because I was concentrating on not thinking about kissing you."

She smiled at him. "My mother has a wonderful saying, Sergeant. You don't accomplish anything by just thinking about it. Let's accomplish something now," she invited softly.

As she watched, the pain in his eyes faded like smoke, leaving only two still pools of liquid silver that beckoned to her, beckoned irresistibly. He leaned closer, caressing her first with a look, then with his voice as he murmured, "Has anyone told you lately what a very special lady you are?"

His nearness was doing delicious things to her senses. "Not convincingly, Sarge," she breathed. "Why don't you give it a try?"

Gently, his lips settled over hers, sending a wave of pleasure rolling through her entire body, making her wish that she had two good arms to throw around his broad shoulders. Gently, his free hand slipped behind her neck and his fingers twined themselves in her hair.

The kiss deepened, joining them in an intimate solitude that erased everything but that moment. Wrapped in the sweet fragrance of flowers and lost in a swell of delightful sensation, Sandy felt herself melting into a steamy hot puddle in the hospital bed....

"Here's that vase," caroled the nurse, bustling back into the room.

Ted froze in mid-kiss and opened his eyes. As he reluctantly released her lips, he whispered, "To be continued, Ms. DiGianni."

"Amen, Sergeant Gaine," Sandy whispered fervently back.

Somehow Ted managed to keep a straight face as he handed the bouquet over to the smirking nurse and left. Joe was waiting for him near the elevators, and together they rode in pregnant silence down to the lower-level parking area.

"Well?" prodded Joe as he unlocked his car.

"She's terrific." Ted sighed.

"Is that what you're going to put in your report?"

"Do I look anxious to have Nielsen pull me off the case?" demanded Ted with mock severity. "How about Dooley? Is he conscious yet?"

"Nope," Joe sighed, turning the key in the ignition. "He's in a deep coma and the doctors don't know when he'll come out of it—if he wakes up at all. Meanwhile, Alf Michaels has been assigned to guard him, and needless to say, he is not a happy camper."

Ted shot him a disbelieving look. "You're joking. Dooley's under police guard, and for Alessandra it's you're-on-your-own-thanks-a-lot-kid?"

"Not exactly," admitted Joe with a faint smile. "I had a little chat with Michaels about keeping an eye on Alessandra, too. Their rooms are on the same floor. I couldn't tell him about Mr. Vanish, of course. So I hinted that friends of Dooley's might take it into their heads to blame her for what happened to him, and if Michaels could arrange to walk past her door every now and then, we'd appreciate it."

"I wish we could do more—it's insane for a seasoned officer like Michaels to be guarding a vegetable."

"Dooley's in a coma right now, but there's a chance he may open his eyes tomorrow and start screaming for a lawyer. In any case, he's a confessed murderer, and regulations state clearly—"

"I know what the regulations say," Ted grumbled.

"If it'll make you feel any better, the hospital administrator isn't crazy about the situation, either." And with that, Joe put the Chevy in gear, pulled out of the parking spot and headed toward the exit.

"Listen, if I'm going to be helping you protect Alessandra from Mr. Vanish, I'll need to know everything you two have dug up on him."

"Sure," said Ted. "I keep all my notes in a folder locked in the bottom drawer of my desk."

Joe frowned. "Just notes? I thought you said you'd found Waldron's file."

"Alessandra's hidden it in a safe place. Don't worry— my notes include everything that either of us has figured out."

"I should look at that file, partner. It could be that I'll find something you both missed. Some vital clue."

"It could be," Ted agreed. "But I honestly don't know where Bert's file is right now, so I'm afraid we'll just have to make do with going over my notes"

Joe shrugged. "Okay, if we must."

Investigative Services was lightly manned at that hour on a Sunday evening. Sergeant Coolidge was in, finishing some paperwork. He glanced up and waved a burly hand as they walked past his desk.

"Hey, look," said Joe, pointing.

Byron was grimly lugging the huge vacuum cleaner into their work space.

Ted glanced ruefully at his brown-bag dinner from Hamburger Harold's. There would be no digesting of food once that monster machine began roaring in his ear. "So much for eating at our desks," he muttered.

But almost as soon as the vacuum cleaner had disappeared through the entrance to their office, Byron reappeared and began strolling happily away.

"Whoa, Byron!" called Joe, striding quickly to intercept him. "Aren't you going to clean our carpet?"

Byron turned and smiled guilelessly at the two detectives. "It's already cleaned," he said with a characteristic shrug.

"Then aren't you going to put away your carpet cleaner?" asked Ted.

Byron frowned, a little confused. "I did put it away."

Ted jerked his head in the direction of their work space. "In there?" he said, fighting to keep his voice free of irony or sarcasm.

It was difficult to know how to speak to Byron in a situation like this, hard to judge at what point expectations became unreasonable.

Byron's brows knitted now, and he reached into his pocket for a well-folded piece of paper. Ted could see that it was a diagram of the entire office, the individual work spaces marked with numbers. Byron ran his finger around the diagram, obviously retracing his route that shift, and ended by triumphantly poking his finger several times into the square that denoted Joe and Ted's working area.

"I was right," he crowed. "It goes in there. See? That's the highest number. Every day when I come to work, Mr. Tyler makes me a di-a-gram, to show me where he wants me to clean. Number one is where I start, and then number two, and then number three—"

"I think we understand, Byron," Joe assured him. "And today he wanted you to finish up here, in our office?"

"It has the highest number," said Byron solemnly.

"And when you're finished, what are you supposed to do?" prompted Ted.

"I put away the carpet cleaner."

Joe and Ted traded long-suffering looks. There had obviously been a misunderstanding here as to the meaning of the phrase "put away."

"Byron," began Joe, "are you sure Mr. Tyler means for you to put away the carpet cleaner in the last office you clean? Doesn't he want you to put all the cleaning supplies away in the same place?"

"No, he told me," said Byron earnestly. "See, I made a mistake today. I had another di-a-gram in my pocket and I got mixed up and started in the wrong place. So I had to keep on until I was finished. Then I looked at the di-a-gram from today and I saw where I was supposed to finish, and I had to bring the carpet cleaner here to put it away."

Joe tried again. "But are you sure Mr. Tyler won't be upset about the carpet cleaner being left in somebody's office?"

"He won't be upset."

Ted sighed impatiently. His dinner, barely appetizing while warm, was congealing in the paper bag in his hand while they word-waltzed with Byron all around the real issue here—the unwanted presence of his vacuum cleaner in their office. He would have to take the bull by the horns—gently.

"Well, Byron," he said, trying to sound like a mildly disappointed parent, "I'm afraid *we're* a little upset. You see, these offices are very small. There just isn't room to store a carpet cleaner. So would you please take it downstairs and put it away in the closet with the other cleaning supplies?"

Byron looked unhappy. "Mr. Tyler isn't going to like it," he warned. "And I won't get my ten dollars this week."

Ted shot him a startled look. "Byron, do you mean you get paid to leave the carpet cleaner inside somebody's office?"

"Sure. Mr. Tyler gives me money for doing it," he explained patiently. "That's how come I know he won't be upset."

"I think I'd like to have a closer look at this vacuum cleaner," remarked Joe casually.

While Byron watched, wide-eyed, Joe studied the evidence from every angle, handling it carefully in order not to smear any fingerprints that hadn't already been obliterated. At last, he turned to Ted and said quietly, "I've found three probable sites. Let's get Surveillance up here to take it apart."

"Byron," said Ted with a friendly smile, "what's Mr. Tyler's first name? Do you know?"

Byron frowned. "I only call him Mr. Tyler. But there's a letter on his shirt."

"Is it a 'C', by any chance?" mused Ted with a calculating glance at his partner.

Joe's eyebrows lifted slightly. "C for Charlie?" he murmured, and shook his head. "I know it's a small world, but . . ."

"Do you know Mr. Tyler?" asked Byron.

Ted smiled. "Not as well as we're going to, Byron."

An hour later the vacuum cleaner lay in pieces all over the floor, and Detective Winters was removing the third and last voice-activated tape recording device that he had found inside it.

"Ingenious," he remarked, holding up a tiny triggering mechanism in a pair of tweezers. "He couldn't get into the computerized filing system, so he simply recorded various investigators discussing the contents of their case files."

"Can I go home now?" pleaded Byron wearily.

"Sure, Byron," said Ted. "We'll just go down to the maintenance office with you to explain to your boss why you're so late finishing up."

"Gee, that's nice of you Sergeant. Thanks."

"Oh, *there* you are, Byron," said the man with "W. Tyler" on his shirt pocket, glancing up from the inventory book. "I was expecting you to clock out almost an—"

"Hello, Tyler," said Ted, filling up the doorway to the maintenance office and wearing his sternest, stoniest expression. "You're under arrest for illegal use of electronic monitoring devices and possession and sale of illegally-obtained information. You have the right to remain silent. If you give up that right—"

In a fit of disgust, Tyler threw his stubby pencil down on the desk and watched it bounce away and clatter on the floor.

IT TOOK AN HOUR to get through the paperwork involved in booking Walter Tyler, during which time he confessed to selling confidential police information to a street shark named Charlie. Detectives immediately went out looking for him. By then, Joe's and Ted's dinners had expired of natural causes, so they took Ted's notes with them to the nearest Submarine Heaven to discuss while eating in the car.

"Have you checked out the content of these classified ads?" asked Joe between sips of cola.

"Not yet. Maybe you could do that tomorrow morning while I'm talking to the security people at the hospital."

"Sure, no problem."

"And then I want to get in touch with Edgecliffe College."

"Ah, yes, Dr. Liszt," said Joe, reaching for the appropriate page in the file folder. "I'm afraid you'll be wasting your time, partner. There was a fire in the good shrink's office shortly after she was killed, and all her notes and records were lost. Burned to ashes."

Ted regarded him curiously. "How did you know she was a psychiatrist? I didn't say she was in my notes."

"I was in Chicago back in 1974 when she was killed. The way she died was so shocking it made the front pages of all the newspapers. The police suspected foul play by one of her patients, but before they could launch a proper investigation, a fire broke out in her office and destroyed all the evidence." Joe shook his head. "Man, talk about frustration. That was when I decided to become a police officer. We moved to Toronto a couple of months later and I joined the Department."

"Interesting, isn't it," said Ted thoughtfully, "how Liszt dies and then her records are destroyed, and Bert dies and his file disappears...and Alessandra found five cases where it's possible Mr. Vanish disguised himself as the victim in order to confuse investigators about the time of death. Maybe there's a pattern to the way he works, after all."

"Maybe," Joe said, then sighed. But he didn't look convinced at all.

Chapter Twelve

Monday, June 18

The IV needle came out in time for breakfast. That was what the nurse's aide who had brought in the tray called it, anyway. As far as Sandy was concerned, plain tea, cream of wheat, and red jelly barely qualified as food.

According to the nurse, she was now on a standard postoperative diet—liquids for one day, semisolids for one day, and finally solid food. According to Sandy's roommate, who was being discharged that morning, the only interesting thing about the standard diet was that you never got the same color jelly two meals in a row.

"Good morning, Ms. DiGianni."

Sandy glanced up and smiled warmly, all thoughts of food forgotten as Ted Gaine pulled the visitor's chair close to her bed. Then she saw the concerned expression on his face.

"Is something wrong, Sergeant?"

He sighed and sat on the bed, reaching out to grasp her hand.

"The job isn't done yet, Alessandra," he said grimly. "We aren't going to have the support and manpower of the Police Department this time—not initially, anyway, but I'm working on it." He rubbed her fingers wearily between his own.

Sandy swallowed hard. She liked the feel of her hand in his large warm ones, but it worried her to see him looking so discouraged. "What's going on?" she asked uncertainly.

"Okay, here's the situation. Obviously, you're safe from Dooley now, and we've arrested the guy who broke into your apartment, so he won't be bothering you anymore."

She eyed him uneasily. "But we still don't have Mr. Vanish?"

Gaine shook his head. "Not yet. My superiors have decided to go on the assumption that Vanish was never involved, that Dooley simply gave you that name so he would have someone else to blame for Vito's murder. I wanted to put undercover detectives on this floor, but Inspector Nielsen wouldn't go for it. So that means it's just you and me and Joe Wegner and Sergeant Michaels, who's posted to the door of Dooley's room at the end of the hall."

Sandy's eyes widened. "Dooley is just down the hall?"

"It's all right, Alessandra—he's comatose, and even if he wasn't, he wouldn't be going anywhere. And Michaels knows where you are, and he's agreed to patrol the floor periodically. Whenever we're off duty, Joe and I will be here at the hospital. I'm going to see if we can work with the hospital's own security people on this." He paused to dig a business card out of his wallet. "Meanwhile, you'll have to keep your eyes and ears peeled for anything unusual, anything that doesn't feel right. If you notice anything at all," he continued, handing her the card, "call me or Sergeant Wegner immediately at headquarters. If we're not there, give a message to whoever is—it'll be relayed at once. If it's an emergency, call

Hospital Security and ask for Peter Haydn. Have you got all that?''

Sandy gazed at him with stricken eyes. A week ago, Gaine's words would only have worried her, for she'd had her health then, and with it the illusion of being able to take care of herself. Now that she was weak and in pain, with one arm in a cast, all her illusions were gone, and Sandy realized that she was terrified.

Sobbing in a breath, she reached out toward him. "Stay close to me, please?"

At once he was bending over her, his arms around her shoulders, his cheek pressed against her hair. "I'm here, Alessandra," he murmured, "I'm right here. Everything will be all right."

"If anything happens to me, the printout is tucked inside the ceiling of my bedroom closet," she blurted. "And if he finds it before you do—"

Suddenly Gaine's lips captured hers, stopping her words and kindling a slow, familiar fire deep inside her. It flowed like lava through her body, burning away her bones, leaving only the hungering of her skin and the quickening of her heart and the urgent certainty that if this man with the velvet voice didn't want and need her as much as she did him, she would surely die. . . .

CAREFULLY, HE PLACED the Webley in Nick Vermeyer's cooling hand and closed it around the butt of the revolver. Then he lifted the hand with the gun and fired a second bullet into the floor beneath the desk, ensuring that there would be a cordite smell on the corpse's fingers. Suicides had to pull the trigger themselves, after all. . . .

Just one thing remained to be done. Mr. Vanish opened the desk drawer and found the suicide note he'd typed earlier. He inserted it into the typewriter, carefully lining up the edge of the page with the mark he'd used while typing the note. Then he stepped back with a faint smile of satisfaction.

There. He'd done what he'd been paid to do. Now he could tie up a couple of nagging loose ends named Dooley and DiGianni.

He stripped off the surgical gloves he'd been wearing, removing them and turning them inside out at the same time, then stuffed them into his pocket. From another pocket he took a fresh pair of gloves and put them on. Cordite could be explained in the study, but not on the handle to the back door.

So they figured they had him pegged, did they? he thought savagely as he let himself out of the house. They thought they'd identified his M.O. from Bert Waldron's files. Well, they had a surprise in store for them....

AT TORONTO MERCY HOSPITAL, the shifts changed at 3:00 p.m. Although there were twice as many nurses and orderlies as usual from 3:00 to 3:15, they were generally unavailable. Keys were being handed over, rosters were being signed, the incoming staff were being brought up-to-date on the patients who would be in their care. And gossip was exchanged, particularly about the behavior of a certain police detective who had brought an impressive bouquet to the young lady in room 921 the previous evening, and had hung out a Do Not Disturb sign on her door for fully half an hour that morning.

Miss Foote, the day charge nurse, had frowned mightily when she heard about this. That young woman had been brought to her floor after emergency surgery; she'd been in only fair condition, with strict instructions from the attending surgeon as to her recuperation. Nowhere on the list of recommended therapy did the words *necking* or *petting* appear.

Obviously, this detective would bear close watching whenever he visited the patient. Miss Foote passed a strong recommendation along to the evening charge nurse, Mrs. Conway, along with her deep reservations about the wisdom of allowing a confessed murderer to occupy an ordinary hospital room not far from his earlier intended victim. Granted, the patient was comatose, and granted, there was a police officer guarding the door, but he paced and fidgeted and grumbled to himself a great deal. He never stood at attention beside the door, the way a police guard ought to stand.

Miss Foote warned Mrs. Conway to keep the extension number for Hospital Security close at hand during her shift, and Mrs. Conway solemnly promised to do so. As the elevator doors closed on the departing Miss Foote, Mrs. Conway smiled and shook her head indulgently.

By 3:45, the shift was well under way. They were going to be a little shorthanded this evening, Mrs. Conway noted. Well, she didn't mind doing the same work as her nurses—unlike some charge nurses she knew—and she was rather looking forward to the next instalment of the soap opera that seemed to be unfolding in room 921.

She didn't have long to wait. Just after 4:00 p.m., she looked up from her paperwork and found a white-clad young orderly leaning across the counter of the nurses' station. He was blue-eyed, of medium height, and wore his light brown hair slicked up in a pompadour.

He had said something to her. "I beg your pardon?" she asked.

"I said, I've come up to check on the gunshot wound that came through the Trauma Unit night before last. I was on duty in Emerg," he explained, "and I saw how scared she was. I wanted to make sure she's okay and maybe say hello to her. A little bit of public relations, you might say," he added with a grin.

Involuntarily, she smiled back. "I don't recall seeing you around, Mr.—" she glanced at the name tag pinned to his shirt "—Storm."

"No, ma'am," Allen Storm replied. "I'm permanently assigned to the Trauma Unit downstairs. I don't usually visit the floors. But I wanted to see this patient again. Is she allowed visitors yet?"

"That depends. Do you know her name?"

"Alessandra DiGianni."

"Ah, yes—the little girl in 921. I might have known," mumbled Mrs. Conway to herself, and she pulled a chart out of the rack and opened it while the orderly craned his neck farther over the desk—trying to read the doctor's scribblings upside down, no doubt. Well, good luck. Dr. Marley had the worst handwriting in the entire hospital.

"Nobody but her family and the police," she said, slamming the chart shut and sliding it back into its slot. Then, seeing the disappointed look in the orderly's eyes, she added, "The patient seems to be making a rapid recovery from surgery, so Dr. Marley may change that order after rounds this afternoon. Why don't you try again later on?"

"Maybe I will," he said with a broad grin. And he winked knowingly at her before stepping into the down elevator.

THE PAIN WAS BACK, but not as strong as before. Sandy wanted to wait until it was unbearable before asking for more medication. The shot she'd received just before lunch had made her dizzy and a little queasy, so she hadn't been able to finish her meal.

Dinner would be served in an hour, if she could hang on until then. Sandy could hardly wait to see what color jelly would be on her tray.

"How are you feeling this afternoon, dear?" The nursing shift must have changed again. This Mrs. Conway was a new face, at any rate. She took Sandy's blood pressure and pulse. "Would you like something for pain?" she asked as she rearranged Sandy's pillows.

Smiling, Sandy shook her head. "I want to stay alert."

"In case that handsome detective drops by again?" teased the nurse.

"I don't think he'll come back again today," said Sandy, trying to sound casual. She was hoping he *would* return, but she knew how much paperwork was involved in wrapping up an investigation.

"Oh, and speaking of gentlemen callers, there's a young man outside waiting to see you. Dr. Marley says you can have visitors now, if you're feeling up to it. Shall I send him in?"

Suddenly tense, Sandy asked, "Who is he? Did he say?"

"His name is Allen Storm, and he's an orderly from Emergency. He says you were admitted during his shift."

Sandy uttered a little gasp of recognition. "*That* Storm!" Her memories of Sunday morning were vague and elusive, but she did recall the sympathetic presence and strong, warm hand of the orderly who had taken her to Radiology and remained with her while her arm had been X-rayed. Sandy owed him a debt of gratitude for helping her through the worst of it. Even though she was weary and in pain, she couldn't just turn him away.

"I'd like to talk to him," said Sandy.

Mrs. Conway left the room, and a moment later a shy-looking young man in a white uniform walked in behind a blue crystal vase containing an enormous bouquet of yellow roses and red carnations.

"Oh," breathed Sandy, "those are beautiful. Is there a card?"

He set the flowers down carefully atop the low dresser opposite the foot of her bed. Then he came slowly toward her, wiping his palms on the sides of his trouser legs.

"They're from me," he said, his voice sounding nervous and hopeful and exhilarated, all at once.

Suddenly her skin began to prickle a warning. He was gazing at her the same way a thief might admire a priceless diamond just before tucking it into his pouch. Ted had instructed her to be alert for things that didn't feel right, and the look in Storm's eyes certainly fit that description, but there wasn't much Sandy could do right now except keep her hand close to the call buzzer and try to get rid of him.

"I asked the nurse to let you come in because I wanted to thank you for your kindness when I was admitted, Mr. Storm," she began stiffly. "Of course, I realize that you were just doing your job—"

"No, ma'am," he interrupted in a husky voice. "From the first moment I saw you I knew you deserved special treatment." Suddenly his eyes were so filled with adoration that Sandy found herself groping uncomfortably for words.

"Mr. Storm," she almost exclaimed, desperately pinning on a sympathetic smile, "I really appreciated your warmth and skill when I was hurt ..."

He seemed to grasp for her arm, but Sandy flinched and pulled away, her alarm rising.

"Mr. Storm, please! I'm grateful for the kindness you showed me earlier, but I really need to rest. Please understand," she begged him.

He shrugged and wiped his hands on his pants legs again. Distractedly, she noticed that his nameplate was crooked. "Maybe I'll drop in later, then," he said, in a voice that forced her heart up into her throat. He looked so young, like a kid with a crush.

"That's fine," she said doubtfully.

"And would you do me a favor? Don't throw out my flowers," he pleaded. "Just keep them here in your room and . . . kind of think of me sometimes, okay? Please?"

He looked so pathetic that she couldn't bear to say no. "All right, Mr. Storm, I'll keep your flowers if you want."

"Promise?"

"Promise," she sighed wearily.

And he blew her a kiss and strutted out the door as if he'd just won the lottery.

Tuesday, June 19

SANDY SAT ON THE EDGE of her bed, trying to do the initial set of exercises that had been prescribed for her by the physiotherapist earlier that morning, but completely unable to concentrate.

After much internal debate, she had decided not to make a big deal out of her strange encounter with Mr. Storm. There was nothing intrinsically dangerous or evil about the man, surely. There was just something in his eyes . . . and the relief she'd experienced as he finally left the room. The possibility that he might come back hung over her mood like a blanket of smog. She really wanted to discuss this with Ted, but she hadn't heard from him since his visit yesterday morning.

And if Miss Foote, the puritanical day charge nurse, had anything to say about it, she wouldn't see him unchaperoned again. Miss Foote had marched into Sandy's room right after Ted had left and had quoted her chapter and verse the hospital regulations regarding police contacts with patients. There would be no scenes of unbridled passion in room 921 as long as *she* was on duty, thank you!

Unfortunately Miss Foote tended to impose her presence on nearly everything Sandy did. She constantly felt the nurse's stiff-lipped disapproval, like a cold draft stealing into the room through an unseen crack in the wall, and it made her angry and uncomfortable, and all the more determined to get well and get home as soon as possible.

Sandy turned to lean back on her bed, and her gaze went immediately to Storm's flowers. She wanted to get well and get home, she amended, without any unfinished business from the hospital following her there. She would have to confront Mr. Storm—if he came again— and make it quite clear to him that she did not want him to try to contact her at any time in the future.

"Lunch," caroled the nurse's aide as she brought in something that looked more like a meal, now that Sandy was nearly on solid food. It was an optical illusion, of course. Nothing that came on a hospital tray really tasted like food.

Half an hour after the tray had been collected, Sandy heard the *ding* of the elevator, and at once her breathing quickened. Was it Ted? Oh, please, let it be Ted. Hastily, she slid herself off the bed, shoved her feet into her slippers, tightened the belt of her robe, and opened the door of her room just a crack.

Allen Storm was standing at the nurses' station. After a second, he nodded to the nurse behind the desk, wheeled and headed down the other hallway, past the elevators.

Sandy gnawed her lower lip thoughtfully. She was being discharged the day after tomorrow. If she didn't confront him soon, she would lose her opportunity. And as long as he was up here anyway... She decided to follow him.

Storm was at the far end of the corridor, making a left turn. Sandy hurried as quietly as she could, past patients' rooms on her right, and showers and a small kitchen and a supply room on her left. Just before she reached the end of the hall, she stopped and peered cautiously around the corner.

He was standing in front of room 943 chatting with a uniformed police officer who Sandy deduced was Sergeant Michaels. The officer was just past middle age, lined and leathery and carrying a bit of a paunch, and he didn't look or sound very happy with his current assignment.

"...baby-sitting. I mean, this guy's in a coma," he was saying. "If there was any chance at all he could escape, they'd have put him under lock and key to start with, right?"

"So, think of it as a paid vacation," said Storm with a shrug.

"I don't need a vacation right now," grumbled the officer. "I'm six months from retirement and I want to go out with a bang, you know what I mean? Listen, Allen, I really appreciate your taking the time to come and visit with an old warhorse like me. The prisoner doesn't talk much, and the nurses are all too busy...."

Sandy pulled back carefully from the corner and returned thoughtfully to her room. So Dooley was in 943, and Allen Storm was cultivating the police officer who'd been assigned to guard him. There was nothing sinister about that, really—was there?

Could it be just an unsettling coincidence? Was Storm in the habit of checking up on patients who had come through Emergency during his shift? Perhaps, but Sandy decided not to take the chance. She picked up the telephone and called the office number on the business card Ted Gaine had left her.

As she'd half expected, neither Gaine nor Wegner was in. She left a message with Sergeant Andover for either of the detectives to call her back. Then she hung up and waited impatiently.

Twenty minutes later, her telephone rang. It was Sergeant Wegner. "What can I do for you, Miss DiGianni?" he asked.

Sandy told him about the Allen Storm situation, and about the orderly's disturbing interest in both her and Dooley.

"You were right to bring this to our attention," he said, "but you mustn't let yourself get all upset over it. Sergeant Gaine and I will look into this Allen Storm right away, and if there's anything to worry about, we'll take care of it, all right? You just relax and enjoy your flowers."

Sandy hung up, feeling a strange mix of emotions. It was reassuring to know that the two detectives were following up so quickly, and at the same time disquieting that she hadn't been able to talk to Ted Gaine. This Mr. Anish investigation must be turning her paranoid. She had clearly heard patronizing undertones in Wegner's voice, as though he thought she was blowing things out of proportion. Maybe she was. Maybe being hurt and in the hospital was warping her perspective. And if it was, how would she know?

ELEANOR VERMEYER had come home after a long weekend at the family cottage to find her husband dead of a gunshot wound to the head and a suicide note in his typewriter. She had immediately called the police.

Now she sat, pressing a white silk handkerchief to a face flushed and swollen from weeping, refusing all comfort as the detectives conducted their investigation.

"Nick became so depressed after Lou was killed," she sobbed. "They were very close, you know, like brothers. When he didn't want to come up to the cottage with me this weekend, I knew something was wrong. But I had no idea he was planning to—"

Suddenly she'd dissolved into fresh tears, and Sergeant Wegner closed his notepad and murmured to his partner, "Let's make this quick. The widow's obviously a basket case, and this was obviously a suicide."

Ted sighed heavily. "I'm not so sure it was, Joe," he replied as they walked back to the study where the body had been found.

Joe glanced at him in disbelief. "You're not sure? How cut and dried does the situation have to be for you? I've got a hundred dollars says Ballistics matches the gun we found in Vermeyer's hand with the slugs that killed Parmentier and Blass."

"And the slug we pulled out of the floor?"

Joe shrugged. "There could be any number of reasons for that. You're trying to second-guess a man who'd already slipped over the edge, remember. Who knew what was going through his mind?"

"It just doesn't feel right, Joe. I say we call it questionable for now."

"Nielsen likes evidence, not feelings," Wegner pointed out, pulling a surgical glove from his pants pocket. "I'd better get that note out of the typewriter for Forensics."

"No, wait a minute. There's something we should check out." Ted pulled on his own glove, pressed the carriage return and proceeded to type a few characters.

Joe's jaw dropped. "What are you doing, Ted? That's evidence!"

But his partner was staring intently at the page in the typewriter. "Look at the left margins—the margin of the note and the place where I just typed," he said.

Joe looked, and his jaw dropped even further. The margins were slightly, but visibly, different.

"No matter how careful you are, once you've taken a page out of a typewriter, you can never put it back in exactly the same place," said Ted with grim satisfaction. "If Vermeyer typed this note, he obviously didn't do it just before killing himself. And if he'd typed it earlier, why would he bother putting it back in the typewriter? More and more, this feels to me like murder, Joe."

"I don't believe this," Wegner muttered to himself. "Next you'll be telling me that Mr. Vanish did it."

"That's not as farfetched as you may think. When we were discussing the Parmentier case last week, what was your only objection to my theory that a lookalike might have attended that party? The Vermeyers would have spotted a ringer. But what if Nick didn't really get a good look at the guy, only said it was Parmentier because it was inconceivable to him that anyone would have been impersonating Parmentier? Or what if Nick was out-and-out lying to us? What if the killer realized this and became nervous that, over time, Vermeyer might have second thoughts, and he decided to eliminate the witness before he could change his statement?''

"There are too damn many ifs in that equation, partner," replied Joe, annoyed. "I think you've got Mr. Vanish on the brain. Let's just stick with the evidence in front of us, all right?''

"And call it a suspicious death?" Ted insisted quietly.

"Okay, it's suspicious," said his partner reluctantly.

BY MIDAFTERNOON, an impatient Sandy had decided to resolve the Allen Storm situation herself once and for all by paying a visit to the orderly on his own turf.

She would be tactful, of course. There was no point in drawing undue attention to her unauthorized presence in Emergency by making a scene. She would tell him calmly and quietly that although she appreciated his attention and flowers, he just wasn't her type. She would ask him to please not contact her again. Then she would return to her own floor and be a model patient until Thursday morning... or until Ted Gaine's next visit, which she hoped would come first.

At 3:00 p.m. sharp, as though drawn by a huge magnet, all the ninth-floor staff headed toward the nursing office for the changing of the guard. As soon as the door closed behind them, Sandy walked to the elevators, pressed the down button and held her breath. Not until she was inside the elevator and moving toward the ground floor did she release it. With luck, Emergency would be too busy for anyone to notice that she didn't belong there. With luck, she would find Allen Storm, deliver her message and be back in her room before the afternoon nursing shift discovered she was gone.

At ground level, Sandy stepped out of the elevator and began following the painted arrows on the wall to Emergency. The bare, pale green corridor opened into a large waiting room with an admissions desk at one end. Beside it was a double door, wedged wide open, through which Sandy could see men and women in white uniforms trotting briskly back and forth with stainless-steel clipboards in their hands. That was where Allen Storm would be.

Striding with a confidence she didn't feel, Sandy passed the admissions desk and entered the nonpublic part of Emergency. Her eyes darted back and forth in search of a medium-tall, brown-haired orderly. A moment later, she found him, parking a gurney in a side corridor.

"Mr. Storm," she called gently.

"Yes, ma'am!" He wheeled around with a half smile on his face, and Sandy froze, struggling for her next breath.

It wasn't the same man. He had the same shade of brown hair, slicked up in a pompadour, and the same cheekbones, and the same lips and jawline, but the eyes were different. Not the color of them, or the shape, but the expression; the personality living behind them and shining through them was radically, terrifyingly different.

"I—I'm sorry to bother you . . ." she stammered.

He cocked his head curiously, trying to place her. Then he remembered her and his eyes lit up with recognition. "Oh, yeah, gunshot wound, early Sunday morning, right?"

She nodded weakly.

"You were in bad shape that night. It's good to see you up and around, Miss . . . ?"

With an effort, she found her tongue and replied, "DiGianni. Alessandra DiGianni. I . . . just wanted to thank you . . . for your kindness."

He shrugged one shoulder. "You looked kind of alone and scared. Next time you can hold *my* hand," he said with a grin.

"Well, thank you again." On legs that wobbled dangerously beneath her, Sandy made her way back to the elevator and pressed the number of her floor.

Allen Storm had never brought her flowers. He'd never even set foot in her room. The man who'd done those things, who'd begged her not to throw out his gift, had been an impostor. And she could think of only one impostor who would be interested in both her and Dooley— Mr. Vanish.

As her mind formed the words, Sandy began to tremble with urgency. The elevator was moving at a snail's pace. She willed it to go faster. She had to get back to her room right away and telephone Ted Gaine. And she had to warn the officer guarding Dooley.

Forcing down a wave of panic that threatened to engulf her, Sandy hurried into her room. Instantly her gaze leapt to the flowers. He'd begged her to keep them. That meant she had to get rid of them right away. There could be listening devices, or timed-release poison gas, or who knew what concealed in that vase.

Sandy ran out of her room again and over to the nurses' station. Miss Foote was behind the desk, putting on a cardigan sweater and about to leave the floor.

Desperately Sandy looked around for Mrs. Conway, but the warm, motherly charge nurse was nowhere to be seen.

"Can I help you?" came Miss Foote's stiletto voice.

Sandy groaned inwardly. She had a better chance of convincing Mrs. Conway... but this *was* an emergency, and Gaine had told her to contact Security in an emergency.

"Please," she begged, "you must call Security up here. The blue vase in my room is police evidence. They'll have to take it out."

Miss Foote drew herself up, one eyebrow raised imperiously. "What kind of nonsense is this?" she demanded. "You want me to call Security to remove a vase from your room? I assure you, Ms. DiGianni, they have better things to do. If you no longer want the flowers, an orderly can move them somewhere else."

The image of Allen Storm carrying the vase flashed through Sandy's mind, and her stomach began immediately twisting itself into a knot. "No!" she protested, vehemently shaking her head. "You can't just shuttle them around. They have to be held for the police."

But Miss Foote stared her down, not deigning to answer, unmoved except for that one superior eyebrow. Sandy wanted to kick herself for even mentioning the vase to this woman. She should have known better. She should have *known*.

"All right, never mind," said Sandy, backing away from the counter.

"No, since the flowers are obviously making you uncomfortable, we'll take care of them now," decided Miss Foote. She signaled to one of the nurse's aides. "The blue vase comes out of 921."

"They're really beautiful," remarked the aide as she emerged from Sandy's room cradling the vase of roses and carnations in her arms.

"I'm sure they'll be just as beautiful in some other part of the hospital," replied Miss Foote, her eyes coldly daring Sandy to object to her plans for these flowers.

Sandy forced down a swelling tide of fear, reminding herself that if Ted Gaine hadn't been able to convince a police inspector that Mr. Vanish was stalking her, then she was wasting her breath trying to get Miss Ice Cold Foote to react to the threat.

"Thank you," she said, as coolly as she could. Then she marched back into her room, found Gaine's business card and called Homicide. Sergeants Gaine and Wegner were both out of the office, but Sergeant Singh was there. He took her message and promised to pass it along at once.

Sandy's hands shook as she replaced the receiver on its cradle. All right, that part was done. Now she had to warn Sergeant Michaels, down the hall. But calmly, she reminded herself. Not like a crazy woman, or else he wouldn't believe her, either.

Suddenly the door to her room opened and Miss Foote came in, followed by an orderly carrying a small tray.

"Lie down on the bed, please," said Miss Foote.

Instantly Sandy was wary. "Why?"

"Your doctor has ordered additional medication." The charge nurse half turned and picked up a syringe from the tray. "I spoke to Dr. Marley just now about the scene you made in the corridor, and he agreed that in your highly agitated state you ought to receive sedation."

And the orderly, no doubt, was there to ensure that the patient cooperated, thought Sandy bitterly. With a sigh of resignation, she leaned back and took the injection, the faster to get Miss Foote out of her room, off the floor, and out of the damned hospital, so Sandy could go warn Sergeant Michaels.

TED GAINE SAT in a corner booth in the police records library, staring alternately at the one-page printout of Mr. Vanish's M.O. that Joe had given him the other day and at the display on the computer screen in front of him.

Joe claimed to have run a comparison of all the unsolved murders in the files in which Mr. Vanish was suspected of being the perpetrator. He'd found a dozen cases, and from them had concluded that Mr. Vanish never used a weapon more than once. And from that conclusion it must follow logically that Mr. Vanish couldn't have murdered Parmentier or Blass.

Now, attempting a similar comparison with slightly different parameters, Ted was discovering that there were no cases in the files in which Mr. Vanish was actually named as a possible suspect.

Not even the Parmentier file, which Ted had assumed would include Alessandra's statement naming Mr. Vanish as the murderer. Joe had never entered it in the records.

Ted frowned and punched up a different set of search parameters, but with the same results: no cases found in which the name Mr. Vanish was mentioned.

Then how could Joe have located the twelve he'd used in his comparison?

Ted stared at the message flashing on the screen as his mind considered possibilities. Joe could have randomly chosen a bunch of cases that had gone unsolved a certain length of time, assuming Vanish had been considered a suspect. Or he could have asked other detectives to name those cases in which they'd even briefly suspected Mr. Vanish. Or he could simply have known that Vanish had committed those murders, using a different weapon each time.

But how could he have known? Unless— No, that didn't make sense. Or did it? Alessandra had pointed out, rightly, that not every police officer was immune to temptation.

And Ragusz had said something, too, that had stuck at the back of Ted's mind—something about being glad that the two of them at least had got together. It didn't feel right. It begged a question, but Ted wasn't sure what question to ask. Maybe Ragusz could tell him.

Ted strode to the main desk and telephoned Dragnet. When Ragusz finally picked up the receiver, he sounded as though the phone call had woken him up. "Yeah," he yawned, "this's Dragnet."

"This is Gaine. What did you mean by that crack about the two of us, Alessandra DiGianni and me, getting together last Wednesday?"

"Last Wednesday?" he echoed sleepily. "Oh, yeah. It was the second time in a week that I'd given that demo. I couldn't figure out why you didn't come in the first time, with your partner, but I was glad at least that—"

"My partner?" Ted cut in, feeling a sudden twist in his gut.

"Yeah. Wegner came in wanting to know about worm programs. Didn't he tell you?"

"I . . . must have forgotten. Thanks, Raggie."

Slowly, Ted hung up. The pieces were beginning to fall into place, but he didn't like the picture they were making.

Uneasily, he realized that he hadn't touched base with Headquarters or with Alessandra all day. He picked up the receiver again and punched up the number for Homicide. Andover picked up the phone at the other end.

"Messages?" said Andover. "Sure, here they are—two messages, both from your Miss DiGianni. Your partner took them and said he'd pass them on to you."

"I haven't spoken to Joe all day," said Ted softly. "What do the messages say?"

"This morning, she called about a problem she was having with an orderly at the hospital. Your partner was already at the hospital, so I passed the message to him. About twenty minutes ago, a second call came in, this one marked urgent. The orderly is an impostor, it says."

Ted swore under his breath. "When did Joe pick it up?"

"Singh forwarded it immediately."

"I'd better get over to the hospital right away."

"Good idea," said Andover. "Your partner could be in big trouble. I'll call Hospital Security and let them know."

Yes, thought Ted as he raced across the parking lot to his car, one of his partners was definitely in trouble. But which one?

SANDY GAVE MISS FOOTE ten minutes to leave the hospital. Then she sat up and swung her legs over the side of the bed, half expecting the room to spin, but grateful that it didn't. She slid down to stand on unsteady legs, her good arm outstretched for balance and support.

The sedative was making her tipsy. Not quite anchored to the floor, she couldn't trust her sense of balance. Fortunately there were walls she could lean against on her way to warn Sergeant Michaels. And she had to warn him immediately.

Sandy made her way to the door of her room and peeked out, squinting in an effort to force things back into focus. It was visiting hour. Patients and their friends and relatives were strolling up and down both hallways. Perfect.

She swung herself around the doorjamb, resting against the corridor wall for a moment as she planned her path past the elevators. Then she pushed off and joined the parade, praying that her own family would delay their visit until evening, as they'd done yesterday and the day before.

Grimly concentrating on keeping her balance, Sandy passed the elevators and headed down the hall in the direction of room 943. Once again, she passed the half-tiled entrance to the showers. Then she came opposite the kitchen, and the sight of Sergeant Michaels lounging against the narrow counter with a mug of coffee stopped her in her unsteady tracks.

"Who's watching Dooley?" she blurted, with a terrible premonition of what the answer would be.

"A friend of mine. It's all right, Miss," he assured her in a gruff voice meant to discourage any further probing.

"Another policeman, you mean?" she persisted.

He uttered a resigned sigh. "One of the orderlies is spelling me for ten minutes. Is that all right with you?"

Sandy's heart almost stopped. "*Dio,* not Allen Storm!"

"Yes, Allen Storm." The officer cocked his head curiously at her. "Are you all right, Miss? You don't look too steady on your feet. Would you like some help back to your room?"

Fighting a wave of dizziness, she cried, "No, listen to me, please! I'm Alessandra DiGianni. Didn't Sergeant Wegner tell you that there's a hit man after Dooley and me?"

Michaels frowned uneasily. "He said there might be. Why?"

"Please, listen," she begged, aware that precious seconds were ticking away. Vanish was already inside Dooley's room, and he wouldn't even have to use a gun.

"He's here. The hit man is in the hospital. I've learned who he is. I was coming to warn you. He's been visiting you, posing as Allen Storm. I met the real Allen Storm today, and they're two different men. Sergeant Michaels, please believe me—you've left Dooley alone with a murderer!" she concluded breathlessly.

Her ears were humming. Sandy shook her head to clear it, willing adrenaline into her bloodstream to counteract the effects of the sedative. She mustn't fold up now, she mustn't!

After what seemed an endless moment, Michaels put his coffee mug down on the counter and unfastened the safety catch on his belt holster. "I think I'd better go and check this out," he said grimly.

Trembling, Sandy followed him to the bend in the corridor and peered around the corner. The door to room 943 was closed and there was no one in sight.

Gesturing to her to be quiet, Michaels crouched defensively beside the door and listened. Nothing. Then he gave it a gentle push inward. Still nothing. Finally, he straightened up and walked inside, letting the door close behind him.

All at once there was a hand clamped tightly on Sandy's right shoulder and a voice whispering coldly into her ear, "Invalids belong in their rooms, dearie."

Frozen with terror, she felt something hard jab into the small of her back. "Don't scream," warned the low raspy voice. "There's a gun in my hand. It can blow a hole in you the size of a pumpkin, and that's exactly what it will do if you let on to anyone we pass that I'm anything but an orderly helping a sick patient back to her room. Nod if you understand."

Somehow, Sandy managed to make her head move up and down. She didn't have to pretend to be unwell. As Mr. Vanish came up beside her, placed his right arm around her waist, and jabbed the muzzle of his gun into her left side, behind the concealing bulk of her cast, her knees almost gave way beneath her.

"Easy now, easy," he said in a louder voice, for the benefit of any bystanders who might be listening. And slowly, as everything inside her twisted sickly with fear, they strolled back along the hallway toward her room, collecting sympathetic glances from everyone they passed.

Just as they rounded the corner beside the elevators, the telephone at the nurses' station rang. Mrs. Conway answered it. "Ninth floor, Mrs. Conway speaking. Who? No, nobody from this unit called Security, unless..."

At the word Security, Sandy paused, a remnant of hope stirring in her heart. But Mr. Vanish jabbed his gun even more painfully into her ribs and muttered coldly, "Keep walking."

Sobbing in a breath, she obeyed. He'd already killed Dooley. Now he was going to kill her. The closer they drew to her room, the more certain she became of that, and the more distractedly her thoughts began to mill around in her mind, faster and faster, until the past was a blur and the present was an icy blanket of pain and fear—and Ted's face.

Sandy felt tears stinging her eyes. The thought of dying without ever seeing him again was like a cold blade twisting slowly in her chest.

Once they were through the door of room 921, Mr. Vanish pressed her to sit on the bed, her back to him. Her left shoulder strained against the edge of the cast as he held her there, his fingers locked painfully around the back of her neck.

"My flowers," she heard him murmur incredulously. "You lying—! You got rid of my damn flowers."

Suddenly he gathered a fistful of her hair and jerked her back onto her feet. When she cried out in surprise, he pressed the muzzle of his gun against her cheek and whispered hideously into her ear, "Now I'm going to have to go to Plan B. I hate Plan B."

Once more, his right arm snaked around her waist and he was walking her out into the hall, the barrel of the gun held firmly to her rib cage.

She was cold. She was numb with the cold and trying not to shiver. In this nightmare, her limbs were turning to wood, and they obeyed him, not her. He told her fingers to push the elevator DOWN button and she watched helplessly as they did his bidding.

"All right, freeze, Storm, or whoever the hell you are!"

Mr. Vanish spun her around. Sandy's eyes widened as another terror was revealed: she was staring down the barrel of a police revolver.

"Drop the gun and let the girl go," commanded Sergeant Michaels.

She felt something cold and hard touch her left temple.

"Drop *your* gun, Michaels, or she dies."

Stiff with apprehension, Sandy held her breath. The police officer hesitated, and finally crouched to put his revolver on the floor. And then, as though it were happening in slow motion, she saw the barrel of the officer's gun bounce back up and spit flame, and Mr. Vanish's pistol floating in front of her face, firing once with a roar like a cannon. And suddenly the officer was writhing on the floor, groaning and bleeding, and Sandy was being dragged backward into the elevator, and Mr. Vanish was issuing a tight, angry warning over her shoulder, to a crowd of horror-stricken onlookers, not to try to stop him.

And as the elevator door closed in front of her shocked face, Sandy thought for a moment that she saw Ted Gaine lying there, his limbs twitching as though to ward off death, a dark red stain spreading across the front of his shirt. Tears welled in her eyes, blurring her vision and sliding hotly down her cheeks. And deep within her, a spark of anger ignited.

"Push P-1," Mr. Vanish rasped in her ear.

The sedative was still in her system, thickening her tongue, making her muscles sluggish. Somehow she managed to say in a voice that sounded as though it were coming from the next room, "Push it yourself."

He was going to kill her whatever she did. Why should she make it easy for him?

Spitting out an annoyed syllable, he thrust her against the far wall of the car. As her legs folded beneath her and she slid slowly to the floor, she was able to look at him for the first time.

He'd been hit. Blood was streaming out of a wound in his left leg and pooling on the floor around his shoe. He'd clenched his jaw against the pain, and now pointed his gun at her and hissed through gritted teeth, "Once this thing hits bottom, you're history."

He needed her alive in case the elevator stopped at one of the intervening floors. He needed someone to threaten so people would be frightened and keep their distance.

With that knowledge, her fear parted like a mist, and she found herself able to see and think more clearly.

When nobody had known where to look for him, Mr. Vanish had loomed larger than life. Seen up close, however, he was just a man, shorter and slighter than Ted Gaine, and hiding behind a mask. He'd been clever in the past, but not this time. This time he'd taken a bullet from a policeman's gun and was struggling just to stay on his feet. Sandy saw the sheen of sweat on his pain-pinched face, outlining the parts he'd added in order to become Allen Storm. When he shook his head to clear it, her heart leapt hopefully in her chest.

He was probably in worse shape than she was right now. His only advantage was that gun. Maybe she had a chance to survive after all—if she could just get closer to him without arousing suspicion.

The lighted panel over the door indicated that they were passing the sixth floor. "I don't understand," she sobbed, eyeing the angle of his good leg.

His face was so tight with pain that it resembled a death mask. "It's very simple, really," he said with a ghastly smile. "Dooley I had to get rid of because he wit...witnessed the Parmentier hit. And also because he tried to blame me...for the job behind the arcade. I can't let every...two-bit punk who wants to do away with someone frame me for his slipshod work. I have...a professional reputation...to think of," he gasped, cocking his pistol with effort as they passed the third floor.

Sandy forced herself to ignore the sound of the gun. She could do it, she told herself grimly. She had nothing to lose anymore, and everything to gain. Wincing at the strain it put on her broken arm, she dragged herself across the floor of the elevator, sobbing and groveling as though in mortal terror, but moving ever closer to his good leg.

"Blass and Vermeyer," he went on, "were strictly business. I don't take the money... without making the hit. She paid in advance... for both of them...."

They were passing the ground floor. She could almost touch him....

"But you... and Waldron... just got too damned nosy... I'm afraid..."

Just as the elevator bumped to a stop, Sandy reached out her good hand, wrapped it around the back of Mr. Vanish's right heel, and yanked as hard as she could, breathing a silent prayer.

His only support gone, the hit man fell backward with a crash, stunning himself momentarily as his head contacted the safety rail on the wall, and firing his gun harmlessly into the ceiling of the elevator compartment.

In that second, the door slid open, revealing the dim interior of a steel-and-cement parking garage. Sandy drew a steadying breath and gathered her legs beneath her again and forced them to carry her out of the car.

The elevators sat on a concrete pedestal in the middle of the parking area. Made clumsy by the sedative still in her system, Sandy stumbled through the facing row of cars and glanced desperately around. There had to be an exit ramp somewhere, a way to get to the street. Her eyes searched the walls, finding shadows everywhere, the umbrae and penumbrae of a platoon of concrete posts, but nothing she could immediately identify as a way out. And all around her, in every direction, she saw cars perfectly set between the straight lines of parking spots, their ends aligned in opposing rows like the teeth of several lengths of open zippers.

Ping! A bullet ricocheted off the post beside her, spraying her with stinging concrete dust. Gasping, Sandy dodged left, feverishly urging her sluggish legs to move faster, faster! Suddenly she was facing a blank wall, and cars were pointing at her like fingers, and the limping ka-*thunk,* ka-*thunk* of her pursuer's footsteps was getting closer.

Her thoughts were getting scattered, but she tried to control them. If Ted had got her message, he was on his way, and she needed to stay alive until he got there. Sandy fought the drug, blinking hard to keep her eyes focusing, visualizing all the strength in her body flowing into her legs.

She glanced left and right, then finally crouched beside a maroon Buick and tried the passenger-door handle. It was locked.

She bobbed quickly up and down, risking a glance over the hood of the Buick, but couldn't spot Mr. Vanish between her and the elevator. Suddenly Sandy realized she couldn't hear his footfalls, either. He'd stopped. Had he lost her—or found her?

Sandy froze, afraid even to breathe. Slowly, she turned her head, her eyes widening in horror as she saw him through the Buick's rear window, leaning against the trunk of a gray Mercedes parked three cars down the line, and staring right at her!

Sandy's heart leapt up and lodged in her throat as he raised the gun, took unsteady aim and fired.

She flinched and grimaced as the bullet creased the Buick's roof. Then, before he could cock the gun and shoot again, Sandy was on her feet and staggering away from him as fast as she could go.

Her body was screaming for rest, but she had to keep going, had to force Mr. Vanish to keep walking on a wounded leg. It was her only chance now—keep moving and hope that leg slowed him down. It was already affecting his marksmanship, but his aim would still be deadly at point-blank range.

She hurried past rows of cars, dodged through them, crept between them, stopping every while to listen breathlessly for the hollow sound of limping footsteps, then swallowing her heart and taking off again, away from them. And as she zigged and zagged, she cast her eye along the outer wall of the garage, searching for the gap in a row of cars that would indicate the entrance to a ramp up or down—either direction would put an additional strain on Mr. Vanish's wounded leg.

At last, she spotted it—the back of a closed garage door, probably triggered from inside by an automatic eye. And beside it was the pedestrians' exit to the street— a long, diagonal run across the open space between rows of cars. And if Mr. Vanish was close enough to draw a bead on her . . . !

Sandy dropped wearily beside a white station wagon to catch her breath and consider her situation.

Suddenly it occurred to her that the garage was unusually quiet. She hadn't seen Mr. Vanish in several long minutes. Only the nearness of his footsteps had repeatedly flushed her out of hiding. And now those footsteps had halted, and she had no idea where he might be.

Her skin prickling icily, Sandy crept forward along the fender of the station wagon until she could see the full length of the row of parked cars in both directions. Empty. Then she crawled backward and scanned the row behind her. Not a sign of him. With difficulty, Sandy lay down on her stomach, wincing as the cast got in the way. The cold of the concrete easily penetrated her thin cotton robe and hospital nightgown as she placed her eyes at ground level and searched vainly beneath the cars for a telltale pair of feet. Puzzled, she resumed her crouching position.

Where could he be? Still not risking a full breath, she mentally counted off sixty seconds, straining her ears to catch the slightest sound, the shuffling of a foot, the rustle of a pant leg. All at once she heard a sharp clicking sound, from somewhere ahead of her. A gun was being cocked.

He had to be hiding in the shadows between the cars and the wall, waiting for her to find the exit and make a run for it right past him at point-blank range. Tensely, she crouched, knowing that if she tried to get out that door she would surely be shot. The elevators? Too far behind her now, and Mr. Vanish was too close to outrun. Whichever way she moved, she was lost.

Suddenly there was a round metallic boom, then a widening slit of daylight as the huge automatic door began to open. Startled, Sandy froze for a moment. A dark green sedan was entering the garage. Was it Ted Gaine's? Her vision chose that moment to blur, and she couldn't identify the driver.

Dio, he'd seen her! Stopping just inside the entrance, the driver got out, staring in her direction, completely unaware of the gunman hidden in the shadows. It was Gaine.

Sandy's heart dropped. He was a perfect target.

"Ted, take cover!" she screamed, then fell to the ground, trying to shield her head with her good arm, as a bullet whizzed past her, ricocheting off the side mirror of the car just behind her.

More shots were fired. She would have to find a safer hiding place. But before Sandy could gather her legs beneath her, she felt a hand tangle in her hair and yank her head backwards, pulling a short, startled scream from her lips as she was hauled to her feet. She felt something hot and hard against the curve of her left jaw. And she knew, as emptiness twisted slowly inside her, that Mr. Vanish had won, in spite of Ted Gaine's arriving to skew his plans.

Just like Sergeant Michaels, upstairs.

Gaine was crouched behind the opened door of his car, his revolver drawn and ready to fire. Behind him, someone else was aiming a second weapon over the roof of the car.

"Drop your gun and let her go," called Gaine, his face a granite mask.

"Drop yours or she dies right here," retorted Mr. Vanish in a hideous, raspy voice.

Sandy's thoughts began whirling frantically. *Dio,* it was happening again. Almost the same players, the same script, the same terrifying ending. Ted Gaine would pretend to put his gun down, bring it up firing at the last moment, and Mr. Vanish would put a bullet into him and leave him writhing on the ground, his limbs twitching in shock, his lifeblood draining out of him . . . !

Her heart was frozen and her mind was screaming in agony, but all that escaped her lips was a quiet sob. *Oh, Ted . . . Oh, no, Ted!*

But Sergeant Gaine made no move to put down his weapon. "Give it up, Joe," he said sadly. "It's all over now. I figured everything out while driving here and got Nielsen on the radio; and Ragusz and Andover know too. And even if you got past the two of us, how far do you think you could travel on that leg?"

Behind her, Sandy felt Mr. Vanish stiffen. She cried out involuntarily as he yanked her head back again, pulling his human shield closer to his body.

"Far enough, Ted," he said.

Horrified, she saw the barrel of Mr. Vanish's gun floating beside her left cheek, aimed directly at Ted Gaine. And in that instant, the anger that had been smoldering inside her burst into searing flame. Sandy hadn't fought this long to survive only to be a helpless witness to the murder of the man she loved.

Without warning, she grabbed for the gun with her right hand, twisting it downward with all her strength. She'd taken the hit man by surprise. Uttering an astonished expletive, he nearly lost his grip on the weapon. But not quite. All at once they were struggling for it, and his right hand was snaking over her shoulder, trying to pry her fingers away.

"No!" screamed Sandy, lashing out reflexively, not even aware until her cast connected with a sickening thud that she had swung her left arm.

As Mr. Vanish dropped to the ground behind her, Sandy felt her knees give way. Sobbing, she sank onto the concrete, cradling her broken arm....

Then the garage was teeming with voices and bodies, most of them in brown uniforms.

"Is that him? He doesn't look dangerous now."

"I'll go get a gurney."

"Better make that two."

"Alessandra, are you all right?"

She could tell from the edge on Ted's voice that this wasn't the first time he'd asked the question. Tears of relief streaming down her cheeks, she looked up and found him kneeling beside her on the ground, a frown on his face and a pleading expression in his soft gray eyes.

Suddenly his arms were around her in a gentle embrace and he was murmuring reassurances as the Hospital Security people darted back and forth. It was all over now. Everything was going to be all right. But . . .

"You called him Joe," she said, dazed.

"Joe Wegner. Here, take a look at the elusive Mr. Vanish."

Carefully, he lifted her to her feet and turned her around. And as they stood staring at the motionless body on the garage floor, Sandy could see that her cast had displaced some of his disguise, revealing the detective's familiar features.

Sandy shivered. "He was the psychopathic child in the article?"

"In public, a charming pretender," Gaine quoted grimly. "He had us all pegged. Knowing how police detectives were trained to think, he was able to get away with murder . . . until an amateur got into the act." He tightened his embrace momentarily.

Suddenly one of the brown uniforms stopped beside them. Sandy glanced up and saw that its wearer was holding a walkie-talkie.

"There's a gurney on its way for her, Sergeant," said the security man. "You ever play pro hockey, ma'am? You've got a vicious left elbow there."

"Hey, what's this in his pocket?" demanded a security officer.

"Don't touch that!" cried the second detective. "My God, Ted, it looks like a remote detonator!"

The security man with the walkie-talkie nearly dropped it. "You mean that clown planted a bomb? We'll have to evacuate the hospital right away—"

All at once, things clicked together in Sandy's mind. "No, I know what it looks like," she exclaimed. "He brought me a vase of flowers. A blue crystal vase. He begged me not to get rid of it. When he saw that it wasn't in my room anymore, he was angry. He said something about having to go to Plan B now.''

"That has to be it, Ted. A bomb inside the vase."

"But she said it isn't in her room anymore," pointed out the security man.

"Miss Foote knows where it is," said Sandy. "She's the one who took it away."

The security man thanked her and rushed off.

"When the gurney gets here, I'll have to leave you for a while," said Gaine gently. "But I'll be back to take your statement. And then you and I have a future to discuss, lady."

Sandy gazed into his face. A future with Ted Gaine? With a stubborn, overbearing, classic textbook chauvinist who would probably never be cured of interfering with her life? He wasn't at all what she had imagined her Mr. Right would be—but there he was, protecting her, holding her, caring about her, smiling at her . . . kissing her.

Suddenly Sandy couldn't think of anything more wonderful than a future with tough, smart Sergeant Ted Gaine.

Chapter Thirteen

Wednesday, June 20

Styling long hair with one hand had to be the toughest job in the world, Sandy decided. She was sitting on the edge of her hospital bed struggling to tame her rebellious dark tresses with only a brush and five hairpins, when Ted Gaine walked in wearing a broad smile.

"Good morning, beautiful," he said, bending to plant a kiss on her lips that made her forget all about her hair, her itchy new cast, everything.

"Mmm, now it is," she purred happily.

"I passed your family downstairs, and they looked pretty grim. Have you told them yet what happened yesterday?"

"I didn't have the heart. Mama is still trying to get over the fact that someone broke into my apartment and shot me in the arm. And Uncle Hugo has high blood pressure and is supposed to avoid stress. And Tommy hasn't quite recovered from the scare you put into him last Friday night. He'd be a basket case right now if Hugo hadn' stood up for him when it counted. So I guess I'll have to break it to them gently—over the next six months or so."

"That sounds like a good plan," he said, sinking onto the visitor's chair beside the bed. "Meanwhile, I have so so news, good news and great news. How do you want it?"

"I already know about Dooley," Sandy sighed. "Well, he did keep saying that Mr. Vanish was going to kill him. What about Sergeant Michaels?"

"That's the good news. He's in Critical Care right now, but the doctors are optimistic that he'll make a complete recovery. He'll retire with a full pension and a citation for bravery, I expect."

"Going out with a bang," agreed Sandy, recalling Michaels's earlier remark.

"And you'll be happy to know that Mr. Vanish was transferred out of here last night to a prison hospital. Security found the blue vase and handed it over to the Bomb Squad, who found enough plastic explosive in the bottom of it to reduce your room and possibly the two adjoining rooms to smoking rubble. Obviously, Vanish intended to detonate it once he'd killed Dooley and got clear."

Her eyes widened with horror.

"But the best news is that we made the final arrest in the Parmentier case last night—the person who hired Mr. Vanish."

Sandy frowned, remembering what he had told her in the elevator. "It was a woman. He said that *she* had paid him for both hits."

"That's right. Your statement was what tipped us off—and the ledger page Blass left you, which proved that somebody high up in Unity Sportswear had been arranging for 'accidents' to befall the company's competitors. Last night, Detective Harding and I went out to the Vermeyer place and arrested Mrs. Vermeyer for nine counts of conspiracy to commit murder.

"My unofficial guess is that Nick Vermeyer hadn't the slightest inkling what his wife was doing, until Vanish turned up in disguise at the victory party. She told us the real Parmentier had been there and bullied her husband into backing her up. Then you came poking around nine months later and Nick started coming unglued. And Blass, who had probably taken that ledger page with him as insurance when he left the Vermeyers' employ, eventually realized that having it made him even more of a target. So he passed it off onto you. But he was too late. She had already hired Mr. Vanish again to eliminate Blass *and* Nick, who had suddenly become a liability."

Sandy couldn't repress a shudder. "*Dio!* What a cold-blooded woman!"

"She and Joe were quite a pair, all right—by my very unofficial and completely off-the-record reckoning, of course," he warned her severely. "Not a word do you repeat until after the trial."

"Yessir, Sergeant Gaine!"

"Anyway," he said, casually moving from the chair to the edge of the bed, "before I buried myself in paperwork, I thought I'd come around and find out how you felt about going to a movie with me this weekend. You're still being discharged tomorrow, aren't you?"

It took a moment for his words to register. "You're asking me for a date?" she said hopefully.

The gray eyes were soft as mist. "I'm asking for a date, yes. And would you do me a favor, Alessandra? I do have a first name. Now that the Parmentier case is wrapped up, would you please call me Ted?"

"All right, Ted," she said, smiling. "I guess I have to get used to the new me and you."

"Is that *all right* to the movie, as well?"

"Convince me."

Chuckling, he gathered her up carefully in his arms and began feathering little kisses across her neck. "I'll pick something light and funny, I promise. No police thrillers. If movies work out, we'll progress to long walks in the park, a moonlight picnic on Center Island..."

His warm breath on the side of her neck was doing indescribable things to her.

"...you can take me to dinner at your mother's place..."

Sandy giggled. "Mama will be ecstatic."

Now Ted was nibbling her earlobe, and tiny hot explosions of pleasure were going off deep inside her.

"...and I'll take you to meet my family. We'll get engaged..."

"Whoa!" she gasped. "Not so fast!"

Obediently, he stopped nibbling, and with a gentle finger smoothed a stray bit of hair away from her cheek.

Sandy turned and faced him. "Ted, I do have wonderful feelings for you. And I want to take the time to explore them and enjoy them. So can we please just take things one step at a time?"

He smiled, a slow, warm, loving smile. "Honey, I'm an investigator. We *always* take things one step at a time." And he leaned forward and kissed her, sending delicious vibrations right down to her toes and leaving no doubt in Sandy's mind that Sergeant Gaine was a very thorough fellow, indeed.

Harlequin Intrigue®

A SPAULDING & DARIEN MYSTERY

Meet an engaging pair of amateur sleuths—
Jenny Spaulding and Peter Darien.

Harlequin Intrigue introduces this daring pair in
#147 BUTTON, BUTTON this month (October 1990).
And once you meet them, you won't want to say
goodbye to Jenny and Peter. They will be returning
in further spine-chilling romantic adventures in
future books. In April 1991, look for #159 DOUBLE
DARE in which they solve their next puzzling
mystery, the disappearance of the star of a popular
TV sitcom.

Join Jenny and Peter for danger and romance....
Look for the identifying series flash—A SPAULDING
AND DARIEN MYSTERY ... for Romance, Suspense
and Adventure ... At Its Best.

IBB-1

H·I·S·T·O·R·I·C·A·L
Christmas
S·T·O·R·I·E·S 1·9·9·0

Once again Harlequin, the experts in romance, bring you the magic of Christmas —as celebrated in America's past.

These enchanting love stories celebrate Christmas made extra-special by the wonder of people in love....

Nora Roberts	**In From the Cold**
Patricia Potter	**Miracle of the Heart**
Ruth Langan	**Christmas at Bitter Creek**

Look for this Christmas title next month wherever Harlequin® books are sold.

"Makes a great stocking stuffer."

HX90-1

HARLEQUIN
American Romance®

November brings you...

SENTIMENTAL JOURNEY

BARBARA BRETTON

Jitterbugging at the Stage Door Canteen, singing along with the Andrews Sisters, planting your Victory Garden—this was life on the home front during World War II.

Barbara Bretton captures all the glorious memories of America in the 1940's in SENTIMENTAL JOURNEY—a nostalgic Century of American Romance book and a Harlequin Award of Excellence title.

Available wherever Harlequin® books are sold.

Win 1 of 10 Romantic Vacations and Earn Valuable Travel Coupons Worth up to $1,000!

Inside every Harlequin or Silhouette book during September, October and November, you will find a PASSPORT TO ROMANCE that could take you around the world.

By sending us the official entry form available at your favorite retail store, you will automatically be entered in the PASSPORT TO ROMANCE sweepstakes, which could win you a star-studded London Show Tour, a Carribean Cruise, a fabulous tour of France, a sun-drenched visit to Hawaii, a Mediterranean Cruise or a wander through Britain's historical castles. The more entry forms you send in, the better your chances of winning!

In addition to your chances of winning a fabulous vacation for two, valuable travel discounts on hotels, cruises, car rentals and restaurants can be yours by submitting an offer certificate (available at retail stores) properly completed with proofs-of-purchase from any specially marked PASSPORT TO ROMANCE Harlequin® or Silhouette® book. The more proofs-of-purchase you collect, the higher the value of travel coupons received!

For details on your PASSPORT TO ROMANCE, look for information at your favorite retail store or send a self-addressed stamped envelope to:

PASSPORT TO ROMANCE
P.O. Box 621
Fort Erie, Ontario L2A 5X3

- ✂ - - - - - - - - -

ONE PROOF-OF-PURCHASE

3-CHI-2

To collect your free coupon booklet you must include the necessary number of proofs-of-purchase with a properly completed offer certificate available in retail stores or from the above address.